'Any man wo...
to have you a... ...

For a long, quiet moment their gazes locked and the grim expression upon Felicity's face finally melted, her heart giving a funny little jump.

'That's better,' Jarle murmured. 'You have a delightful smile. You should use it more often. A grumpy wife is no asset to anyone.'

She was on her feet in an instant, facing him with a proud, pink-cheeked defiance. 'An asset. Is that all you seek? Someone to host your table and smile upon your guests? You could get such a creature from one of the new mail order catalogues, I am sure.'

He laughed as if she had made a joke. 'But they would not be half so much fun as you. It is a pity, in a way, that we could not make a go of it, for I admire your spirit tremendously,' he said with playful good humour. 'I think we'd make a good team.'

She was insulted. 'A good team? What do you take me for? A horse?'

But he shook his head vehemently. 'Good lord, no. Perhaps I should have said partner. I believe we could make quite a good alliance, Felicity, you and I.' And as she made to speak again he placed the tip of his finger on her soft lips to silence her as he continued, 'Perhaps you should not dismiss it quite out of hand.'

Born in Lancashire, Marion Carr has spent many years in the Lake District, but now lives in the West Country with her lawyer husband, younger daughter and two dogs. She has been a teacher, bookseller and smallholder, but writing ever since she could hold a pencil. She enjoys travel, old books and talking to people. With over forty articles and short stories published, this is her second Masquerade Historical Romance.

Previous Title

MADEIRAN LEGACY

A PROUD ALLIANCE

Marion Carr

*First published in Great Britain 1990
by Mills & Boon Limited*

© Marion Carr 1990

*Australian copyright 1990
Philippine copyright 1990
This edition 1990*

ISBN 0 263 77080 X

*Masquerade is a trademark published by
Mills & Boon Limited, Eton House,
18–24 Paradise Road, Richmond, Surrey, TW9 1SR.*

*Set in Times Roman 10 on 11 pt.
04-9012-81508 C*

Made and printed in Great Britain

CHAPTER ONE

THE HONOURABLE FELICITY TRAVERS stepped lightly down from the omnibus and strode out with vigour along the busy street. A man jostled her shoulder but she continued purposefully on her way with scarcely a pause. She dared not hesitate for a second or her courage might fail her entirely.

She had rehearsed what she was to say a dozen times. It was perfectly simple. Merely thank him for taking care of the business since her father's death and declare that now she and Mama had returned his services were no longer required. The sooner they were rid of Blakeley, the better.

Lifting the skirt of her tropical white dress which, having come straight from the ship, she had not had time to change, she circumnavigated a large puddle, only to be splashed by it as a cart drawn by a pair of Clydesdales rumbled by. Stacked high with women in wide hats, purple banners, streamers and posters declaring the delights of a weekly paper out this very day, the thirteenth of April, 1909, the vehicle looked as if it might topple over at any minute.

'Votes for Women.' The cry went up and Felicity tightened her lips with fresh determination. How dared she quail at her duty in the face of such fervour? She had never been one to do so in the past and had no intention of starting now.

For a moment, the pain of memory blotted everything else from Felicity's mind as she recalled the dear face of her father and compared with disfavour the chill greyness of the Manchester street about her with the recollected

heat and bustle of her beloved Calcutta. How she wished
he were still with them, but he was gone and they must
face life alone in this new drab world. She shivered. The
importance of duty had been instilled in her ever since
they had first gone out to India all those years ago. Papa
had been happy then, and Mama's talent and beauty had
charmed everyone, making it a great honour to be invited to one of her many social gatherings. How different from the wan, pathetic figure she now presented.
But Lady Travers had protested vehemently that Felicity
should make no move until after their appointment with
the lawyer.

'Dearest Mama, it will take no more than a half-hour,'
Felicity had countered as she was hustled aboard the
hired brougham which was to take them to their hotel.
'And I shall feel so much better prepared if I have at
least lifted the curtain a fraction upon this mystery.'

'I do not understand,' Carmella, Lady Travers had
moaned, not for the first time. 'I really do not see how
he could do it to us,' she said again for good measure,
punctuating her words with tiny dabs of a lace handkerchief to her swollen eyes, causing the mingled scents of
sal volatile and eau-de-cologne to waft across the carriage, thus depressing Felicity's spirits still further. 'I was
ever a good wife to him. Why could he not take me into
his confidence?'

Felicity privately thought that she could guess very
easily why Papa had kept such information to himself
but deemed it wise not to say so. 'Indeed, you were the
very best of wives, dearest Mama, do not distress
yourself.' Felicity exchanged yet another anxious glance
with the loyal Millie who sat stroking and patting her
mistress's hand as if calming a child. They shared concern
for Lady Travers's health. The shock of losing her beloved husband had been followed swiftly by the mys-
tifying information that, not only had Sir Joshua
surprisingly owned a Manchester fashion emporium of

which they were in total ignorance, but also their lawyer had grave misgivings about the way it was being run. All of this had grievously affected her health. Felicity was anxious to learn the whole truth with all speed so that she could spare her mama further distress.

And so here she was, tingling with nerves but none the less determined, gazing curiously across the street, wishing her eyes could penetrate the darkened interior behind the over-ornate façade and with it the mystery which shrouded its very existence.

She knew that Manchester, as the heart of the booming cotton industry, was a prosperous and hard-working city. On her short journey through its bewildering network of streets, she had seen numerous warehouses and manufactories, handsome Gothic churches, theatres, an opera house and the famous Exchange Building where all the financial dealings in the textile world took place. It was undoubtedly impressive. Yet in the narrower streets, glimpsed from the major thoroughfares, she had caught a very different picture of the other side of life in this bustling city. She had seen bare-footed children, weary work-worn women carrying bundles of laundry or hurrying to their shift at the mill, their grey faces swathed in shawls against the biting north-east wind. Now, as she stared up at the four-storey building which towered over its neighbours, rows of tiny windows glinting in contrast to the grim stone walls darkened by time and the all-pervading smoke that filled the city, she had a sudden and inexplicable urge to turn and run away. But the noisy crowd in the street pressed in upon her, filling her nostrils with strange, not altogether pleasant scents and her mind with more images than it could assimilate.

'Votes for Women,' came the cry once again. 'Come with us to Albert Square.'

If Felicity had known the profound effect the pamphlet was to make upon her life she would not have accepted it with such carelessness. But as her mind was fully engaged elsewhere her fingers closed upon it without question as she smiled vaguely at the purple-sashed figure, almost welcoming the distraction. No. There was no going back. Besides, once having decided upon a course of action, she disliked prevarication of any kind.

'No doubt Mr Blakeley is merely a foolish old gentleman, when it comes to it, who will be only too glad to go,' she said into the general hubbub, and, jauntily adjusting her new hat to a more becoming angle, she started to cross the street.

It was a particularly delightful model of drawn chiffon in her favourite apple-green with a gauze ribbon of darker green wound about it and tied under her chin. A bunch of saucy yellow cowslips bobbed merrily at one side. The colour contrasted well against the glossy honey-gold of her hair and sun-bronzed skin unfashionably glowing with health and vitality. But then she had ever held scant patience for parasols, always finding far too much to occupy her outdoors to worry overmuch about keeping her fair skin modestly pale. Much to her poor mama's despair.

'Travers and Co. Drapery and Linen Goods,' she read out loud. Curiosity, together with the first tinge of excitement, stirred within her. She didn't have to find a new manager. It might be fun to...

At that moment a window was flung noisily open in a house opposite and Felicity's eyes widened in astonishment as she saw a woman start to toss small paper packets on to the unsuspecting occupants of a passing motor car.

'Oh, no,' she cried, slapping her hand to her mouth to suppress the gurgle of laughter which rose in her throat at the comic spectacle of the Liberal Member of Parliament dropping his electioneering megaphone in consternation as the packets burst forth clouds of white flour over his head and festooned the unremitting black of his morning coat with a snowy shower. Roars of laughter from delighted spectators filled the street and unexpectedly Felicity caught one of the packets in her own hand. Her softly rounded cheeks coloured with excited confusion. The next moment half a dozen police constables were forcing back the door of the house, eager to climb the stairs and arrest the sole female perpetrator of this outrage against masculine dignity. Somewhere in the background, Felicity heard a window smash and the mêlée of women on the pavement surged forward, taking her with them.

'Don't be turned back. We have still to reach Albert Square.'

Jostled and jabbed by the eager crowd, Felicity struggled to free herself, perplexed and instantly concerned by the implications behind the scene as the woman was marched firmly, though it seemed unprotesting, to a waiting black van where several others with no apparent connection with the incident were already being thrust urgently aboard. The noise grew deafening as the watching crowd jeered and at the same moment a band rounded the corner loudly playing the 'Marseillaise'.

The crowd surged forward, and, clutching frantically at her new green hat, Felicity almost lost her balance, stumbled over a child and knocked him sprawling to the ground.

'Oh, are you hurt?' she cried, quickly setting him safely on his feet again. The feel of the scraggy, ill-fed figure beneath the inadequate clothing grimed with long wear brought a pang of guilt to her sensitive heart. How could she be so concerned over her own petty problems when she was indeed fortunate in comparison with the sufferings of others? 'You should not be out here alone. Where do you live?'

She never heard his reply for to her incredulous horror she found herself lifted from her feet by a pair of strong arms and forcibly catapulted through the air, all sight

of the child gone. As her shoulder hit the corner of the
shop window, jarring every bone and nerve in her body,
startled tears blurred her eyes and she slid to the ground
in a jangled heap of pain and shock.

For long seconds she was quite unable to move,
stunned by the violence of her fall.

'A remarkable fine shot, ma'am,' came a deep-
throated growl somewhere above her, and, as soon as
she was able, Felicity lifted her head to look at its owner.
Through the iridescent blur of startled tears she focused
upon a grey waistcoat. Once dashingly patterned in silk
brocade, it was now feathered with thick streaks of flour.
As her gaze trailed higher she found an equally thorough
dusting upon thick dark hair and long sideburns. Worse
still, it lay on the high cheekbones and on a slightly
crooked nose, looking disconcertingly like snow on
mountain tops.

But any nervous inclination to giggle quite deserted
her as she met the full impact of his deep-lidded gaze,
brown eyes, darkly fringed with lashes, menacingly narrowed. She urged herself to stand and face her accuser
on an equal level but her shaking legs refused to comply,
so she continued to sit on the pavement in a crumpled,
undignified heap, acutely aware that she was showing
far more ankle than convention allowed. Closer in-
spection, however, informed her of the futility of trying,
for he was the quite the largest, brawniest man she had
ever clapped eyes upon. Even on tiptoe she would come
no further than the top button of the catastrophic
waistcoat.

'Is this woman troubling you, sir? I'll have her
removed.'

The police constable coldly gripped her elbow and
Felicity gave an instinctive cry of alarm.

Jarle, looking on, felt the anger churn within him.
This had been one of the worst demonstrations yet. A
plate glass window had been broken, goods ruined, trade

lost and now this foolish female had attacked him with flour. A night in a cell would soon cool her zeal. Pity, for she was pretty enough in a way. She reminded him of a Renoir painting with those flushed cheeks and that white summer dress. But then the hat spoiled it.

'Not in the least,' he calmly told the constable. 'This young lady is one of my assistants and has no connection with the suffragettes so far as I am aware.' He saw she was as surprised as he was by this statement. Well she might be. It was not at all what he had meant to say.

But Felicity's relief was short-lived as she found herself being passed from hand to hand, like a parcel, she thought crossly.

The constable, satisfied that his duty had been accomplished, saluted politely and discreetly departed. The crowd sauntered away, looking for fresh excitement elsewhere.

But Felicity's saviour was by no means so easily satisfied. To her acute embarrassment she found herself propelled through the great doors, almost frog-marched between a bewildering array of high-topped counters, before the goggle-eyed stares of a host of shop assistants, to be thrust into a small, untidy office. Anger burned through her with such ferocity that she could feel its radiation right down to her toes.

'Take your hands off me,' she gasped, wrenching her arm free with such vigour that her hat wobbled off her head and plopped upon the floor. 'I am most certainly not one of your shop assistants.' Her tone said Heaven forbid! but she regretted the haughty note upon the instant for it made her sound an insufferable snob, and she was surely not that.

'No, indeed. My shop assistants display better manners,' said he with a mendacious calm. 'And have more useful occupations to fill their time.'

'No doubt you keep them chained to their counters,' Felicity retorted with some warmth. But her rescuer only smiled, his eyebrows twitching with an unexpected show of humour.

'That's what they are paid for.'

She had a sudden longing to prick the core of his amused arrogance and inform him of the years she had spent working in the medical mission with the sick and the poor, administering what simple relief she could to the women and children of India. But she bit it back, feeling sure he would dismiss such a catalogue as mere good works with no sincerity attached. Having decided what she must not say she was left totally speechless, forced to examine his decidedly handsome features in silence for a full half-minute. He seemed content to do the same to her before drawing in a deep breath and adding, somewhat brusquely, she thought, 'Would you have preferred to be taken in hand to the lock-up? I'm sorry if I offended your sensibilities.' He spoke as if she were not capable of owning any. 'But it was the first thing which came into my head. You have my permission to leave now.'

Turning his back upon her, he opened a drawer in a large walnut desk, and, withdrawing a white cotton handkerchief, began pointedly to dust away the flour from his face and the spoiled front of his waistcoat.

Felicity gasped. His permission, indeed. Who did this man think he was? Some clerk from her father's accounts department, no doubt.

'And take this ridiculous hat with you,' he said, sealing her opinion of him and turning the rose to scarlet in her cheeks. If he knew that it was the owner of the store, his own employer, whom he was treating with such disdain, that would soon wipe the complacency from his tone. She could hardly wait to tell him. Felicity chose not to recall that he had in fact saved her from the arms of the law.

'I am not what you think,' she began as she looked up at him, clear grey eyes opening wide with entrancing gravity, experiencing a delicious satisfaction from seeing him finally lost for words.

But not for long. 'I can't imagine what your family is thinking of to allow a young lady such as yourself to comport herself in this fashion. A political demonstration is not the place to be wandering abroad,' he said curtly.

Felicity was outraged. He spoke as if she were no more than a child and she was all of two and twenty. 'I was not wandering. I had a most specific purpose in mind.'

'I saw the evidence of that purpose with my own eyes,' he said drily. 'I must congratulate you and your colleagues on effectively silencing the voice of an obstinate government, if but temporarily.'

'You misunderstand, sir.'

'My name is Jarle Blakeley,' he coolly informed her. 'And I do not possess a title, I'm glad to say.' And those that do, he thought irritably, often do not deserve one.

Felicity very nearly gaped at him. Jarle Blakeley? Her late father's manager? Not a gentle old man at all, but an arrogant boor of little more than thirty years who seemed to think he knew it all. She was about to inform him that she did possess a title and it was her ardent pride in that noble lineage which had brought her to call upon him in the first place when he took her completely off guard by intercepting her thoughts with the most incredible observation.

'Contrary to what you may suppose, neither the waif you so brusquely cast aside, nor his poor starved family, if indeed he has one, hold the vote either. His interests lie purely with filling his empty belly, though I doubt a fanatic such as yourself would be able to appreciate that.' He flung the soiled handkerchief in the waste-basket, feeling his irritation grow. It had been a bad enough day but now this campaigning female, no doubt from some modern-thinking middle-class family who had never known need or hunger, thought herself fit to speak for those who scarcely had time to lift their heads from counter or loom. Women like his own mother, for instance, who had brought up seven children chiefly by the sweat of her own brow and would not have had a moment spare to use her vote had she possessed one.

Felicity, meanwhile, was stinging from the seeming injustice of this attack. Yet even as she drew breath to retaliate a small voice of caution within bade her to take care with this man. He was not at all what she had expected and her mission loomed ominously.

'The waif, for your information, Mr—Jarle—Blakeley—sir,' she began, taking childish pleasure in the pedantic enunciation of his name, 'cannoned into me and not me into it—er—him.' She felt a hot tide of colour stain her cheeks at the slip but resolutely continued, 'Surely it will only be for the good of such children if women are granted the vote? Will it not at least give them a voice in the care of their own families?' she finished crisply.

It was not a question to which she desperately demanded an answer yet she saw him consider it with a surprised attention.

'I find your argument interesting. Pray be seated, Miss—um?'

'I prefer to stand,' she proclaimed, zealously ignoring her aching feet and feeling irrational fury as he abruptly sank into a deep leather armchair. The gesture was an open rebuke. No gentleman would ever seat himself while a lady still stood. Yet it proved preferable to standing beside his towering height which gave her a greater sense of inferiority.

He emphasised the insult by resting one long leg across the other knee. He had quite the shapeliest, most muscular thighs she had ever seen and she blushed to find herself so engaged in their scrutiny.

'Do you believe it wise for issues concerning women and children to come into the political arena?' he asked interestedly, as if they were engaged merely in a mild debate. Jarle was indeed enjoying the combat. He hadn't felt so alive in months. Her figure too was not displeasing despite its rather dusty, unkempt appearance following the disturbance. Let her try to convince him if she so wished. He was content to enjoy the view.

Felicity was frantically searching her mind for a sufficiently informed answer. Though her sojourn abroad, and sheltered upbringing, ill equipped her for this kind of verbal sparring, she was determined not to be outshone.

'I believe that women should be free to be themselves and not depend on any man for permission how to spend their purse, how to live their lives, nor how to govern their country. Women are taking more of a control over their own lives than ever before and choosing for themselves when or even if they will marry. Many are choosing careers or limiting their families to allow them greater freedom. I applaud such a movement even though I am no militant. We have a voice and should be heard,' she finished rather grandly.

'Well spoken,' he quietly remarked and she quickly searched his face for any sign of condescension, surprised when she found none. 'But many men honestly believe that women and children should be protected from politics.'

'Kept at home as slaves, you mean,' she retorted rather crossly.

'Not necessarily. Many women do not have a choice of career, as you call it. They simply have to earn their bread.'

He had a way of turning her own argument upon her, but she was not so easily put down. 'Then it is all the more important that they have an equal say in matters which affect their livelihood.' Got him, she thought and was again proved wrong.

He was on his feet, stabbing the desk top with a blunt-tipped finger as if to emphasise his point. 'If we clutter the statute books with the question of women's franchise there will be no time to put essential social reforms into effect. It will come, in good time. In the meantime there are more important issues at stake and women can be cared for by their menfolk, who very much enjoy doing it. Particularly...' he paused, and the seriousness in the brown eyes softened with a lively humour, as they moved slowly over the neat lines of her body, lingering for a second on the firm, rounded bosom before dropping leisurely downwards over trim hips to focus on a slender ankle charmingly revealed where she tapped her foot impatiently upon the carpet '...if the woman in question is a pretty woman.'

Her cheeks flamed and she jerked the foot back beneath the hem of her gown, away from his bold gaze. 'You go too far, Mr Blakeley. I take no political stance whatsoever but reserve the right, as a woman, to fight for my rights. However, enough of political argument. What I have to say to you——'

'I have heard many times before,' he interrupted, and, as if suddenly bored, got to his feet and strode to the door. 'And have no wish to hear again. Ladies dressed in green and white can scarcely claim to be taking no political stance since these are well known to be the colours of the suffragette movement. I can only be grateful you chose not to wear the hideously purple sash, since the colour would not suit you.'

'I—I did not realise...' Felicity spluttered.

'That I was so well informed?' came the infuriating and inaccurate response. 'If the pamphlet you so conspicuously carry did not declare your allegiance, the hat certainly tells all.'

Her hand flew involuntarily to her precious hat which she had attempted to reinstate and as she did so she watched with dawning horror as the half-crumpled, long-forgotten paper sailed zig-zag fashion downward to land at Jarle Blakeley's booted feet. Its title, 'Votes for Women', blazed across the top of the single sheet, followed by the name of the author, none other than Christabel Pankhurst herself.

Oddly discomfited beneath his assessing gaze, it was the hat she felt moved to defend. 'I do not understand how it could possibly give offence,' she declared, disappointment uppermost in her voice for of course she hated it now and would never feel able to wear it again.

He positively snorted his derision. 'It gives a good deal of offence when damage to person and property is perpetrated by selfish violence,' he growled, meaning the paper, and, rolling it into a ball, tossed it into the far corner of the room where it fell amid a pile of other papers. 'I recommend you fill your time more productively.'

'Doing what?' Felicity raised her small chin in defiance. 'Producing babies, I suppose.'

There came a dangerous sparkle in his eyes that for a moment robbed her of breath.

'Report here first thing on Monday morning. I will try to ensure that you not only learn the benefits of honest toil but come to understand more about those less fortunate than yourself.' He held open the door for her. 'It will also serve to keep you from further mischief.'

Felicity was astounded. Had she heard right? Was her own manager actually offering her a job? 'I beg your pardon?' she said in a tone meant to freeze but which brought only a smile to his wide lips.

Unperturbed, he continued. 'Naturally if you are already in employment you have only to say.' He paused for her reply, lifting one eyebrow in quizzical enquiry. When she did not answer he merely nodded and said,

'The wages I pay are not high, but then they are no lower than any other store of a similar nature. You may start at eleven shillings a week.'

Felicity gasped. Though she held a healthy respect for the world of work and had intended to find some useful duties to occupy her time when their affairs were more settled, this proposition was positively ludicrous and she would waste no time in telling him so. She looked up into those deep brown eyes, meaning at once to set him straight upon the matter.

'What time would you wish me to start?' she asked, quite putting herself out with the shock of it.

He was ushering her through the door and his brows lifted in surprise. She had spirit, he'd grant her that. 'Monday morning at seven sharp. We open at eight-fifteen and there's much to be learned the first morning, so don't be late. I trust you will find no difficulty in rising at that hour for once? Have your maid call you. Assuming you are not arrested in the meantime,' he finished with asperity and closed the door upon her strangled exclamation.

Out on the now quiet pavement, some piquant elf of humour rose in her mind and she almost laughed out loud. The absurdity of the situation at once incensed and captivated her.

With steady hands she adjusted the green hat, pulling down the gauze ribbons to tie them firmly beneath the small pointed chin. She had no intention, of course, of taking him up on the offer. Such an idea was quite unthinkable. Though a part of her mind acknowledged that the prospect was tempting. But no. She had other plans for Mr Jarle Blakeley. Plans she would take great pleasure in executing. Smiling reflectively, she turned upon her heel and walked briskly down Deansgate, a decided lift to her step.

CHAPTER TWO

JARLE BLAKELEY unrolled the sheet of parchment and stared at it with unseeing eyes.

His long fingers slid across its shiny surface, weighting down each corner with paperweight, inkstand, book. But still he made no effort to study the plan. Instead he turned his back upon the wide walnut desk as if wishing to dissociate himself from it and what it held. Hooking his thumbs into his waistcoat pockets, brow creased in thought, he began to pace restlessly, striding back and forth in the small room with a kind of contained athletic grace as if at any moment he would break into a run and quit its close confines.

There was certainly little enough space for such an activity. The panelled walls were crowded with all the paraphernalia requisite for running a large business, though the thick coating of dust lying upon cupboards, shelves and piles of ledgers that leaned drunkenly about the floor suggested it had not been run too well of late. Jarle took in the depressing scene with nothing more than bleak disinterest. Men were sailing the oceans, experimenting with tangled wires and tiny engines high in the sky. New industries were being born. Opportunities were passing him by and he was doing nothing about them. He felt jaded, lacking any appetite for life.

He must pull himself together. For a few moments the girl had brought fresh life to the gloomy office and to himself. The wide lips curled upwards in a self-mocking smile. At least it proved he was still alive in one direction. Staring down at the plan, he suddenly put out a hand and swept all the props away. The sheet of paper immediately curled in upon itself and rolled off the edge of the desk. Jarle made no move to retrieve it. Usually bursting with energy and ideas, he still lacked any zest for this latest enterprise, even after six whole months. Wrinkling his brow with self-loathing, he snatched up the telephone.

'Are you there?' he growled into it as if the unhappy person who received his call were quite deaf. 'Jarle Blakeley. You asked me to contact you.'

He listened in silence for a moment, then his whole body jerked and he almost dropped the mouthpiece. 'Tomorrow? Impossible.' Again silence as the lips gradually tightened. 'Very well. I'll be there.' As he thrust the mouthpiece back upon its hook, the usual satisfaction he felt at possessing such a modern instrument was absent.

Glowering dark eyes swivelled relentlessly round, fixing themselves with fascinated anguish upon the sepia photograph, already beginning to fade at the edges. He gazed at it for a long silent moment. 'It was a mistake, Tom.' He gave a snort of self-derision as if amused by his own folly. 'When will I ever curb my impulsive nature? I should have learned that lesson long since. But it is done now and there is an end to it.' Then, without a flicker of expression upon his face, he turned from the photograph and, opening the door, he called across the floor to where two young girls were tidying boxes of ribbons.

'Amy. Fetch me a cup of tea, will you, love? I feel as if I've been in a desert.'

She looked up and her eyes kindled merrily. 'Looks more like a salt-mine to me.'

He grinned at her, though without his usual good humour. 'And a clean jacket and waistcoat.'

'Right, Mr Blakeley.'

He closed the door and went back to sit behind his desk but he did not pick up the ledger upon which he had been working before the commotion in the street had disturbed him. He sat staring into space, his mind whirling.

And what would the plain, homely daughter make of his strange agreement with her father? The wry smile dissolved into a frown as he picked out a steel pen and absentmindedly began to polish the nib. One thing was certain. She must never learn the truth. He rather thought that would be far too much for a gently raised female to bear.

'Here y'are. I've brought you a nice cup of Indian. That'll perk you up,' Amy said presently. 'Give me your jacket and waistcoat, and I'll sponge it down for you.' She gave a little chuckle as she left. 'Sorry it had to be you at the end of that. I can think of plenty who deserve it more.'

As Jarle put on the fresh jacket and waistcoat she had brought he shook his dark head in despair. Even young Amy seemed to be in sympathy with the suffrage women.

His gaze was drawn back to the tea by a thin curl of steam emanating from the spout of the brown teapot. Indian tea. A frown puckered his brow and his mind leaped back to its earlier musings. There was something wrong somewhere, more than even Sir Joshua had realised, and come what may he would get to the bottom of it. But he had not expected the family to return so soon, no doubt the result of that interfering old busybody Redgrove.

Jarle stared down at the flowing handwriting scripted in stark legal terms with many heretofores, parties of the first part and inasmuches, but the essence of it was that the time had now come for him to fulfil those terms. What would they be like? A tweedy, loud-voiced dragon of a mother and a weedy scraggle of an unmarriageable daughter? He'd promised to do his best by them and he would, for was he not a man of his word? Shuddering with distaste, he started to pour out his tea.

* * *

Pushing open the faded maroon door of Canning, Lee
and Redgrove, Solicitors and Commissioners for Oaths,
without troubling to use the brass knocker which looked
in dire need of a good polish, Felicity felt ready for anything. Since her encounter with Jarle Blakeley, an idea
had formed in her mind. Whatever reasons Papa had
had for keeping all knowledge of the shop from them,
no doubt nothing more than foolish pride on his part—
ever a family failing—Felicity was certain she could learn
to run it herself. Why ever not? Women were taking vast
strides forward as the suffragette movement so ably
demonstrated. Her heart gave an odd little jump at the
prospect of working in close proximity with Jarle
Blakeley. She had quite forgotten her intention to dismiss
him and now wondered if he would accept her as an
employer.

'I am so sorry to have insisted on your coming to my
offices,' intoned Mr Isaiah Redgrove as Lady Travers
and Felicity seated themselves as comfortably as they
might on the hard chairs in the lawyer's inner sanctum.
A reed-thin man, he seemed as musty as the premises
he occupied, his black cloth suit quite green with age.
'Only I wished most particular to speak with you before
you returned home to Hollingworth House, ma'am.'

He cleared his throat and, drawing a black silk
handkerchief from the top pocket of his morning coat,
dabbed at his lips and then at his brow. Felicity watched,
fascinated. Never had she seen such a funereal handkerchief before, and it sent a shiver down her spine, for
it seemed to presage ill tidings. Yet what could be worse
than the death of a much-loved father?

'Pray tell all, Mr Redgrove,' she said firmly, tilting
her small pointed chin upwards and smiling at him most
charmingly. 'I am sure we are quite able to withstand
it.' She was wrong, for by the time Mr Redgrove had
finished his tale Felicity had grown quite pale and her
mama had pitched forward into a dead faint right on to

the poor man's blotter. It took two restorative glasses
of his best port before they were quite the thing again.

Once Carmella was duly installed in prickly conva-
lescence upon Mr Redgrove's horsehair sofa, Felicity
turned to him, her expression grim. 'Are you trying to
tell us there is no money, no money at all?'

'As I said, Miss Felicity, Sir Joshua was in deep
financial difficulties with considerable debts.' As a groan
emanated from Lady Travers he hurried on desperately,
'He was a most generous man, as you will be only too
well aware. Sir Joshua chose to sell the farms and cot-
tages and most of the land over the years for far less
than their market value, to the sitting tenants, thus relinquishing all hope of further rents for himself in order
to give them the security he believed they needed.' Mr
Redgrove looked faintly disapproving at such philanthropy. 'I warned him at the time of the effect such an
action would have upon his investments but his mind
was set.'

Felicity linked her fingers together in her lap and let
out a small sigh of resignation. How like Papa. She could
not quarrel with his principles, even though it now left
his own family in a decidedly precarious position.

Sir Joshua Travers had been a delightful combination
of qualities; a proud but caring man. A man of honour
and tradition, content to neglect his own affairs and his
ancestral home in the service of his country. For as long
as Felicity could remember he had acted as emissary and
later ambassador to the late Queen, from Ireland to
Africa and countless places in between. More recently
he had proved particularly successful in assisting the
Viceroy of India with the reform of the administration
in its task of increasing association with Indians. His
love of India had been intense and had inspired Felicity
to leave her boarding school in England before the appointed age to share in India's vivacity and colour and

take her own useful part in the family's efforts to serve their adopted country.

But Papa had given no indication that money was in any way a problem. In comparison with most of the populace of that country how could they fail to feel wealthy? And there was entertaining to be done, servants, regal apartments to be kept, and all the panoply of pomp and fashion that accompanied such a lifestyle. Sir Joshua was also one of the most generous donors of funds to every worthy cause that sought his aid and had never refused Felicity in any of her schemes. On the contrary, despite his somewhat narrow views of women, he had always been most insistent that she perform her duties conscientiously.

He had been a good, kind father, albeit with exacting standards, and she had loved him dearly.

Mr Redgrove gave a small, polite cough. 'It was at my request that Sir Joshua made what sadly turned out to be his last visit to the mother soil, but I was most concerned about his financial position. And there was, of course, the question of the shop.'

Jolted from her reverie, Felicity brushed the start of tears from her eyes and shifted forward in her seat, eager to learn all she could, for this piece of property could well prove to be their salvation.

The lawyer lowered his voice, for he felt sorry for this delightful girl and her mother. Living a life in India he could not begin to imagine had undoubtedly undermined the poor lady's health. 'Some time ago, Sir Joshua purchased a large drapery and fashion emporium which he intended to extend by adding further diverse departments. Quite the rage now, I understand.'

'My husband made no mention to me of this draper's shop,' burst in Carmella in hurt tones.

Mr Redgrove tutted consolingly and shifted some papers unnecessarily upon his desk. 'You might well look shocked, Lady Travers. Yet I sympathise with Sir

Joshua's motives in keeping the matter hush-hush. Had it been generally known that your husband was so thoroughly embroiled in trade...' Isaiah Redgrove studied the grain of the leather-topped desk. He did not relish what he had to tell these good people. 'His social position would undoubtedly have been in jeopardy, his immediate resignation would have possibly been demanded from every club of which he was a member. It could well have jeopardised his entire career.'

Carmella wailed into her handkerchief with great energy.

'But I'm afraid he paid the business scant attention and it became far from profitable. So it was perhaps for the best that you were saved from the taint of trade.'

'I see no "taint" in trying to earn an honest living,' retorted Felicity hotly.

'I am sure you will think so since you are a very modern, democratic young lady.' The solicitor made it sound as if she had a disease. 'Nevertheless, however estimable you might think it, for a man in your father's position, employed as he was by the Crown, to be involved in trade to that extent could only be viewed by his peers as dubious.'

Felicity cringed but offered no further argument, knowing it to be very likely true. Old ideas died hard.

'You said it was not profitable. Why was that?' Lady Travers intervened with a return of her accustomed shrewdness which Felicity could only envy. She had quite overlooked the point.

'Ah.' Mr Redgrove steepled his fingers reflectively. 'Now that is the puzzling part. The annual accounts appeared to be perfectly in order yet Sir Joshua's overdraft grew beyond all expectation.'

'Overdraft?'

'It is painful for me to say it, ma'am, but the situation was dire. Sir Joshua obstinately refused to discuss the

matter with me; none the less, extreme remedies were
called for if the ghoul of bankruptcy was to be avoided.'

'Bankruptcy?' Carmella could scarcely utter the word
between lips gone suddenly dry. It was far worse than
Redgrove's first intimation of huge outstanding debts
had intimated. How were they to survive? She glanced
across at her daughter, so proud, so strong, if decidedly
too homely-looking for her liking. Then she thought of
Gilbert Farrel, long picked out as a husband for Felicity
and soon to follow them from India. Would he still want
her without a penny to her name and the debtor's prison
a step away? And if he did not, who else would? It was
all too terrible to contemplate. 'I cannot bear it,' she
cried, rocking her ample figure back and forth upon the
sofa.

Concerned that her mother might swoon again,
Felicity hastily intervened. 'What is to be done, Mr
Redgrove?' she asked practically, grey eyes wide with
fright. 'I am strong and could work, pay off the debts
as soon as prudent, but b-bankruptcy?' Her lips faltered
over the word for the prospect was fearsome.

Mr Redgrove leaned forward and touched the smooth
slender hand with an avuncular pat from his paper-dry
fingers. 'Now, do not distress yourself, my dear Miss
Felicity. The matter has been well taken care of.' He
would have taken care of it himself if he'd been able for
one smile from those lovely young lips.

Carmella gave a little cry. 'Do you mean we are not
to be destitute after all? There, I knew Joshua would
see us safely placed.' The tears were rapidly drying upon
Carmella's cheeks and she was all attention. There must
be some way to save them from the shame of privation.

'You are little more than a child, m'dear,' Redgrove
was saying. 'And exceedingly pretty with your honey-
brown hair and candid charm. Most valuable assets.
Many a gentleman would welcome a helpmeet such as
yourself upon life's journey.'

Felicity froze with a new fear. 'I am not in the market for a husband and if Mama were not in shock she would vouch for it. I can work. I do assure you that, no matter how long it takes, all debts will be settled, including, Mr Redgrove, your own legal fees.'

'Ah,' said that gentleman with a philosophical smile. 'They never are, m'dear. They never are. Except, of course, in this instance.' There was something dangerously close to a twinkle in his faded eyes and Felicity's suspicions grew.

'Are you funning us, Mr Redgrove? Did Papa settle his debts before his death, after all?' She held her breath as she waited for the reply. 'Please come to the point, do,' she cried.

He was startled by her vehemence and the yellow cheeks took on an almost pinkish hue. 'I am coming to it. Legal matters cannot be hurried,' he said ponderously, wishing the whole interview were done with and he could slip round to the Wheatsheaf for his usual lunch of pork pie and pickles. 'It was not your poor dear Papa who saved you from the courts, but Mr Blakeley, an extremely wealthy, self-made man who bought Sir Joshua out, lock, stock and barrel.'

'Lock, stock and . . . ?'

'Barrel, Lady Travers. It is a business expression, I believe, ma'am. It means——'

'I know what it means,' she thundered, and both Redgrove and Felicity started. The latter hid a smile for Mama, it seemed, was coming to herself again. 'Presumably this does not include my home, Hollingworth House?'

There was the most dreadful silence. The leather in the old chair creaked ominously as Redgrove tried desperately to sink back into it. The conversation was not going at all as he had planned. 'I—I'm afraid so, ma'am,' he spluttered, gasping for breath like a stranded fish before hastily continuing in a gabbling tone, 'But it is perfectly possible for you to continue to live there.'

'How so?' she demanded in ringing tones, making the lawyer cringe. 'Does this Blakeley fellow intend to charge us rent?' The voice was awesome, that of a woman who had ridden on elephants through primitive mountain villages without a word of complaint. A woman who, despite a tendency to vanity, had followed her husband up river and down valley, often with wet feet and a pounding headache, and had returned at the end of the day to smilingly host a seven-course dinner for twenty without turning a hair.

Judging by her hysterical manner that afternoon it was not surprising that Mr Redgrove had underestimated her. Now he gave a high strangled croak which might have turned into a laugh were it not so ill advised to do so just then. All his carefully rehearsed speeches were in tatters and he blundered on, every shred of tact gone from his head.

'No, indeed. It was agreed that should Miss Felicity still be a spinster on his death and without provision, Sir Joshua ensured you would both be able to remain at Hollingworth House as Mr Blakeley's wife and mother-in-law. It was a clause in the contract, a necessary provision, if Mr Blakeley was to take him over. Do you see...?' His voice faded into pained silence.

If Felicity had grown pale at first mention of a serious financial crisis, she now turned deathly white. Grey eyes stood out dark and frightened and she swayed slightly upon her feet so that she had to reach out and grasp the corner of the lawyer's desk.

Carmella was not so overcome and sat straight and alert as a cat which had just been shown a jug of cream. 'You say this Blakeley fellow is wealthy?'

'Exceedingly.' Mr Redgrove did not miss the change in her tone and almost fawned in his eagerness to please. 'A very fine man, Lady Travers. Owns various prop-

erties. Mills, hotels, houses. And sold land for a huge
sum to the Great Western Railway Company.' He leaned
closer to whisper confidentially. 'No one can put a figure
to his fortune but it is undoubtedly immense.'

The silence which followed this statement sent the
blood roaring through Felicity's head as she stared in
horror at her mother's enraptured face.

'Mama?' she croaked.

Lady Travers got up from the horsehair sofa and,
smiling, crossed the room to take Felicity's hands between her own. 'My dearest daughter. This gentleman
clearly requires a wife, as you do a husband. And I think
we have little choice but to at least consider his suit.'

Spinster was such a horrid title and one Felicity had never
thought to attach to herself. Now she did so and it made
her feel distinctly unhappy. The alternative, however, was
even less palatable. Yet she was haunted by the memory
of a pair of serious brown eyes so strangely at odds with
the mocking tone and she groaned out loud.

'Are you feeling ill?' Carmella enquired solicitously,
and Felicity assured her that she felt quite herself, which
was the greatest untruth she had ever told.

They were travelling by hired chaise to Hollingworth
House but any pleasure of a homecoming in the fresh
spring morning was quite spoiled as far as Felicity was
concerned.

Felicity stared unseeing at the rolling Pennine hills
which lay like a humped green velvet carpet down the
centre of England. She gave none of her usual attention
to the flower-decked hedgerows filled with the white
blossom known mysteriously as 'bread and cheese' in
those joyous days of her childhood. Not even the rus-
tling charms of the tall horsechestnut trees, bursting into
pink budded glory, could splinter the shackles of her
misery.

'You must say at once if you do not like him,' said Carmella decidedly. 'I am sure I would not have you marry with someone you detest on sight. Though I confess I thought Joshua a poor weed when I first saw him. But we came to make a good enough pair in the end. It will be a little difficult to explain it all to Gilbert, I dare say, but we shall think of something. Besides, he has had ample opportunity over the past years. I cannot imagine what held him back,' Carmella tutted and looked to her daughter for a response but Felicity only returned her abstracted gaze to the passing scene, a blur before her dazed eyes.

She had forgotten how green England was, and how beautiful. Her vision focused momentarily on a family of hedge-sparrows noisily squabbling over living space in the crowded hawthorn. For some reason it only increased her sadness.

Gilbert Farrel, wealthy businessman and socialite, was considered quite a catch by most of the mamas of the British contingent in India. Felicity had known him for a long time, and, despite his careless idle ways, which tended at times to irritate, she liked him well enough. They had talked of marrying, possibly next spring when he would join her in England, after a suitable period of mourning had elapsed. Yet she had had her doubts, and perhaps Papa had had them too in the end. When Sir Joshua had returned from that last visit to England, the mark of death already upon him, he had been most insistent that Felicity did not rush into a hasty marriage with Gilbert. She had wryly thought it could hardly come into that category, but since her father's sick-bed had not been the place to discuss such matters she had simply set his mind at rest. Believing his concerns to be motivated by the fact that he did not wish his beloved daughter to leave him, she had stayed by his side even as he slipped into the coma that was to claim his life. Now an altogether different liaison was being forced upon her, one she dared not even contemplate. She could not imagine why her father should consider marriage with Jarle Blakeley preferable to her long-standing engagement with safe and reliable Gilbert.

'Ah, the market cross. See, Millie, we are almost home,' cried Carmella, leaning forwards in her seat, her pale cheeks quite pink with excitement, and Felicity sighed resignedly.

Ever one to take on the shackles of duty, the prospect of that duty's including marriage to a man she despised was more than she could bear. She had certainly never intended a stern, self-seeking businessman for a husband, one who was bent only on buying himself into the British aristocracy by way of a wife. She shuddered, filled with a bitter nausea. But what other course was open to her? She could not forsake her family's honour and her father's wishes, nor abandon poor Mama, and of course Millie, to penury. The prospect was quite unthinkable.

Casting a sideways glance at Carmella, Felicity noted the lines of tension around her small, once pretty mouth. Despite her tendency to fluster, and her obvious disappointment that her daughter had not turned out to be as stunningly beautiful as she would have wished, Felicity knew she was not nearly as selfish as she made out. There would be sulks, of course, if she refused to marry him, but Carmella might come to accept it. Yet there was no denying the inherent fear of destitution, no matter how well hidden. And, worse, Felicity knew that her mother dreaded the prospect of being foisted upon some reluctant relative as companion, to end her days as an ageing burden propped in the corner to read newspaper clippings or serve tea.

Felicity sighed again and blinked back the unwished-for tears as the chaise bounced over a ridge and passed between two familiar tall gateposts. And as the vehicle bowled along, she looked about her with a new interest. The rough grasses had been cut and become rolling

parkland. The old yews had been clipped into fine
examples of formal topiary they had not resembled in
many a long year. Leaning forwards in her seat, she examined with startled surprise the sweet-scented order of
the rose gardens, almost restored to their former glory
with even the broken sundial replaced. The orchard was
thick with blossom and the herbaceous border already
stood proud, promising to be a riot of colour when
summer dawned.

'Are you quite all right, darling?' Carmella asked,
giving her daughter's hand a small squeeze.

Felicity swallowed the sudden constriction in her
throat. 'Yes, Mama. Quite all right.'

She could remember the mellow charm of the house
which had grown over the centuries from a modest
country manor to one of sprawling dimensions. Vastly
extended during the Georgian era when Joel William
Travers had been rewarded with a baronetcy for his part
in the Seven Years War, the projecting wings and the
grand curving exterior staircases on the central block had
replaced its homeliness with a bolder, almost palatial
composition. She recalled games of hide and seek along
its endless corridors, listening to the cooing of wood
pigeons in its acres of woodland and roaring log fires in
the depths of winter. But then she recalled her parents'
exclamations of dismay whenever they returned from a
sojourn abroad to find a carpet quite worn through or
a banister needing replacement.

'If only my ancestors had left me the funds to feed
the monstrous appetite of this beast,' her father would
moan. 'Everyone will simply have to stop walking about
the place, then perhaps it won't fall down,' and the child
she then had been had laughed, not understanding.

But whatever the inconvenience of its outmoded
grandeur it had been her home, solidly in the background, a security waiting for them to return to when
the days of service and duty were done. The Travers

family had built Hollingworth House and lived in it for more than five centuries. She could scarcely contemplate the prospect of entering it as a guest of a new owner.

And what would be Jarle Blakeley's reaction when he saw that the bride he had acquired in his iniquitous business takeover was the very same suffragette who had splattered his handsome face with flour?

CHAPTER THREE

FELICITY and Jarle glowered at each other across the hearthrug in what had once been her papa's study. For a brief moment, Felicity had enjoyed a delicious sense of superiority at the sight of the mouth dropping agape in the handsome face. The recalcitrant suffragette had been the last person he had expected to see step in upon his mat that day.

'Mr Blakeley,' she murmured, giving a gracious inclination of her head, aware that on this occasion every neatly brushed hair was in place and her suit of cobalt blue set off her colouring to perfection.

'What the d——?' The gape was replaced with a tightening of the wide lips, cutting his own words sharply in mid-sentence, though they were both well aware that by now he had guessed exactly who she was.

Tossing her head, she gave her most winning smile, which, as Millie had so often said, would freeze the whiskers off the next door's cat. 'May I introduce my mother, Carmella, Lady Travers?' Felicity said, trying to disguise the slight tremble in her voice. She had forgotten how good-looking he was. But she must strive to hold to her carefully nurtured confidence and not be overset by such a trifling matter as money. After all, when did the aristocracy ever consider it?

There was a moment's frigid silence as his glare cut into her own but then he blinked and, swinging upon his heel, extended a hand to the small but elegant lady smiling innocently up at him. 'Lady Travers. I am delighted to make your acquaintance.'

Carmella flushed like a girl as she allowed him to kiss her hand. How charming he was. How handsome. She could hardly believe their good fortune. If only Felicity would stop sulking darkly in that foolish way they might swiftly come to a most agreeable arrangement. 'Allow me to introduce Millie, my one-time nanny, now our dear friend and companion.'

Jarle stuck out a hand which Millie took in her forthright way and gave it a good shake. 'Good afternoon, lad,' the old woman said and Jarle's grim face suddenly relaxed.

'You from the North too?'

'Aye. One time I was, long ago in the distant past.' Millie beamed at him. 'Still shows, does it?'

The great man suddenly gave a spurt of laughter. 'Aye, lass, it still shows.'

'Eeh, nah then. You sound proper North country yourself.'

'I was born and brought up in the wilds of Lancashire. My mother was a weaver,' he saïd with evident pride in his voice, 'and a fine one at that.'

The two grinned at each other in a companionable way and Felicity felt oddly discomfited. It did not seem right for Millie to be so friendly with this man. It was rather like consorting with the enemy. Yet she supposed he had saved them from ruin so perhaps she should temper her own natural instincts of animosity a little. Under different circumstances she might even... She cut the thought off abruptly before it entered dangerous ground.

'No doubt you will wish to freshen up,' he said. 'May I show you to your rooms?'

'I dare say we can find our own way,' said Felicity cuttingly. 'After all, I was born and brought up in this house.'

He regarded her thoughtfully for a moment before answering. 'But now it is mine,' he said very quietly.

'And, though I have tried to keep things much as they were in your own time here, you will undoubtedly find some changes. The place was in a sorry state, to be truthful, and in need of much work. To date I have done little more than clean it up and make structural work safe. The next task is complete refurbishment.'

'I was quite happy with my bedroom the way it was,' said Felicity frostily, causing Carmella to glance nervously at Jarle Blakeley, half expecting him to react badly to this remark. But he said nothing, merely smiled and held out his hand to indicate they should precede him up the stairs.

Feeling faintly piqued, with a flounce of skirts and toss of her head, Felicity did so. Carmella placed her hand upon Jarle's arm and they followed together at a more sedate pace.

'How very kind you are, Mr Blakeley. Pay no heed to Felicity. She tends towards belligerence when she feels insecure. It will pass. I declare we do not mind in the least which rooms you give us, though I would prefer Millie to be close by, if that is not too much trouble?'

Blakeley smiled. 'Of course it is not, Lady Travers. I trust you will soon feel quite at home. At dinner I will introduce you to my own family. My sister, Kate, is looking forward to meeting you. As is Uncle Joe, though you may find him a trifle eccentric. He prefers to dine in his own quarters.' He offered a rueful smile and Carmella laughed. She liked this young man.

'I'm sure we shall rub along famously. I didn't realise you would have such a houseful.'

'My family is extensive. I hope you are not too alarmed but I feel it only right to offer some of them a home.'

'Most commendable.' Carmella squeezed his fingers playfully and, reaching up on tiptoe, whispered against his ear. 'I, for one, am not sorry to be free of the responsibility of this mausoleum, so put away your guilt, young man, and save your charm for those who need it.'

They both glanced instinctively upwards and for some seconds Jarle was mesmerised by the sway of trim hips even if the booted feet did slap down rather crossly on the polished boards. She was really quite pretty, in an individual sort of way. Pity she was so ill tempered.

Felicity, however, could not fault him on his choice of apartments, which proved a further source of irritation to her. Even more vexing, the rooms looked considerably better than she had ever seen them. But they did little to lift her spirits and she decided to leave her unpacking until later when she felt more rested. Secretly, she was hoping for a way out, a miracle which would release her from her duty, and then she could go away again without bothering to unpack at all. Putting a cold cloth upon her head, which was beginning to ache, she lay down upon the bed.

Carmella found her there an hour later, which put that good lady into quite a fluster. 'Whatever is the matter with you, girl? Why are you not dressed?'

Felicity did not open her eyes. She did not wish to look upon the world. 'I do not feel very well,' she said limply.

'What nonsense.' Lady Travers, already splendidly attired in vivid purple, sailed across the room and flung open the wardrobe doors. 'Why, you have not even unpacked. You must endeavour to look your best, Felicity, and do try to be more agreeable.' She came to take her daughter's hand and put on what Felicity recognised as her wheedling voice. 'Do you not think that Mr Blakeley is a most attractive man? I declare I do not understand your sulks. Many a young lady would give a good deal to be in your shoes. Now, please put on your sweetest smile and your prettiest dress.'

'So that he can better inspect the merchandise?'

'Do not condemn him before you have scarcely spoken two good words together,' said Carmella briskly.

Felicity decided not to enlighten her on the fact that they had in fact spoken many words together, and none of them good. 'How can you take it all so calmly?'

'Because, my dear daughter, I learned long ago the inestimable value of one of Millie's many sayings, "bear and forbear".'

'And "what can't be cured must be endured",' quoted Felicity grumpily. 'I know. But I swear I could not endure marriage with Mr Jarle Blakeley for even a week.'

Lady Travers, however, had heard enough, and was whisking out dresses with abandon as she called out in her stand-no-nonsense voice, 'Millie, Millie, come.'

And Millie came.

In no time at all Felicity was washed, powdered, brushed, and dressed in petticoats and lacy chemise.

'Now, which shall it be?' said her mama thoughtfully, rifling through dresses. 'The green or the pink?'

Felicity almost opted for the green but thought better of it. 'Perhaps the pink. Somehow I do not think Mr Blakeley will care for green.' She had bought the dress on a whim and had not yet found an occasion to wear it, for it seemed so utterly frivolous with its french knots and tuck pleats upon the most flimsy of fabric.

Millie curled and patted her hair, puffing it out in the manner dictated by the fashion magazines without recourse to hot waving irons or aids to beauty optimistically termed 'transformations'. She then tied a small bunch of matching pink ribbon at the back and suggested a black velvet choker to finish the picture. But Felicity opted for her silver locket which contained a tiny photograph of her father. Millie fastened this about her throat and stood back to admire the effect.

'There, you look a real bobby-dazzler.'

Even Felicity had to admit the result was most flattering, the soft colour of the dress highlighting the silky bronze glow of her skin, and she gave a small smile at her reflection in the glass.

'That is much better,' said Lady Travers, clapping her hands with delight. 'Now keep that smile safe, darling. Remember, we have no dowry for you now and our situation is grave, to say the least. I'm afraid beggars——'

'Can't be choosers,' finished Felicity, and they both burst out laughing.

He was not sure how he had expected her to look. But not like this. Privately astonished by the change in her, he could scarce take his eyes from her throughout dinner. She looked somehow smaller, gentler than he remembered, more fragile, despite the healthy outdoor glow of her fine skin which he did not find at all unattractive. Perhaps he hadn't made such a bad bargain after all, if he could only coax away that sullen pout.

Dinner was a carefully courteous affair, the conversation skilfully led by Lady Travers, who was well accustomed to avoiding difficult subjects. The two main protagonists were no more than coolly polite to each other.

The only other person present, Jarle's younger sister, Kate, seemed to be a shy, retiring sort of girl and scarcely opened her mouth, except to eat, throughout the entire meal.

Felicity did ask her if she had any kind of job at the emporium but she shook her head, looking faintly shocked.

'Oh, no. I leave all that to Jarle. I only help in the house and look after Uncle Joe.'

Felicity ventured an encouraging smile. It would be pleasant, after all, to have a friend. 'Then I dare say you busy yourself enjoying dances and musical soirées and such.'

Again the vigorous head shake with wide, frightened eyes. 'No. I should not enjoy that at all.' Whereupon she turned her attention so firmly back to her plate that Felicity abandoned the effort.

The meal at least was excellent, consisting of baked trout followed by lamb outlets and finished with the most delicious custard tart. It appeared to be both cooked and served by one robust personage named Jessie who cheerily told them that she and Millie would enjoy a good chin-wag later when they had time to sit down with their own meal. Intrigued by the seeming lack of servants, unusual in a house of this size, Felicity ventured a question as soon as Jessie withdrew.

'If you are experiencing any difficulty acquiring staff to help your housekeeper, I am sure Mama could be of assistance. It may well be possible to find some of our old servants. They were always loyal,' she said, making a point.

A pair of deep brown eyes studied her gravely for a moment. 'Thank you, but I have not looked for servants because I have no intention of living here.' Turning to Carmella, he continued, 'Forgive me, ma'am, but I consider this house belongs to an age now past. In this new century life becomes too hectic and a smaller, more comfortable home would be more practical for me.'

'Oh, I do so agree,' said Carmella, helping herself to a second slice of tart. 'You can burn half an acre of woodland keeping this place warm. Josh used to suffer apoplexy at the bills.'

'I have had central heating installed.'

'Good gracious, what an expense!' Carmella regarded him with new respect.

'Coal is easily had these days,' he smilingly told her. 'And it is essential that the place is kept warm. I have certain plans for it.'

Felicity glanced up from her intense study of the tablecloth, interested, despite herself, in what these plans might be. But she waited in vain as he calmly continued, 'I am having the lodge house prepared and, when the builders return on Monday to start the second phase, you will find it more comfortable, and certainly quieter, to remove to there.'

'That is most kind,' said Carmella agreeably. 'I must say the house is much improved already, and certainly warmer.'

At the end of the meal, Felicity was surprised to find Jarle Blakeley did not follow the normal custom of staying on to enjoy a brandy and cigar in the dining-room. Instead he repaired with the ladies to the library and took coffee. He chose to drink it, however, while pacing the hearthrug which left everyone feeling vaguely unsettled. At length he set down his cup, and, turning to Carmella, cleared his throat.

'Forgive me, Lady Travers, but I am a plain man and can only speak plainly.'

'A quality I admire,' said she.

Felicity's heart seemed to freeze in her chest and her breathing became excessively painful. She could guess what he was about to say. The word 'duty' resounded in her head like a bell toll.

'Your husband, Lady Travers, as you may be aware by now, was in deep financial difficulties and I was able to—well, to bail him out.'

'For which I am most grateful.'

Felicity ground her teeth but said nothing.

'I admit I was not unwilling. The emporium has great potential and I was interested in venturing into the retail market. But Sir Joshua did insist upon certain conditions, special clauses in the take-over contract, to which I was obliged to agree. It is not difficult to make such agreements from a distance, if you understand me.'

'I dare say it must be,' she said, most agreeably, and Jarle wondered how this gentle, smiling lady would react if he bluntly told her of his general distrust of those of

her class. Yet how could she understand? Privileged and
cosseted as her life had been she knew nothing of ex-
ploitation, nor of the spectre of poverty which in his
worst nightmares still stalked his coat-tails. Nor had he
the appetite at present for long drawn out explanations.
A wife had always figured somewhere in Jarle's plans
once he found the time and inclination to look for one.
But he'd kicked himself a dozen times for allowing
Travers to win that particular part of the agreement, and
foist upon him some female he had never even seen. Now
he was not so sure. Looking at Felicity as she sat across
from him, ankles demurely crossed, the glow from the
crackling log fire softening her face and burnishing her
hair almost to hot pepper, she looked as unlike the dull,
faded spinster he'd anticipated as she possibly could. She
bore little resemblance either to the militant, flour-
throwing suffragette, a side to her nature he'd do well
to keep in mind. Even so, he was not against spirit in a
woman.

But the girl looked pinched and downright miserable
and it occurred to him then for the first time, and with
some surprise, that she might well be less happy about
this arrangement than himself. If that were indeed the
case then best to have it out in the open. He had no
intention of forcing himself upon her.

'There is no necessity to proceed with this marriage
if it makes you unhappy,' he said to Felicity, with a di-
rectness which caused her to start and look up at him
for a moment before jerking her gaze back to the spurting
flames.

Her eyes were a most unusual shade of grey, he noticed, at complete odds with the hair. In fact everything
about her was unpredictable, from her varied tastes in
clothes to the seeming deviousness of her nature.

'Now that I have met you both, I feel I must say that
so far as I'm concerned the contract need not be considered binding.' Jarle paused, studied Felicity's silent

profile for a second, then firmly brought his own gaze back to Lady Travers. 'You will be very welcome to make your home in the lodge house for as long as you wish, and an allowance will be made available to you both as I promised your husband, ma'am. But I'm sure your daughter has her own ideas how she wishes to spend her life, and need not feel bound to keep to the terms of the contract simply for your sake. As I said, you will be provided for in any case.'

It was a generous offer and one Carmella met with tears falling from the blue eyes as she searched for the lavender-scented scrap of lace to mop them up.

But if Felicity had expected to feel a surge of hope at this offer of freedom, she experienced instead quite the opposite effect, much to her dismay. The provoking thought uppermost in her mind was that he did not want her. He did not like her. What could be wrong with her? Probably she was too plain for his taste, homely, as Mama often said, and far too unfeminine. The prospect of their marrying must be even more abhorrent to him than it was to her, she thought, her stomach sinking with depression.

'There is surely no need to come to any hasty decision on that score,' Carmella was saying—with some haste. 'Quite frankly, I do not subscribe to over-organising parents on such a delicate issue, not in these modern times.' She smiled lovingly at Felicity, who sat stony-faced. 'I recommend you talk the matter over with my daughter first, in your own good time, of course, and she can relay to me any decision which is reached.' She smiled up at Jarle with undoubted charm and he saw the echo of the beautiful woman she once must have been. 'The idea is new to her and she may need a little time to consider. I thank you for your kindness on behalf of both of us, and you are quite right. Felicity is well able to earn her own living, I am sure, and we simply must not think about the shame of it all. I can always hem handkerchiefs or some such, for the last thing we wish is to be a nuisance.' She gave a little laugh, trillingly feminine.

It was a clever move and both parties recognised it as such. No pressure was to be brought to bear, other than that of loyalty, duty, honour and most of all, family pride. For any financial assistance Jarle Blakeley offered would clearly smack of charity and be despised by the independent-minded Lady Travers as much as by Felicity herself.

Felicity watched in despair as her mother swept from the room, followed by the scurrying figure of Kate, with the agony of one who knew herself abandoned to her fate.

There was a long unearthly silence, then, seating himself opposite to her and resting his elbows on his knees, he leaned towards her. 'Why did you play that foolish trick on me?' he softly queried and saw her inwardly squirm at the question.

'It was unintentional,' she said, so quietly he was compelled to lean even closer to hear. 'The flour packet was thrust into my hand before I realised.'

His eyebrows quirked upwards, though whether with disbelief or amusement she could not tell. 'Then you do not follow the suffragette creed?'

She was instantly on the defensive. 'I did not say that. Women have a right——'

He held up one hand, palm flat to halt any further speech. 'Spare me that argument again, after such an excellent dinner. I think it would give me indigestion.' He smiled at her and she felt the muscles at the corners of her mouth quiver an unexpected response. 'Would you object if I partook of a small brandy?'

She shook her head, feeling suddenly shy. Uncoiling his long legs, he moved over to a small table where a tray of glasses and bottles had been set. She watched as he poured himself a measure, the only sound in the room

that of a softly ticking clock and the burning logs settling in the grate. A peace descended upon them and she
found herself surprisingly comfortable in this room, with
him. 'Will you answer me a question?' she ventured.

'If I can.'

'If Papa was in such dire straits that he had to sell,
why did you feel it necessary to agree to that particular
clause?'

He regarded her steadily for a moment. 'I'll be honest
with you. I was afraid he would opt for an alternative
buyer. I wasn't the only one interested. This emporium
may not seem of any great importance to you but it has
undoubtedly the best position in town and the space
necessary to build it into a fine department store, which
I fully intend to do.'

It was not a particularly flattering remark and she
found herself wincing involuntarily, yet was determined
to pursue the point. 'But you had never seen me. I could
have been awful.' Realising the immodesty of her remark,
she flushed more charmingly. 'Sorry, what I meant
was——'

He took a step towards her. 'No, don't apologise.
You're quite right, you could have been awful.' He
paused significantly and smiled down at her. 'But you
are not. Any man would be proud to have you as a wife.'

For a long, quiet moment their gazes locked and the
grim expression upon Felicity's face finally melted, her
heart giving a funny little jump.

'That's better,' he murmured. 'You have a delightful
smile. You should use it more often. A grumpy wife is
no asset to anyone.'

She was on her feet in an instant, facing him with a
proud, pink-cheeked defiance. 'An asset. Is that all you
seek? Someone to host your table and smile upon your
guests? You could get such a creature from one of the
new mail order catalogues, I am sure.'

He laughed as if she had made a joke. 'But they would not be half so much fun as you. It is a pity, in a way, that we could not make a go of it, for I admire your spirit tremendously,' he said with playful good humour. 'I think we'd make a good team.'

She was insulted. 'A good team? What do you take me for? A horse?'

But he shook his head vehemently. 'Good lord, no. I'm not in the least interested in horses, foolish, unpredictable creatures prone to easy panic. Perhaps I should have said, partner. I believe we could make quite a good alliance, Felicity, you and I.' And as she made to speak again he placed the tip of his finger on her soft lips to silence her as he continued, 'Perhaps you should not dismiss it quite out of hand. Is the idea quite so unthinkable?'

His eyes glowed disturbingly as he moved nearer and she felt the heat from his lean body perilously close to her own. She pushed his hand aside and squared up to him, back ramrod-straight. 'I am already engaged, as a matter of fact, to——'

'Gilbert Farrel, I know,' he said, quite taking her by surprise.

'How did you...?'

'Know?' He gave a lazy smile, and his gaze moved over her face as if he studied every feature. 'I know a good deal about you, Felicity. More than you know about me.'

Unsure how to take such an enigmatic remark, she felt quite at a loss for words, but, though he was not touching her and she longed desperately to break away from him, she found to her chagrin that she could not. Finally she said, very quietly, 'You don't know me at all, and by the sound of it have no wish to.'

'How many years has this so-called engagement lasted? Is it two or three?' he mocked, ignoring her comment.

'Had I the good fortune to be the recipient of your love, I would not wait two or three months.'

'You would wait in vain,' she told him through gritted teeth, hating him for touching upon her one raw spot, Gilbert's apparent lack of urgency for consummation of their betrothal. 'For I could never love you, never in a thousand years.'

Capturing her chin in his hand, he stroked his thumb upon her lips, pushing them open a little in a movement that was unashamedly sensual. 'Oh, I think you could be persuaded,' he whispered meaningly and her heart squeezed with embarrassment, and something else she dared not put a name to.

'I suppose you want me to grovel my thanks to you for your generous offer of release but I swear, Jarle Blakeley, that I will find some way of caring for Mama and of gaining Hollingworth House back from you.'

'Your mama very sensibly does not want it. She is content to stay in the lodge house.'

'As a guest of charity?' Felicity flung the words at him with a bitterness she could not disguise, and finally managed to free herself from the hypnosis of his hold.

'Do you have a viable alternative? If you will not accept the provision your father arranged for you, which you dismiss as mere charity, how then will you live? On eleven shillings a week as a shop girl?'

She felt dangerously close to tears but would not for a moment let him see that. 'Hollingworth House has been in my family for generations; how dare you steal it from us?'

'I did not steal, I bought it. I am considering making it into a hotel.'

The effect of this statement upon Felicity was shocking. She stared at him as if he had suddenly grown two heads. To lose her home, their security and honour had been awful enough to contend with, but this was even worse. The thought of a constant stream of strangers parading through the corridors of her beloved home, sleeping in their bedrooms, her own bed even, made her go hot and cold with fury. 'I do not believe you would do such a thing,' she said in a hoarse whisper.

He shrugged his shoulders with an easy nonchalance. 'Why not? It is set in beautiful countryside and more and more people are becoming interested in their health and taking to holidays for recuperation. It's a growing business and one I intend to be in. I expect to make good profits.'

'Profit.' She almost screamed the word, backing away from him as if he were unclean. 'Is that all you think of? I would never marry you, Jarle Blakeley. I release you from your promise to Papa. It wouldn't surprise me in the least if it wasn't you who drove him into bankruptcy. I am certain somebody did and who better to gain from it? I'd sweep the streets sooner than be your wife.' Thrusting her head high, she almost ran to the door, and, wrenching it open, half turned to make her parting shot. 'But do not think you are rid of me so easily. I shall take you up on your challenge. I shall report for work on Monday morning to your precious store and fight you every inch of the way. One way or another I will win back what is rightfully mine or at the very least restore Papa's good name.'

Jarle did not reply. He looked on in open admiration as, leaving the door to swing wide, she flounced across the hall, small feet clicking angrily upon the marbled tiles. For a whole long moment he stood rooted to the spot, brows creased in thought. Then he was striding in her wake and from the foot of the stairs he called up to her, his voice carrying to the far reaches of the domed ceiling.

'Here is another challenge for you. You have one month to prove me guilty. If you succeed, everything will be returned to you, house, shop, land, everything. If you fail you must accept your father's solution.' His words echoed around the empty hall. 'Do you hear me? Felicity?'

She gripped the banister rail with both hands to stop herself from falling. 'I hear you,' she said, and her soft words floated down to him.

'Is that a deal?'

Always the businessman. Always making deals. She looked down the well of the stairs at his upturned face, boyishly eager and alert with his challenge. Then she looked upwards and thought of Mama in her distant bedroom and the future which faced her living on charity, owning nothing, not even her pride. But it was the touch of her fingers on the silver locket which reminded her of her true purpose, and, as they tightened, so did her lips with fresh resolution, so that when she uttered the single word of assent he wasn't sure at first that he had heard correctly. Then as she marched primly up the remaining stairs a slow smile spread across his face. This could prove to be the most interesting deal he'd ever struck.

CHAPTER FOUR

'*FIDES SUPRA OMNIA.*' Felicity murmured the family motto
to herself, like a benediction, as Jarle drove her into
town. She must never forget her purpose in agreeing to
this wild challenge. She was quite certain that she would
succeed. Hadn't Redgrove indicated there were puzzling
features in the shop's lack of profit? It would have been
perfectly simple for Blakeley to undermine the efforts
of an absent proprietor and, having reduced him to the
verge of bankruptcy, find him more than willing for a
take-over. Moreover, the very idea of Papa selling her
off as a chattel, when he was most happily disposed to
her betrothal with Gilbert, was utterly ridiculous. The
idea made her go hot and cold all over. Poor Papa. She
must be excessively vigilant. Somehow she would discover the truth, she was sure of it. Then, and only then,
would their future be secured and their rightful heritage
restored.

Casting a sideways glance at Blakeley's impassive
profile, half hidden by the French driving goggles he
wore, she noted the solid squareness of the chin beneath
the high cheekbones. Was that a sign of a ruthless
nature? The mouth was wide and she recalled its sensual
quality with a slight flutter in the pit of her stomach.
Yet it was ever turned down, emphasising an inherent
sadness in the face, and for a moment she speculated on
the reason. Then, to her supreme embarrassment, she
found he was returning her stare.

'Are you cold?' He spoke loudly over the sound of
the engine and she shook her head, trying to smile in a
natural manner as if she had not just been examining

his face. 'It's a Renault Landaulette, shaft drive, six-cylinder,' he told her.

'I'm afraid I know nothing of motor cars.'

'It's a symbol of the new age, of which I intend to be a part. Great things are expected of the combustion engine. Queen Alexandra herself is a great devotee of the horseless carriage.'

'Indeed?' she shouted back, but she was paying little attention to his words. Instead, her mind was asking how she would feel if she failed the challenge, or merely succumbed to her father's will, and the obvious answer obstinately refused to present itself.

'Though it seems to me,' he continued conversationally, 'that no sensible woman, whatever her nerve, would care to use the fastest make of automobile.'

'Why ever not? Do you think women such insipid creatures?' Felicity was indignant.

He turned his face to grin at her. 'Don't bark at me, Felicity. You must admit that when a car is mechanically more complicated it would not be at all suitable for a lady. Driving a motor car is considerably more difficult than pushing a perambulator, you know.'

Felicity held on to her calm with some difficulty. 'Then what are the requirements of a good driver?'

'A steady nerve, good eyesight and plenty of sense.'

'In which you presumably find women singularly lacking?'

'I didn't say that,' he protested. 'But I wouldn't want any wife of mine driving a car alone and risking being stranded on an open road.'

Felicity paid no heed to this natural concern. 'Since you are so fond of challenges, then I will issue one to you. I am not your wife, so show me the controls and I'll prove that I can drive this car as well as any man.'

To her astonishment, the seriousness in his face vanished and he chuckled with laughter. 'Not yet, you are not. What a woman. But no, wife or no wife, absolutely not.'

'Then I shall find someone else to teach me one day,' she retorted recklessly. It was only as she flounced back into her seat with a self-satisfied sigh that the nervous butterflies began to beat their wings in her stomach. What had she said? Must she always be trying to prove herself? Too used to trying to please Papa, that was the nub of it, but she had no need to impress this man. The thought of handling a huge, evil-smelling machine filled her with utter terror. Biting hard upon her lower lip, she determined no more rash words would issue forth.

To her intense annoyance, Jarle was still chuckling. 'I fancy you'll have enough new skills to learn to keep you more than occupied over the next week or two, so put away your feminist sword and pick up your duster.'

If they had not been negotiating a rather tricky corner into Deansgate, trying to avoid barrow boys setting out their wares, hansom cabs, omnibuses, and a surprising number of people despite the early hour, she might well have found a suitable rejoinder to this inflammatory remark. As it was, the nearer they came to the huge emporium, which seemed now to glower in the grey morning light, the more her confidence gradually seeped away.

Once inside, she followed his long stride on scurrying feet to the small untidy office where she had faced him before. He at once seemed to forget her presence and busied himself pulling out papers from commodious drawers, and opening enormous ledgers. She stood irresolute before the wide desk, a small, insignificant figure feeling very much the new girl and not liking it one bit. She was dressed in a quarter-length coat and skirt of Saxe blue with a draped waistcoat of blue-spotted white silk over a lacy chemisette of lawn with the highest boned neckline which was all the vogue. High upon her coif of hair sat a matching hat with two quill feathers in blue and white which bobbed lightly to and fro as she twisted her head this way and that, watching him at work, waiting for him to attend to her. At length she could stand it no longer.

Clearing her throat noisily she addressed him in a voice which sounded more confident than she felt. 'Where would you have me start?'

He glanced up at her, a blank expression in his eyes. He had forgotten I was here, she thought, feeling piqued.

'Ah,' he said unhelpfully and looked at her for a moment, his brow creased in thought. 'We must find you something more suitable to wear,' he said.

Defiantly she raised her chin, which was a feat in itself since that part of her anatomy was already held aloft by the uncomfortably high collar which pinched alarmingly. 'What is wrong with the way I am?'

He gave what sounded very like a snort of derision. 'For Ascot possibly, or even tea with your maiden aunt. For a working day it is entirely impractical.' He strode to the door.

'In your opinion,' she ventured, rather daringly, as he did not at all seem the kind of man used to being thwarted.

'While I accept that you have excellent taste, so long as you work here you will be treated the same as everyone else, which includes a uniform.'

Her heart sank. If she had a weakness, she realised, it was to be smartly dressed. She had always enjoyed fashion and did not care to look a dowd, not for anyone. She was about to tell him so, but he had already left the room, calling for someone called Amy.

For a long moment she stayed where she was, uncertain whether to be angry or agreeable. After all, there were more important matters at stake than her costume. Then a natural curiosity asserted itself and she began to look about her. Here she was, alone in his office. What better opportunity to take a quick look about?

Glancing covertly at the closed door, she slipped quickly behind the large walnut desk, its polished surface littered with books, ledgers and papers.

Heart beating painfully, her fingers shook as they turned over crisp pages in the red ledger. What should she look for? What kind of evidence did she need to prove that Jarle Blakeley had cheated her father? Columns of figures blurred dazedly before her eyes, making not one jot of sense.

The other items on the desk seemed to offer no scope at all. There was a seal with a lever to impress it upon the wax, a blotter, a silver paper cutter and an ivory shoe horn. Blakeley clearly appreciated beautiful things for all the chaotic disorder. She adjusted a brass-framed daily calendar to show the correct day. There was a pair of letter scales with brass weights marked with weight and price of the stamp on one side and on the other, in place of the expected letter, was a small heap of tea leaves. A leather envelope-box shaped like a small portmanteau held a small sack of tea, some of which had spilled out upon the polished surface of the desk. Hardly the way to treat a good Darjeeling, she thought, folding the sack up to stow it neatly away.

'Have you concluded your search?'

She started guiltily, much to her dismay, spilling more of the tea as she quickly withdrew from behind the desk. His thick black brows were drawn together so tightly that they looked like one and certainly set Felicity quaking but she had no intention of showing it. 'I was merely tidying your dreadful muddle.'

'I don't believe I asked for your assistance in that department,' he said coldly.

Felicity rubbed kid-gloved fingers together to brush away some tea-leaves, irritated at finding herself at a disadvantage. 'I was trying to preserve the flavour of your Darjeeling, which had been left open, but it was quite unnecessary. It is a most inferior quality,' she finished, rather priggishly.

His brows lifted a fraction in surprise, eyes glittering with sudden interest. Mama was right, Felicity thought with surprise, there is a certain attractiveness about him despite the slightly crooked nose.

'How do you know about tea?' he asked in clipped tones.

She could still smell the delectable scent, for all it was not of the best quality, and instantly she was reminded of her trip into the Himalayas with Gilbert. Together they had toured the tea plantations which clung to the terraced sides of the steep mountains. Had it been only last summer? How safe and well ordered her life had been then. Now it was as muddled as this room. 'It is not possible to live in India and not learn about tea,' she told him, as if he were some kind of fool.

He did not answer her immediately, merely stood there, chewing upon his lower lip in a most odd way, and she began to feel uncomfortable. What was it about this man which goaded her so? She became aware that she was still holding the small leather box in her hand and she set it hurriedly back upon the blotter. Only then did she become aware of another person in the room.

A girl dressed in a black stuff dress had come to stand beside Jarle. She had fair hair screwed up into a bun and Felicity was relieved to see that the pale blue eyes held a warmth and a sympathy which at that moment were more than welcome.

'I would be obliged, Amy, if you would direct Miss... I beg your pardon, the Honourable Felicity Travers, upstairs and find her some suitable working clothes.'

Felicity turned crimson to the roots of her burnished hair. It was a deliberate attempt to embarrass her by using her full title while immediately humiliating her by referring to the working clothes. He had certainly succeeded.

'Thank you. I should like that,' she said politely, smiling at Amy with a rather tremulous stiff-lipped smile.

Blakeley gave a brief nod. 'I'll leave it to you then, Amy, to direct our new assistant in her duties.'

'You can that.' Amy paused as they were about to leave the office. 'And is she to start in the usual way?'

The mobile eyebrows lifted with a quizzical expression for a brief moment. 'But of course. We can make no exceptions, not even for a young lady with a fine taste in hats and a very long name.'

As soon as the girls had climbed the narrow wooden staircase, worn smooth with countless pairs of feet, Felicity hastened to rectify any ill opinion Amy might have formed as a result of Blakeley's taunts. 'My name is Felicity. I should prefer it if you simply used that and didn't mention to—to anyone else about the title.'

Amy looked at her consideringly, then beamed cheerfully. 'That's all right by me. Bit of a mouthful anyway.'

Amy hid a slight smile as she led Felicity along a dark corridor. Bit of spunk, this one. Mr Blakeley might well find he'd met his match for once. Felicity fortunately did not notice as she was too busily occupied looking about her and wondering what exactly was meant by starting off 'in the usual way'.

They emerged at length into a long, high-ceilinged room divided into several cubicles, and, as Felicity looked down the length of it, she was frankly appalled by what she saw. Each cubicle contained two, sometimes three iron bedsteads crowded together, a single chest of drawers and a wash-stand. There was scarcely room to stand between these stark pieces of furniture, let alone wash and dress. Nor was there any window in the cubicles. The only source of light and ventilation came from a single window at the far end of the room. A threadbare strip of carpet ran between the two rows of beds but the floorboards in each cubicle were bare.

Felicity shuddered. 'Do you live here?' she asked, regarding Amy with genuine compassion.

Amy gave a philosophical smile. 'This isn't half as bad as some places I've worked in, I can tell you. Here we do at least have a separate dining-room, a sitting-room and a tiny room with a shelf of books, albeit a small one, that is known as the library. That's a laugh, anyway. Who has time to read here, even if they all could?' But she wasn't laughing, Felicity noticed, and nor could she. Fresh stirrings of anger kindled to life within her against Jarle Blakeley. How dared he treat her father's employees in this heartless, uncaring manner? In all her years of experience with servants, she had never seen staff so thoughtlessly and inadequately housed.

'Where do you girls bathe?' Felicity enquired, glancing about, for she could see no further door which might lead to a bathroom.

'If you're lucky and can get your hands on enough hot water, and it's not Saturday or Sunday night when there's none at all, you washes yourself here,' she said, a touch of asperity in her voice. 'So long as you don't mind an audience, that is. There isn't much privacy hereabouts, as you can see.'

'Couldn't you live at home?' Felicity asked.

'If you want to work, which we need to do, you don't have much choice but to live in. Bosses prefer you to be handy for an early start and at least it saves long walks home in the dark through the city streets.' Felicity conceded this was an advantage. 'Course, it also means you can be worked overtime at a moment's notice, if someone's sick or it turns extra busy, say.'

Felicity recalled the brightly lit paradise she had glimpsed in the main part of the shop below and could not help wondering what the customers of this wonderful emporium would think if they could see what lay behind its magnificent façade. She decided at once to try to bring about what improvements she could. 'Presumably you get paid extra for overtime?' she enquired, genuinely concerned about the well-being of her new colleagues, but Amy, taking a black uniform identical to her own from a large cupboard set in the wall, only laughed.

'Chance would be a fine thing. Old Bridget rules with a rod of iron. She decides who gets extra. And who doesn't,' she added ominously.

'Bridget?'

Amy started down the length of the room, 'I'll tell you about her presently. For now, get yourself into this.' She handed over the uniform as she stopped by an unmade bed in an end cubicle, a plain pillow and a small pile of blankets neatly folded upon the mattress ticking. 'This'll be yours.'

'Mine?' Astonishment made Felicity's voice sharper than she intended.

'Your things are being sent on, Mr Blakeley said,' Amy told her as she began to unfold blankets. 'Unfortunately this cubicle's next to the sick bay, which is why no one has chosen it. Still,' Amy shrugged her shoulders, 'you won't be here for life, will you? Not like some.'

There was a small awkward silence. The thought of the future was not a prospect which Felicity cared to pursue, so she stuck to more practical matters. Offering a smile to her guide, and glancing about her, she asked, 'Where do I hang my things?'

'In the big cupboard down there. Everyone uses it.' Amy looked apologetic. 'There's nowhere else. When you've changed, come straight downstairs. I'll wait for you.'

Swallowing hard on the lump that had risen in her throat, Felicity peeled off her fine new clothes and began to dress in the long black stuff skirt and blouse, relieved only by a plain white stand-up collar. She felt almost unreal, as if she were watching from outside herself, and, as she hung her own clothes in the big cupboard as directed, she wondered when she would next be able to wear them. She had to admit she had not fully considered what working at the emporium would involve. Certainly it had not entered her head that she would have to live here. But, as Amy quite rightly pointed out, she had little cause for complaint, for her position here was merely temporary. When she had regained her rightful inheritance as she fully intended to do, sweeping changes would be made. Stowing the hat on a top shelf and giving it a last regretful pat, she started down the stairs.

'Now I'll take you to the dreaded "haby" counter,' said Amy as soon as she joined her. Pulling a face, she explained that this was short for haberdashery. 'There are several hundred items in stock for which you need an excellent memory and endless patience. It can take a quarter-hour for milady to choose the right size of elastic.' Both girls collapsed in giggles at this but then Amy was instantly serious again.

'The worst part of it is that you'll be apprenticed to Miss Bridget. I hoped to get you out of it but Mr Blakeley says, no, same for you as everyone, so there you are. She always deals with new apprentices and if you survive her you can take anything. She's a devious old coot and that's putting it kindly,' stated Amy bluntly, then added, 'Can you reckon?'

'Reckon?'

'Add up and take away?' When Felicity smilingly assured her that she could indeed do simple arithmetic, Amy gave a sigh of relief. 'Well, that's all right, then. She hates mistakes in the bills.' Amy hesitated at the door before entering the main shopping hall. 'I'll fill you in on the rules for living-in and meals and such this evening but there is one golden rule which you must learn right away. Never allow a customer to leave if she has not made a purchase.'

Felicity was dumbfounded. 'But how can I do that?' She had an instant vision of herself physically restraining large ladies who were obstinately determined to stalk from the store unsatisfied since she had failed to suit them with just the right shade of blue ribbon or whatever.

'With tact and diplomacy,' instructed Amy. 'You must call the floorwalker, Mr Reynolds, and ask him to help. Miss Bridget is most particular about it, so see you remember.'

'It all seems very silly,' scoffed Felicity. 'How can you possibly satisfy every customer?'

But Amy looked anxious. 'Fail in this and you will be instantly dismissed. You must take care. They don't call her the "dragon" for nothing.'

Stricken into silence, Felicity obediently followed Amy into the shop. It was not going to be at all as she had imagined.

In this, at least, she was absolutely correct. At first sight of the formidable lady herself, dressed in the regulation black—although it was clasped at the neck with a small cameo brooch in place of the white starched collar—Felicity trembled. The black eyes were like small jet beads set in the flat cushion of an impassive face and Felicity very much doubted if it ever showed any expression, let alone anything as reckless as a smile of welcome.

Resolving not to show her apprehension, Felicity folded her hands at her waist and prepared herself for the worst.

'Come here, girl, let me look at you.'

Felicity dutifully allowed herself to be examined from the top of her neatly confined hair to the toes of her very sensible boots. 'Humph.' As if disappointed at being able to find no fault, Miss Bridget proceeded to deliver her usual lecture. 'There will be no transgressions on my counter, gel, no gossiping, lounging about in an unbusinesslike manner, no flippancy, slip-shod work-manship nor wastefulness.'

'I shall do my best to please,' said Felicity, anxious indeed that she should do so. The last thing she wanted was to cause offence to such as Miss Bridget. She had quite enough on her mind.

'Humph. See that you do,' said Miss Bridget again, and, hooking a pair of wire-framed spectacles upon her narrow nose, she glared at Felicity from above them, which seemed rather to defeat their purpose. 'Young gels need discipline as they are too well endowed with evil propensities, particularly in the mass,' Miss Bridget informed her rather mysteriously. 'It is my sad lot to eradicate such ill-considered behaviour at the outset. It saves a good deal of trouble later. Do I make myself clear?'

Felicity ventured a smile which melted the iron frame not one jot. 'Perfectly,' she conceded. But if she thought this would be the end of the subject she was instantly disabused. Adjusting the spectacles, Miss Bridget began to read from a card.

'Fines instituted in this establishment are as follows. For gossiping, and suchlike reprehensible behaviour, threepence. Likewise for bringing a newspaper into the shop. I will endure no such vulgar rubbish. For not re-turning string, paper or scissors to their appointed place—threepence. For neglecting to date a bill for a customer—twopence. And sixpence for being late on duty.'

Felicity listened with increasing incredulity as the list went on, including a forcibly worded version of the 'golden rule' already outlined to her by Amy. She wondered anxiously if she would ever succeed in treading a safe path through this jungle of pitfalls.

But if she had anticipated any introduction or de-scription of the goods she was to sell she was soon dis-enchanted. Miss Bridget had her own ways of dealing

with newcomers which were clearly her only source of
entertainment. Stationing Felicity well away from the
counter where she might contaminate any passing customer, Miss Bridget bid her learn the contents of the
haberdashery drawers with all speed. Mindful of her
status as humble apprentice, Felicity made no protest
and began at once to read the neatly penned labels de-
scribing her stock-in-trade, as willingly as she was able.

It reminded her rather of a joke played upon her on
one occasion by the Indian mahouts who had challenged
her to mount an elephant without first telling her the
instructions needed to bring it down to a level necessary
to accomplish this seemingly impossible task. Now she
resolved yet again not to be daunted. She had succeeded, eventually, with the elephant by judicious use
of a small baton, her limited knowledge of Bengali and
her own innate charm. Charm, she suspected, would be
of little use with Miss Bridget, nor did the woman show
any vestige of a sense of humour, quite unlike the
Bengalis.

Feeling increasingly bewildered, she tried to commit
to memory what sounded very like a foreign language.
Bone casing, busks, marking cotton, ferret cotton, crape
cords, hat bands and guards, pendants, tassels, linen
buttons, madapollams and puggarees. Whatever were
they? Such a profusion and variety of goods in all sizes,
shapes and shades it would take ten years at least to learn,
she was sure.

'Miss Travers,' called the 'Dragon', interrupting this
litany, much to Felicity's relief. 'Please attend to this
lady.'

Her first customer caused no problems, requiring as
she did only two yards of navy ribbon. Aware of Miss
Bridget's beady stare, Felicity directed the customer to
the chair provided while she measured out the required
length and cut it with the silver scissors which hung from
a tape on the edge of the counter. Her fingers shook as

she carefully wrote out the bill, placed it in the cash container that hung from the Lamson's overhead railway and pulled the cord. Felicity and the customer, much impressed, watched it zoom across the hall on the miniature cable, where unseen hands at the cash desk withdrew the bill and the customer's note and sent the correct change swishing back to her.

Flushed with this small success, Felicity returned to her daunting task with renewed fervour. Braids, buttons, buckles and beads, casings, chois skins, edgings. The day wore endlessly on, broken by a brief half-hour at midday to take a meal in the staff dining-room for which she had little appetite. But she was thankful for a sitdown upon the wooden bench, for sitting was absolutely forbidden behind the counter.

'How shall I survive?' Felicity groaned, rubbing the calves of her legs to restore circulation.

Amy smiled sympathetically. 'You'll grow used to it. We all do. Give it time.'

Time was something she had little of. If she was to be so well confined to her counter how would she ever have the opportunity to carry out the necessary investigations to save Mama from penury and herself from an unwished-for marriage? And how would she find the energy?

At tea Amy insisted she eat a slice of bread and butter, which was far from fresh, and a lukewarm cup of tea.

'Does Mr Blakeley ever come into the shop?' Felicity enquired, thinking that perhaps if she watched him at work, learned something of the routine, she might discover how he had perpetrated his fraud.

'Often. He is most diligent,' said Amy, and Felicity wasn't sure whether to be pleased or not by this declaration.

Felicity watched for Blakeley all afternoon and was disappointed when he did not appear.

It was almost seven-thirty and even Felicity, exhausted as she was, felt ravenous for her supper. Perhaps after she had eaten she would feel restored to normality, but somehow she doubted it. Early to bed was the only prospect which appealed.

At the last moment, just when Felicity had finished the tidying and dusting executed at the end of the day, and probably repeated first thing the following morning, a new customer appeared, demanding a length of sprigged muslin from a roll on the topmost shelf. Almost weeping with tiredness, Felicity pulled out the ladder and climbed stiffly up it for the umpteenth time in that endless day. Balancing the roll of cloth precariously on her shoulder she climbed slowly down and placed it on the counter. Fortunately it wasn't heavy as there was little fabric left on it.

'And what would madam require?' Felicity politely asked, holding the scissors aloft as she smiled in her most courteous fashion at the large lady seated at the opposite side of the counter, privately thinking the material could not be for her as it would not suit her. In this she proved correct.

'Two yards, girl, no, wait a moment. It is for a blouse for my niece and she is but a sprat. We'll say one and a quarter,' decided the doyenne of fashion, settling her net purse upon her ample lap and preparing to be waited upon.

Felicity's lips gave a betraying twitch, then, pressing them together, she measured and snipped with deep concentration. Aware throughout the transaction of Miss Bridget's coldly distant scrutiny, Felicity gave what she felt to be her finest performance, discussing the inclement weather and the difficulties of obtaining servants these days. But scarcely had the customer vacated the premises, and before Felicity had stowed away the remaining roll, the wrath of judgement fell upon her. So angry was Miss Bridget that if she had actually breathed fire, Felicity would not have been in the least surprised.

'And what *do* you think you're doing, gel?' the 'Dragon' demanded and Felicity froze, hating herself for the fear the woman instilled in her.

'I—I b-beg your pardon. I—I was merely putting this muslin back upon the shelf.'

Miss Bridget's clawlike fingers grasped the roll and plucked it from Felicity's hands. It fell with a bump upon the floor and rolled away, leaving behind one short length of fabric which was instantly snatched up and waved in Felicity's face. 'Of what use is this? You foolish girl. You have sold the customer such that the amount left is quite useless. We will never sell such a small piece.'

'I sold her exactly what she asked for,' Felicity protested, feeling rather unjustly accused.

'You are not paid to simply sell the customer what she wants. Any fool can do that, gel. You are paid to sell her what we want her to buy, therein lies the skill of the job. In this case a little attention on your part could have sold her the extra yard and a three quarters. As it is we will be forced to sell it off cheaply for a remnant.'

Felicity felt quite unequal to the argument and bleakly accepted the scolding which followed for some further moments before Miss Bridget concluded with the assertion that since the firm could not afford such losses, she would be charged a sixpenny fine.

'Sixpence? But I have not yet received my wages,' Felicity protested in horror.

'Nor will you at this rate, gel,' came the unforgiving reply. 'I could easily have taken another threepence off you at lunchtime for leaving a portion of mutton upon your plate. But since it was your first day I chose to be generous.' The jet eyes glittered. 'I will not always be so.'

Felicity swallowed hard on her misery, unwilling to risk any reply in case further retributions were exacted. Watching the ramrod back stalk away, she thought how easily the hard-earned wages, low as they were, could swiftly dwindle to nothing. And she and Mama needed those shillings, there was no doubt of that. She would evidently have to give more concentration to this iniquitous fine system. But worse than the money aspect was a general feeling of disappointment and despondency. She had put so much effort into this her first day. She had been patient and polite, kept her sense of humour with the most trying of customers and succeeded in making some very satisfactory sales. But not a word of praise or support had she received from anyone.

The gas lights in the shop had been turned down low and it was almost empty as hungry assistants hurried to their evening meal. Folding away her duster, Felicity set off in that direction herself, surreptitiously brushing the tears from the corners of her eyes as she did so when a figure stepped out from the shadows, startling her.

CHAPTER FIVE

'AND how has your first day gone, Felicity?'

'Very well, thank you.' Why could she never speak the truth with this man?

Jarle raised dark brows in a speculative query. 'I thought I saw you talking to Miss Bridget just now. Was it about anything in particular?'

Still stinging with humiliation, Felicity met his question with total frankness. 'She tried to fine me sixpence for not selling a precise amount of fabric.'

Jarle's dark brows drew together in a frown. 'And what did you say?'

'What can one say against such blatant unfairness?'

His lips tightened momentarily as he raised his gaze over Felicity's head to follow the wake of the stiff-backed figure. 'I thought I'd put a stop to all that,' he said, half to himself, through clenched teeth. Then, returning his gaze to Felicity, he continued with an evident attempt at patience, 'Miss Bridget's puritanical zeal sometimes exceeds the bounds of reasonableness. She believes mortification to be good for the soul. I will speak to her. In the meantime, you might choose to reconsider your decision to stay?'

Felicity tilted her chin in proud defiance. 'No, Mr Blakeley, not at all.'

He looked irritated by her denial and reached out to grasp her arm as she made to pass him. 'Confound it, can't you see this is no place for a lady such as yourself?'

She looked at him in some surprise. 'Why ever not?'

'This is a hard city, built on grit and backbone. There is no room for softness here.'

'And you think me soft?'

'I think you've led a sheltered life. These girls don't have aristocratic backgrounds,' he said bitingly. 'They come from poor homes where they were often starved or beaten. They're not polite, genteel gels, brought up to pass plates of cakes and do embroidery.'

Felicity could scarcely take in his words for the remarkable sensation it was having upon her being held so close to him, albeit by a grip oddly gentle despite the firmness of its hold. 'Can this be your prejudice showing?' she blithely enquired and was satisfied to see her shaft strike home as his dark eyes flickered with anger.

'No, dammit, it is not. These are not diplomat's daughters brought up to a life of luxury, but working girls, many with family problems,' he finished, with pedantic patience.

'I too am a working girl now, Mr Blakeley,' Felicity said, gently releasing her arm with some relief. 'And I have family problems of my own, so we should understand each other well.' Striding past him, head held high, she started up the stairs. He watched her go with a thoughtful frown before automatically going about his tasks, locking the great glass and mahogany doors and turning out the gas lamps one by one. He really ought to set about modernising the place. There was no excuse for living in the past. Some shops even had electrically operated moving staircases to take customers from one floor to the next. He gave a tired sigh. He had once had such dreams for Travers Emporium. His ambitious plans were all drawn up ready but somehow the heart had gone from him.

Jarle had first put in a bid for the shop some years ago but had lost out against Sir Joshua's larger bid. That was before his beleagured family had been touched by tragedy yet again. He'd resented it at the time so when Sir Joshua, a broken man, and Jarle had finally come to terms, he'd hoped that this new, once much desired acquisition would revitalise him. The remedy did not seem to be working.

Joshua's daughter, however, was a different matter. A dozen times he'd asked himself why he'd ever agreed to this crazy marriage contract. Had it been as a favour to an old man he'd pitied, or as some kind of penance to his own family? If that was the case then it showed how flawed had been his reasoning at that time. It was not possible to mend broken lives by taking on the responsibility of another. It merely added to his problems. He could kick himself for not grabbing the opportunity to be rid of this promise. Instead, he had embroiled himself further. If he could think of a way out without either of them losing face he would do so. But Jarle recognised in Felicity a proud stubborn streak very like his own. He guessed that if he insisted on releasing her from the obligation of marrying him or even handed her over the shop, house, the whole darned lot, pride would forbid her to accept. They'd got on each other's wrong side from the start somehow.

Perhaps if he talked to Lady Travers, made better provision, tried to prevent them from viewing his financial assistance as charity. There must be some way out of this predicament or he would be stuck with the Travers family, and Felicity in particular, for life. This latter prospect he viewed with mixed feelings. She was not unattractive by any means, and he had always admired a strong woman with a bit of spunk to her nature, but she was the most cussedly independent female he had ever met. Whatever he did, she would be bound to put the worst possible construction upon it. She was probably at this very moment plotting some scheme to best him. Giving his head an angry shake, rather like a dog ridding itself of water, he stalked back to his office. It was such a darned waste.

Felicity for once, however, did not have her mind on Jarle Blakeley. Taken aback by the number of shop girls filling the dining-room, she felt overwhelmed by the noise. The loud scrape of benches, the thump of plates on wooden tables and the loosening of what seemed to be hundreds of female tongues caused her to feel sick with tiredness. She drank some water and chewed at a thick, if slightly stale piece of bread and felt slightly better. The sight of the watery stew, however, made her feel distinctly worse. Consisting chiefly of cabbage and rather grey potato, a few scraps of unidentifiable meat floated in it, covered by a thin film of grease. Wrinkling her nose in distaste, Felicity pushed it away untouched.

The other girls didn't seem to notice, readily tucking in to the unappetising mess, talking all the while.

'Who is going to the meeting next month in the Free Trade Hall?' one thin, red-headed girl called out, receiving a varying degree of interest from the assembled company. 'Come on, some of you must be,' she persisted, and raising her voice continued. 'We've an important guest speaker this time. Annie Kenney herself has agreed to come and say a few words. So, come on, girls, what d'you say? She's a working girl like yerselves. Who's fer coming with me? We can't let the middle classes do all the flippin' talking.'

Several voices were raised in assent. 'No danger of that, Dora, with you around.'

'Which meeting is she talking about?' queried Felicity half under her breath to Amy.

'The suffragette meeting,' Amy informed her. 'Annie Kenney was a factory girl who started to follow the Pankhursts and is now nearly as famous as them and she certainly makes more sense to folks like us, being more down-to-earth, like.'

'Aye,' Dora butted in, green eyes ablaze with passion. 'It makes a change to have a celebrity at one of our meetings. I'm not interested in holding jumble sales to

raise funds for that London lot.' She gave a bitter little
laugh. 'Money's hard enough to come by fer ourselves
round 'ere. But I do want to see some action. Bring the
bosses into line if nothing else. Stop these crippling fines.
Give women the vote so we can look out fer ourselves
in future, eh? So, come on, girls, what d'you say?'

'That's right, our Dora, you tell 'em,' came a ribald
rejoinder and some of the girls cheered, but there were
one or two dissenters quietly grumbling about not
wanting to risk losing their jobs.

'Are you a suffragette?' Felicity asked, grey eyes wide
with surprise.

'Let's say we give our support when we can,' murmured Amy.

Dora grunted in disgust. 'She means we don't have
enough spare time to really make our feelings known,
not while we work twelve hours a day with scarcely time
off to draw breath. The middle classes now, have plenty,
and yet know nowt about our problems.'

'That doesn't mean that they don't care,' objected
Felicity, 'nor that they aren't entitled to want the vote
for all women. If they have the time, let them fight, for
you as well as for themselves. It's only fair.' Felicity
turned impulsively to the listening girls. 'But Dora's right.
You should go to the meeting. All women should speak
up for their rights. How else will we make progress?'
Her voice had become unusually vehement as she spoke,
and, when she realised everyone had grown quiet to listen
to her, she let it fade away into silence, instantly
embarrassed.

'Eeh, listen to her. Hoity-toity.'

Felicity felt very keenly the outsider as she returned
the hostile gaze of dozens of pairs of eyes with her own
less confident one. They were wondering who she
thought she was, this new girl, to tell them what to do.

'And would you be going yourself, then?' challenged
Dora, and the hush deepened as they waited for her re-

sponse. 'We've had plenty of ladies such as yourself here, who work only for pocket-money. But they don't really need to bother themselves about such matters, do they though?' she mocked, and, despite the warning pressure of Amy's fingers upon her arm, Felicity simply could not let that pass. If she was ever to have any credibility with these girls and be able to improve their living conditions, she had to be accepted as one of them. She had to show she was on their side.

'It may surprise you to know that I need every penny of this money I earn, as much as you do, if for a different reason.' She glanced around the tables at the attentive, honest faces. 'And I too would like to see changes, both in this shop and for women in general. I'll be there, Dora,' she said, quite quietly. 'At the front, with you.' There came a small cheer and even Dora looked pleased.

'Right. You're on,' she said with a grin. 'It'll be nice to have someone else besides me who'll speak up round 'ere.' She paused thoughtfully. 'At any rate, we'll soon find out if you mean what you say or whether you're all windbag and hot air. But if you're going to keep your strength up to fight, you'd best eat your supper.'

Felicity glanced down at the dish in disgust. 'This stew is perfectly dreadful. How can anyone be expected to eat it?'

'Perfectly dreadful, is it?' minced Dora, cruelly mocking her accent. 'If you'd been raised in a damp tenement with eleven brothers and sisters all fighting over every morsel, as I was, you'd be thankful enough for it. There are times even now when me mam will pop her own clogs to buy bread for 'em all. Aye, you can laugh, but it's true,' she retorted, red-faced.

'I may well have had a more privileged background but I do understand, Dora, and I assure you no one is laughing, least of all me,' Felicity gently told her. 'But that does not mean that you should eat what is obviously bad food.' The smell of rancid fat assaulted her nostrils and nausea threatened to overwhelm her. She could not possibly bring herself to eat it, not even to become one of their coveted circle. She pushed the plate away and Dora gave a snort of derision.

'Mutton stew too common for milady's delicate palate, eh? Oh, dear, oh, my. I feel so faint, I swear I shall swoon any minute.'

The bench rocked as the other girls roared with laughter at Dora's parody of a 'lady of refinement', touching her forehead with the back of a limp hand as she reeled in a supposedly delicate fashion.

'Why don't you complain?' asked Felicity in a tight little voice.

'Because we'd be out on our ears if we did,' said the reasonable-voiced Amy. 'For every troublemaker, there are two or more willing workers waiting to be taken on.'

'But if you *all* complained together,' protested Felicity in bewilderment, appalled to find this gruesome evidence of Blakeley's lack of concern, 'then someone would surely have to listen.'

'You'd never get the girls to do that,' said Amy. 'Dora's right in many ways. Most of them are too scared to risk losing their jobs. They daren't even get married or else they'll be dismissed.' She shrugged her shoulders. 'Anyway, you get used to it. There's plenty worse places.'

'Aye. Paradise Street, down by the canal for one,' quipped Dora. 'A misnomer if ever there was one.'

But Felicity sat staring at them both in horror. 'Dismissed, simply because you get married?' The more she learned, the worse it got and all because of fear. 'Something must be done.'

'Aye, happen so, but I'm not the fool to do it,' Dora said with a vigorous shake of her head.

'Then I shall,' said Felicity, quite taking herself by surprise. But having said it there was no turning back and she suddenly knew exactly what she must do. Getting to her feet, she took hold of the plate containing the offensive mixture, and, holding it well away from her nose, proceeded to walk down the length of the hall between the trestle tables. The noise and clatter in the long dining hall seeped away as word of her gesture flew in whispers about the room.

There was a rustle of skirts, then Dora was beside her, eyes burning fiercely bright. 'Here, he'll need a spoon,' she said, thrusting the implement into Felicity's hand.

Felicity exchanged a speaking glance with her erstwhile enemy. 'So he will, Dora. So he will.' Without a pause she stalked down the stairs and headed for the office. He was in there. She could see the light below the door. Without stopping to knock she turned the knob, flung open the door, and marching straight in thrust the plate of congealed stew on the blotter right beneath Jarle Blakeley's nose.

She stepped back to await his reaction, hands clasped behind her back so that he would not detect how they shook with nerves. She wasn't so very different from Dora and the other girls, after all. She had never felt so scared in all her life.

She thought of Mama, indefatigable, ready to abandon the security of a fireside to travel through the jungle on a chair slung between poles on long tours of the Indian Empire. She thought of darling Papa, ready to invest a little of his meagre fortune into a fashion emporium so that she and Mama would have a safe future, even if, through no fault of his own, he had lost it. Yet even to the end he had fought, however misguidedly, for their security. That was the kind of spirit which flourished in her family and it lived on, in herself.

She waited for him to speak. Why did he not? He was staring down at the stew as if he had never encountered such a thing in his entire life. Unable to contain her patience any longer, heart hammering most disconcertingly, she launched into a comprehensive roll-call of the shortcomings of his kitchens.

'These hard-working girls are given nothing but stale bread, sour milk, cold meat with more fat than mutton on it, and lukewarm dishwater that passes for tea. Now we are expected to eat tainted stew that is quite unfit for human consumption, let alone for hungry, hard-working men and girls after a long day's work.' Her anger grew apace with each itemised detail till her breathing was so rapid in her breast it pumped up and down like the bellows on a street organ. 'Try it for yourself if you don't believe me,' she cried, slamming down the spoon with a clatter.

The brows had drawn together over the crooked nose, while the devastatingly brown eyes darkened ominously as he regarded her for a long moment.

'Is this your latest campaign?' he said at last, quite illogically in Felicity's opinion. Her temper mounted and she just prevented herself in time from stamping her foot.

'Someone must speak on your workers' behalf, for they are too terrified of you to do it themselves,' she told him most fiercely, and then stepped back instinctively at the explosion of anger which met this apparent truth.

'Too *what*?' His whole awesome frame seemed to quiver with restrained rage. 'You storm in here with your suffrage pamphlets, and now on your first day don the role of Little Miss Goody Two-Shoes to help my workers as if they were the exploited poor. You dare do that to *me*?'

'Would you have offered to solve the problem otherwise? Were you aware of how your workers live?' she retorted and was pleased to see a crimson stain slowly rise upwards over the tightly clamped jaw.

'If action is needed regarding the food which my staff eat, I am perfectly capable of dealing with it myself,' he said icily. 'When I require your opinion on anything, Miss Travers, I will ask for it.'

He had always called her Felicity before. For some reason she grieved the loss of this little familiarity. Tossing her head, she moved to the door, deeming it wise to withdraw. While she still could, she thought. 'Whether you ask or not, I shall continue to give it,' she retorted, recklessly risking his further displeasure. 'I trust now that it has been brought to your attention something will be done to improve the situation.' She heard his teeth grind together and glancing back over her shoulder she saw him glaring at the plate as if for two pins he would fling it across the room. Hurriedly gathering her skirts in one hand, she pulled the door open with the other, anxious suddenly to be gone. When his hand closed upon her arm she started as if he had scalded her.

'Felicity. Am I truly such an ogre that my staff will not speak to me?'

She swung around, nonplussed by the apparent appeal in his voice, only to find her eyes on a level with the top of his waistcoat. Carelessly unbuttoned, it was of blue silk with a tiny imprinted check and the crisp white shirt he wore beneath was open at the neck, the sleeves rolled up above strong bare forearms. She could see a pulse beating at his throat and she scented the exotic tang of an after-dinner cigar. It had evidently been a working dinner, for there was still the day's shadow of bristle upon his chin. She gained an instant impression of loneliness and had the unwished-for regret come into her head that they should be on opposing sides in this battle. Why, she wondered, did there have to be a war?

She knew the reason and she must never forget it. She concentrated on the waistcoat.

'Perhaps you do not show enough that you care,' she gently suggested. 'It is surely important for an employer to be available to his staff.'

He drew in a deep breath. 'I suspect you are right, Felicity.' Perhaps it was this inherent sadness and not the return of his familiar use of her forename which caused the old sensation to flutter somewhere deep within her. 'It is true that I have spent too much time away, on the Continent, in recent months. Time I should have devoted to this shop. Now I see the result of such neglect.' He seemed to focus his gaze upon her, and it was soft and warm like velvet, yet it made her shiver. 'I should thank you, not scold you. I assure you, Felicity, that I have made improvements since I took over, and fully intend to make more. But there is a limit to what can be achieved here. Sometimes I feel as if I am ploughing a quagmire. The harder I push, the less progress I make.'

'Then you must try harder,' she said firmly, trying not to notice how the tip of one finger was sliding beneath her chin to tilt it upwards. But she could scarce fashion the words upon her tongue. Unable to resist him, she dragged her gaze from the waistcoat, and raised it to meet his. She was quite unprepared for the effect this seemingly simple action would have upon her. She felt quite light-headed and yet oddly stilled, as if he cradled close something he found in those grey depths. 'I-it is simply that I am concerned for their welfare. It is my duty,' she said at last rather weakly, wishing she had the strength to step back from his hold. She yearned for the security of her anger, yet it had quite gone.

He moved fractionally closer and for one terrifying, heart-stopping moment she felt sure he was about to kiss her, but then his hand fell away and he gave a dry, brittle little laugh. 'But of course. Behaviour one would expect from a committed suffragette.' And whatever spell had been present a moment before was now broken.

'Most certainly,' she agreed, moving away with mingled relief and regret from the magnetism of his hold. 'In fact, I have every intention of attending an important meeting with Dora, Amy and the rest next month when Annie Kenney comes. They have asked for my support and I shall give it,' she said, with some degree of exaggeration. 'None the less, I feel bound to say, Mr Blakeley, that it does not take an Act of Parliament to provide decent food and living conditions for your own workers. I trust you will attend to the matter with all speed.' Whirling upon her heel she left him. She was halfway up the stairs when she heard the door slam.

Jarle took his opportunity to speak to Carmella a few days later when he found her clipping sprigs of May blossom from a hawthorn tree in the garden.

'I hope you're not intending to take those indoors, Lady Travers,' he smilingly asked. 'It's considered bad luck in these parts.'

'Oh, dear, is it? I'd quite forgotten,' she said, faintly flustered, and he laughed.

'I can't say I believe in it, but Jessie most certainly does. Put them in the conservatory, then you can enjoy their heady scent without offending her country superstitions.'

'Thank you. I will do that,' she agreed. 'I am most grateful for your kind advice for I should hate to offend dear Jessie, she has been most solicitous of our comfort here.'

Jarle cleared his throat. He would never have a better opportunity. 'I was wondering, Lady Travers, if we might have a little talk?'

Carmella was all attention. 'But, of course, dear boy. Let us sit here beneath the cherry tree. I'd forgotten too what a very delightful garden this is.'

Once they were seated within the shelter of the arbour, Jarle half turned to her, concern imprinted on his face. 'Does it hurt a great deal to find yourself a stranger in your own home, ma'am?'

'Heavens, no. I will let you into a little secret, Mr Blakeley. After years of living in large, some might say palatial apartments, with countless rooms and formal gardens, I am more than ready to forsake them in favour of this delightful bower set so charmingly around the lodge house. Such places can be very impersonal, almost lonely at times.' She blinked rapidly for a moment then smiled at him with all the fresh enthusiasm of a child. 'I wonder, though, if you would mind if I make a few alterations to the garden? I should so love to have a small pond, and perhaps a walk set between that spinney of sycamores?'

Jarle responded with a warm smile. 'You must make whatever changes you wish, ma'am. Uncle Joe will help you. I know nothing of gardens. Besides,' He cleared his throat, wondering how to proceed. Best to be plain, he'd only make a worse mess of subterfuge. 'I was meaning to speak with you concerning your stay in the lodge, about your future. I should be honoured, ma'am, if you'd consider the property as yours for the remainder of your lifetime. I'm sure that is what your husband would wish, and it is what I wish also.'

'But where would you live?' interrupted Carmella, quite astounded by this generosity.

'I'm having a house built for myself, closer to town. If you wouldn't object to Kate staying with you here for a while, I'll bunk at the shop until it is ready.'

'But of course. Kate is shy, but an absolute darling. I am teaching her to play backgammon, and she is teaching me the intricacies of crochet. We grow very comfortable together.'

Jarle, thinking how eminently more amenable the mother was than the daughter, began to feel easier in his mind. Though he had to confess the daughter was more intriguing. 'Darn it, I know you've no taste for charity but I hope as you won't look upon it as such. When I took over your husband's empire, I had never any wish for his family to suffer. Quite the opposite, in fact.'

Much touched by his little speech, Carmella patted his hand in an impulsive show of affection. 'Then I shall accept, if only because you offer it so delightfully.' And the two smiled at each other, well pleased.

'I'm relieved to have this matter settled between us, ma'am, because it has caused me some concern. There is, however, another matter upon my mind.'

Carmella gave a knowing nod of her neatly coiffured head. 'Felicity?'

Dark eyebrows twitched upwards as he acknowledged that she had guessed correctly. 'I'm in something of a quandary, for I've made a bit of a fool of myself.'

'Indeed? I cannot imagine anything less likely,' said Carmella with a touch of amusement in her voice.

Jarle told her then of Felicity's determination to regain her father's honour by attempting to restore the family fortunes, and of his own challenge, recklessly issued in the heat of argument. 'I fear she has cast me in the role of villain, not unnaturally in the circumstances.' He decided not to elaborate on her latest attack upon him, stinging all the more for its being partly justified.

Carmella shook her head in sad resignation. 'She has ever been one to rise to a challenge. Loves nothing better than a good cause. Well meaning, you understand, but stubborn.'

There was a betraying tightness to the corners of the mouth, but, as Carmella did not notice, Jarle pressed on, much encouraged. If he could free himself at least from this guilt, he would be thankful. His burden was heavy enough. 'Lady Travers, I feel I owe it to you to tell you a little about myself, so you will better understand how this situation came about which can only lead to disaster for your daughter in some form or another.'

Carmella was all polite interest, showing nothing of her private misgivings and fears that dear Felicity's best chance of a good marriage was fast slipping away before her eyes. She could see it in the anxious crease of his brow. Felicity was proving to be a problem of which he wanted rid. She smiled up at him.

'As I mentioned earlier, I come from a large family. My father and mother were both employed in the textile trade, as a spinner and weaver. Conditions in the mills were appalling in their time. The working day was long and gruelling in ill-ventilated factories, the air filled with cotton lint and with the constant risk of fire. The factories were only warm enough to keep the cotton happy and the older workers would crowd into the boiler house to eat their lunches among the coal dust in order to get warm. Like many another working in these harsh conditions my father contracted a lung disease, byssinosis, from which he did not recover.'

'I am so sorry. How old were you when your father died?'

'Thirteen. I was one of nine children originally but two died of the same complaint as my father. And one of my other brothers lost the fingers of one hand while cleaning the cogs of the looms which were never stopped, however dangerous to life and limb.'

Carmella was startled. 'However did your poor mother cope?'

Jarle looked Carmella straight in the eye. 'I was proud of my mother. She struggled with scraps of candles, ate fat dripping on her bread, scrubbed her own steps and white-stoned them so they were the finest in the street. We had known hardship all our lives. We never expected to have much money but we always had food in our bellies and warm clothes on our backs, and we were loved. She did not ask for sympathy and would not have thanked you for it if you'd offered it.' He paused momentarily as his mind roved back over the years. 'My father was a self-educated man. He believed in book-learning, as he called it. He also believed in hard work and thrift. The puritan work ethic if you like. On his death I discovered that over the years he had made various investments. Some of them were not particularly profitable, but others included some valuable stock in the railways and in a shipping company. The income from these was used over the following years to set each of us on our way. Through hard work and careful saving, and a few strokes of good luck, I managed to add to mine. Most of my brothers went overseas to start new lives in a new world. My sisters, save for Kate, married. Which left my mother, and my youngest brother, Tom.' There followed a long silence which Carmella judged it wise not to break.

'I burned with anger. Can you understand that? I seethed at those who had made their fortunes from the misfortunes of families such as ours. While our mill boss was knighted for his services to industry, my family suffered only injury and death. My mother too died before her time, of course, worn out by the effort. I almost hated my father at first for wanting to ape his betters by buying into their capitalist industries. I spoke out at meetings, joined the new union and helped to win small victories here and there, like longer lunch breaks and warmed factories, but it was not enough. Then I saw that my father had been right. In order to fight the bosses, I needed to be more powerful than them. Do you see?'

'I—I think so,' Carmella ventured, not really seeing at all.

'That is when I followed his lead, worked double shifts, intrigued and manoeuvred, saved every last penny I earned and started to buy stock myself.'

'A wise move, I am sure,' agreed Carmella pacifyingly. 'I can see now why you are so well set up.'

He looked straight at her but Carmella gained the distinct impression that it was another he saw, and not herself at all.

'Oh, I was successful, but things do not always turn out as you imagine,' he said and she found herself nodding in agreement. 'Being rich, and therefore powerful, was the only thing I cared about.' He paused, tightening his jaw. 'But there is a price to be paid, and I am paying it.' Carmella shivered at his tone, wanting to offer comfort yet knowing instinctively it would not be welcomed. With an effort Jarle Blakeley seemed to collect himself. 'I will not bore you with all the painful details, ma'am; suffice it to say that when my family needed me I failed them. I'll not have your daughter's misery on my conscience too. I am not a fit person to make her happy. I have problems enough, not least at the shop. Get her out of it.' He meant out of his life. 'Since she cannot return to India, find her a charming husband from among your aristocratic acquaintances, for if she continues on her present course I fear for what might become of her.'

CHAPTER SIX

MUCH to her delight, Felicity found that the food improved beyond recognition. There was hot porridge for breakfast, thick slices of fresh bread and butter and as much strong tea as they wanted. She became the heroine of the hour, which was in itself rather embarrassing. But she was none the less pleased at having achieved so much and was not at all in a frame of mind to be persuaded to abandon her job at the emporium.

'But whatever should I do all day?' she cried in dismay when Carmella suggested it.

'You could keep me company,' came the unconvincing reply. Carmella held hopes that if Jarle saw Felicity against a more homely background, he might soften his attitude towards her and reconsider.

'But you have Kate, why should you need me?' Felicity stubbornly protested. 'Not to mention Uncle Joe.'

Carmella clicked her tongue. 'He is quite a sweetie but he does do the oddest things. My dear, he spends most of his time knee-deep in mud looking for worms, would you believe?'

Felicity said she would believe anything of that family, if Jarle was anything to go by. 'They are all quite mad.' She glanced swiftly across at Kate ensconced in the window seat, to see if she had heard, but she appeared to be totally absorbed in her needlepoint. Felicity pulled a face.

'Mama, do not ask me, I beg of you. *I* should go mad if I did nothing but sit here all day.' She hurried on, kneeling at her mother's side, afraid she might have given offence. 'Not that I don't adore you—I do. But I'm really

84

beginning to enjoy my job at the shop. I meet so many
different people. It is far more exciting than I expected.'
She might have added that she had not yet achieved what
she set out to achieve and had no intention of leaving
until she had done so. Instead she let her grey eyes shine,
as if with happiness, and Carmella began to relax. If her
daughter found life exciting within the dull brown walls
of an old-fashioned shop, there could be only one reason
and she was certainly not one to put at risk anything
which might come to pass as a result. She would leave
matters as they were at the moment and let events take
their course. And so Felicity moved the rest of her things
to her new quarters, and though she continued to visit
her mama at every opportunity there was no more talk
of her leaving.

And it was true that she did enjoy her work. Surprisingly she had established a routine which was not
only tolerable but satisfying. She found she enjoyed the
challenge of discovering the right piece of frippery
needed to set off a gown, or the perfect knot of flowers
to trim a hat. And she had become an expert at matching
ribbons, braids, frills, lace and suchlike gew-gaws with
every shade and hue.

Each day the emporium was invaded by a horde of
aloof, overdressed ladies who sailed majestically forth,
and, with a delicate wave of a gloved hand, ruled the
waves of floor walkers and assistants who jostled to obey
them. Thanking her stars for a sense of humour, while
keeping it safely hidden, Felicity learned not to hurry
these paragons as they stretched patience to breaking
point over some apparently trifling matter.

And in the midst of all this bustle, at regular and frequent intervals throughout the day, stalked Jarle
Blakeley. Tall, commanding, purposeful, he made many
an ambitious mama turn her head as he strode about
the shop floor. He missed not one jot of the business

that was carried out around him and was quick to point out any assistant neglectful of his or her duty.

Try as she might, Felicity could not rid herself of the feeling that he watched her more than he did the others. Whenever he was present, she was acutely aware of him. Noting every move he made from the corner of her eyes, she believed his gaze to be likewise constantly turned in her direction. Now she sensed, with an odd bleakness that gripped her heart, that she had been right when she'd suspected him of fraud, for he showed every sign of guilt, even to flushing quite scarlet on one occasion when they almost bumped into each other in the corridor.

But time was growing short and there was none to spare for sentiment. If proof existed that Blakeley had swindled poor dear Papa, then she must make haste to find it. She vowed to start that very night.

Felicity lay in the narrow bed listening to the snuffles, hiccups and soft snoring of her fellows. Her over-sensitised nerves thought they took longer than usual before a satisfying silence fell upon the dormitory.

But Felicity's tiredness had vanished and she was alert and eager to be off. Somewhere on these premises was hidden the proof she sought. *'Fides Supra Omnia'.*

Pulling a shawl about her shoulders over her nightgown and pushing her abundant curls impatiently back from her face so that they hung down her back, a ripple of colour, she crept across to the door. Try as she might she could not recall the creaky floorboards she had so meticulously noted earlier, and, despite her bare feet, with every sound they made she expected half the dormitory to awaken. She carried no light but as she groped her way down the winding staircase, slipping occasionally on the polished treads, her eyes gradually grew accustomed to the darkness.

She paused at the foot of the stairs to steady her breathing and listen intently for any slight sound which might indicate that Blakeley was still in the building. But no light showed beneath the office door, and, holding her breath in a vain attempt to subdue the noisy clamour of her heartbeat, she grasped the brass knob with chilled fingers, turned it and slipped quietly into the room, closing the door quickly behind her.

In her mind she could feel Jarle Blakeley's presence in the room and her eyes searched the darkness as if to locate him. Illumination, she decided, was imperative if she was to decipher any information at all from the ledgers and if she was to gain control of her excessive imagination.

Seconds later she had located a small electric desk lamp. Switching it on, she blinked in the green glow of its sudden light, but at least it brought the room down to manageable proportions and no hobgoblins lurked in the corners.

Undoubtedly a man's room, if only by its untidiness, she thought. One wall was lined with bookshelves which were stuffed not only with books but with red leather ledgers, swatches of cloth and bills stuck on spikes. Upon the other walls were plans and drawings which on investigation proved to be of the shop itself and of departments yet to be added. Blakeley's plans were evidently well advanced.

To the left of the single window hung leather bags in which the post was delivered and beneath stood a letter press with its gelatinous pad where letters or catalogues for mail order customers could be copied.

Behind the wide, double-sided desk stood a matching walnut bureau and it was to this that Felicity directed her attention. But she was at once distracted from her task by a photograph. Young men in white trousers and blazers, their stiff collars making them stand unnaturally straight and with boaters set at suitably rakish angles upon their heads. Girls in pretty print frocks and wide straw hats. Though the photograph dated from some years previous, perhaps taken at a summer picnic, she had no difficulty in picking out Jarle Blakeley in the centre of the back row. She experienced the strangest uplifting of her heart as she closely scrutinised the smiling face, which even on so short an acquaintance had already grown familiar. In the centre of the front row sat a woman, a look of quiet pride upon her pale face and with one hand resting possessively upon the shoulder of a young boy seated crosslegged on the floor in front of her. It was a pleasant photograph, without doubt of Jarle's family, and she set it back with reluctance as she turned to the task in hand.

Her heart started to hammer in her breast, and, feeling more like Sherlock Holmes every minute, whose adventures she loved to read in *Strand* magazine, she silently set about opening and searching the many drawers in the bureau. Guilt, coupled with the fear of discovery, made her clumsy as she swiftly scanned papers, notebooks, invoices, receipts and bills of lading. She found a list of employees in one ledger, with her own name marked in fresh green ink at the bottom of the last written page. Yet the more she read the less sense it all made, and the more the stillness of the room pressed in upon her. She would need the expertise of an accountant to perceive any fraud. Sitting back on her heels, she considered her problem.

Everything she had so far seen indicated that Travers Drapery was a thriving establishment. There appeared to be no long-standing debts, no threatening letters, no unpaid invoices. The cash book was up to date and each and every paper was precisely docketed in its appointed place. Jarle Blakeley might display a tendency to carelessness in his domestic life but his business habits were immaculate. There was nothing that hinted at fraud or dishonest dealing. Did this prove his innocence or merely that she had found, as yet, no evidence to convict him? The fluttering of a pulse in her throat became suffo-

cating as she baulked at the word 'convict'. She glanced
again at the happy young people in the photograph and
tried to picture the one at centre back in prisoner's garb.
Misery engulfed her.

Yet Mr Redgrove had spoken specifically of debts, and
of an overdraft. Feeling suddenly sickened by what she
was about, she began slamming bureau drawers with
more haste than care. Tears burned the backs of her
eyelids. How foolish she was. It had been her poor father
who'd acquired the debts, not Blakeley. Yet stubbornly
she remained convinced that somehow or other Jarle
Blakeley had been responsible for causing her father's
bankruptcy and premature death. Who else could have
been so? He'd also worsened her mother's already ill
health as a result and deprived herself of her true
heritage.

'Whatever is needed to bring about his downfall, I
will not hesitate to do it,' she said through gritted teeth,
firmly blotting out the image of doe-brown eyes. Her
conscious mind cried out for retribution and any
emotional murmurings from her softer heart must be
firmly quashed.

Somewhere in the far reaches of the building she
thought she heard a sound. She listened intently, like an
animal whose senses were quickened by the imminent
approach of danger. She was sure she would faint away
with fright if the door, upon which her gaze was riveted,
actually opened.

Exiting the office on swift, silent feet, every breath
seeming to echo noisily in the emptiness, she cried out
in startled alarm when the lacy wool of her shawl snagged
around the doorknob. Chiding herself for her fool-
ishness, she made her way to the main part of the shop.

Mahogany counters stood like dark sentinels, their
mirrored eyes throwing ghostlike visions which re-
kindled her fear till she realised each apparition was a
reflection of herself creeping about in her long, flowing

white nightgown. She gave a nervous little laugh and felt better.

With renewed resolve she located and opened a set of double doors which led to the store-rooms. Perhaps here would lie the key. She passed through the dressmaking departments where shadowy mannequin figures with wooden knobs for heads sported corsets, hand-made riding habits or tulle blouses cascading with snowy lace. Through the mail order and examining rooms where each garment was inspected before dispatch, and on to the main stock-room and unpacking department.

Lighting a single gas lamp, she surveyed the room, which was crammed from floor to ceiling with goods of every description, and experienced instant despair.

'This is hopeless,' she gasped. 'Where to look? And for what?'

Bleak with failure, dropping from fatigue, she wandered listlessly down the narrow aisles, the chill of the night striking through her thin nightgown. She hugged her shawl closer, and, reaching the end of one aisle, she started up the next. If Jarle Blakeley were capable of fraud, and siphoning off her father's profits for his own benefit, he was hardly likely to leave evidence of his villainy for all to see. She would need to be much cleverer than this if she was to defeat him.

Twitching the problem back and forth in her agile brain, she came to a table piled high with bolts of silk and muslin. Fingering the fine soft sheen of the fabric she was carried back in an instant to the Indian natives who wove with such skill and dexterity, remembering how often she had watched and chatted with them. Jewel greens, oranges, magentas, and brilliant reds were piled before her dazzled eyes. Unrolling one of bright peacock blue, she traced the design with a probing fingertip.

'Oh, what is this?' She gave a little cry of disappointment as her fingers encountered a rough flaw in the fabric. 'How dreadful. This beautiful fabric is marred.'

Pulling more material free, she bent closer to examine it. The first length of the role was of excellent, first class quality, but this later portion was of an inferior standard. 'How sad,' she mourned, draping the shimmering blue fabric about herself, enjoying the luxurious softness of the silky folds. Perhaps it was the release of the high nervous tension which made her reckless, but, tossing aside her shawl, she draped the silk about her body and over her head in sari fashion, transported back in time to the wonderful, hectic streets and bazaars of India. 'It is such a delightful blue.'

'And much more becoming than green,' said a low voice from the shadows. She spun around, the silk slithering to a heap at her bare feet, and colour shot her cheeks like madder.

'I—I was examining the fabric,' she stammered and instantly clicked her small tongue with irritation at such a ridiculous excuse. She lifted her eyes, ready to meet the full fury of his glare. If the young man of the photograph had been summer, the visage before her must surely be winter. To describe his expression as chilling would be to gravely undervalue it. Yet his voice when he spoke was calm and rational, as if they had indeed met in the park upon a summer's day. Only they had not.

'It is becoming an infuriating habit of yours to put me in the worst possible light, but on this occasion you must permit me the advantage,' he said with measured patience. 'The time wants ten minutes before one o'clock in the morning and I'm blessed if I can conjure one justifiable reason for your presence in my stock-room at such an hour. However, I await your explanation with interest.'

How cold her feet were, how deep the blue in the silk where the flaw had absorbed too much dye, how his dark brown curls appeared almost black in this light. How cross and irritable she felt, but not with him; with herself, for being caught. She had grown careless and he had heard her.

'I c-couldn't sleep, so I—I took a walk.' The excuse sounded limp and incredible even to her own ears. She did not expect him to believe her. Nor did he. She could tell by the unmistakable glitter in his eyes.

She hated him. That explained the turbulent emotions he invoked in her and which now cascaded through her like a douche of icy water. Hate, born of utter dislike and frustration by his behaviour. That was it exactly. How could a man be so gracious and so provoking all at the same time? Even now he was smiling at her.

'Do you always swathe yourself in finest silk as a cure for sleeplessness or simply as a means of enjoying your early morning somnambulations?' The man was enjoying himself hugely at her expense. 'Or is that all part of your plotting to discover the wicked truth about me?' he teased. He was quite insufferable, no matter how he might pretend to disguise it. But she would soon prick the balloon of his arrogance.

'You would do well to examine your silks with more care, instead of mocking me,' she said, as briskly as she dared, and had the satisfaction of seeing his brow crease in puzzlement. 'Or are you only too aware that you sell faulty merchandise?'

They both seemed to hold a shared breath for one long frozen moment. Then, moving closer to tower over her in a most threatening manner, he spoke in a voice that was a long way from gentle.

'What in damnation do you mean by that? Quality is the byword of this store. I'll not have it said otherwise. Have a care, Felicity, where your fertile imagination leads you. A man has only so much patience and you are trying mine sorely.'

She could smell the cigar upon him again, and something else. Brandy? Her heart began to patter all the more. What if he were drunk? And here she was all alone with him in the middle of the night. Instantly she became aware of her dishabille, of the loose abandonment of her hair and the dusty bareness of her feet. The cold sensation vanished, to be replaced by a latent heat that crept over her body beneath her nightgown. Her only protection now was the truth.

'Let me show you,' she said, with only the slightest tremble in her voice to disprove her apparent confidence.

Slipping past him, she retrieved the silk from where it had fallen. 'Look at this,' she said, smoothing the fabric out upon the table so that he could clearly see what she meant. 'It is flawed, which you must admit is most odd. The best silk comes from the inner part of the cocoon spun by the doomed silkworm about itself. The outer threads are twisted and rough and must be loosened in hot water to allow them to be removed so that the inner smooth thread can be wound on to a reel. A single cocoon can produce a length of thread three hundred yards long and can be woven at once without any further treatment.'

'I understand all that,' he remarked, carefully examining the extent of the flaw. 'But mistakes can happen. Careless workers, not properly checked.'

'It shouldn't. Not to this extent. It's the amount of waste product from the silkworm which has to be discarded which gives silk its high market price, apart from its having to be woven with great skill and care, of course,' she continued thoughtfully. She struggled with her memory to recall anything which Gilbert might have said which would explain it. As a merchant he dealt in many fine cloths, including silk. 'Broken threads can be used, of course, by spinning them together to make them strong, and so you have spun silk, inferior to pure silk but still marketable. But this material cannot even be classed as such.'

They were standing close together now, animosity forgotten as they bent over the fabric. 'You think it has been manufactured with the waste product?' asked Jarle in surprise, instantly following the drift of her thought processes.

'Yes, I do.' She looked up at him challengingly. 'Anyone who wants to make extra profit can easily do so by passing off an inferior fabric as best Indian silk, or an adulterated tea as a quality Darjeeling. I think, Mr Blakeley, that I need look no further for my proof. I believe I have it all.' She began to walk from the room but he was too quick for her, and, catching her at the door, spun her round to face him.

'There you go again,' he growled. 'Jumping to conclusions and blaming me for everything. All right, so you have proved that some goods in my shop have been tampered with or are not what they purport to be. But does that prove it was I who made them that way?'

'Who else?' she tartly retorted. 'You are surely not saying that my own father was responsible for cheating himself?'

Jarle gave a weary sigh. 'In many respects your father was an innocent, especially where business matters were concerned. He had no experience of them. But I agree that someone was cheating him. Since Sir Joshua's death I've found some evidence of fraud.'

'Why haven't you done anything about it?'

Jarle hesitated, and, as he did so, a look of disbelief crept across Felicity's face. Jarle saw it and felt his reply to be equally damning. 'I believe in justice, so am not prepared to make accusations without solid proof.'

'How very convenient,' she said.

'I have given priority to making this store profitable, for the rest I watch, and wait.' Jarle paused significantly. 'Building the complete picture before I act.'

'And no doubt when you do it will be devastating for the poor miscreant,' Felicity mocked.

'You can be certain of that,' he said in a manner which even Felicity could not doubt. 'I am unused to being crossed and someone is thwarting me at every turn. I have half the puzzle, but I need the rest.'

'Then I trust you find it soon, and save poor Papa's honour?'

Jarle dropped his head for a moment as if overcome by despair or perhaps some private tussle for patience. When he spoke again it was in a softer, gentler tone. 'Felicity, one day you will have to relinquish the past and look to the future. You are no longer a little girl seeking to bask in Papa's adulation.'

'That isn't true. I didn't,' she said.

Dark eyebrows lifted in surprise. 'Are you saying that Joshua did not adore you? I can hardly believe that.'

She shifted uncomfortably beneath his probing stare. 'I didn't say that.'

'You implied it. What kind of a father was he, Felicity, if not adoring? Are you suggesting that he too was flawed, like this silk?'

'No, I am not.'

'But he was human.'

'He was wonderful,' Felicity retaliated energetically. 'A gentleman, not like some I could mention.'

'But he spent too much time away from home and you longed for more of his attention?' His voice was so soft it almost made her want to cry, to lean on him, to lay her head upon his broad shoulder, to lift her face to his and . . . Before she knew it, that was exactly what she was doing. And he was looking down into her eyes with an expression which perplexed and delighted her all at the same time. When his lips closed upon hers she felt she would dissolve from the pleasure of it. The blood rushed in her head and her heart pounded against his, yet she wantonly wrapped her arms about his neck and returned his kiss with not a whisper of shyness, nor an echo of lingering pride.

After he had released her, she tried to recall what it was they had been arguing about, but it had quite deserted her. Her mind was a whirlpool of conflicting emotion quite out of control. Slowly it came to her that he was speaking again, stroking back her hair, touching her lips, trying to make her listen, to understand.

'Unfortunately I can see no other explanation. I hate to say it, but he must have known about both of these products because he is the supplier of both. It is hard to imagine they passed through unchecked.'

She felt bemused, unable to concentrate, her lips still stinging from his kiss. 'Unchecked by whom? What are you saying? Who are you talking about?'

His eyes were dark pools of chocolate and she was drowning in them. 'I've just told you, Felicity,' he said gently, fervently wishing he did not have to hurt her yet again. 'These goods all came from one supplier. Gilbert Farrel. Your fiancé.'

She was shaking her head in disbelief, slapping his restraining hand away, backing through the door. 'You're lying. You're making it all up,' she cried.

'Felicity, don't. Don't hurt yourself by defending him. It must be true. Why should I lie?'

But Felicity was not prepared to listen. 'That is the craziest notion I ever heard. Gilbert is...was my father's friend. You are simply determined to blame everyone but yourself. What kind of a man are you?' She almost shouted this last at him as, spinning on her heel, terrified the tears might break, she fled to the sanctuary of her bed.

Jarle Blakeley watched her go with a deep sadness. Why did she have to be so meddling? Why could she not be content to remain at home like her mother, or Kate, and do whatever women did at home? He absolutely refused to be held responsible for her happiness.

He'd issued instructions for her employment to be terminated, so, whether she liked it or not, she would be forced to curtail her snooping. Turning down the light, he strode back to his room in ill temper, his last thought on the brandy bottle which he knew still stood upon his side table.

Miss Bridget prided herself on never being lily-livered when it came to her duty and she was particularly pleased in this instance. Proper little madam she was, and quite out of place here. And so Miss Bridget bluntly informed Felicity that her position was terminated and was not in the least perturbed by Felicity's fury.

'But why? What have I done?' Felicity could scarce believe her ears. Only a few hours ago she had been in his arms, stunned by an unexpected kiss. Though she supposed it would be more truthful to admit it had been she and not he who had instigated it. She tried not to think about that since it confused her.

'It is not for you or me to question Mr Blakeley's reasons,' Miss Bridget tartly informed her. 'He wishes you to leave, therefore you will collect any pay owing to you, and do just that.'

Felicity was astounded by the depth of her own disappointment. Had it something to do with Gilbert and this ridiculous accusation Blakeley had made against him? Surely not. She could see no connection at all, but Jarle Blakeley evidently devised his own rules. 'He can't turn me out without at least an explanation,' she persisted. 'I refuse to go.'

Miss Bridget looked over her spectacles at Felicity as if she had announced that she no longer believed in the British Empire. 'There can be no question of refusing,' she said in a high taut voice. 'See that you and your belongings are removed from the premises by the end of the week.'

'No fault has been found against me,' Felicity cried, grasping the astounded Miss Bridget by the elbow as she moved away. The woman gave a frozen little smile.

'If that is the only thing troubling you, we can soon put that right. I am sure that a reason can be found.'

For the rest of the day she never took her eyes from Felicity. And halfway through the afternoon, when Felicity was dealing with a particularly difficult customer, Miss Bridget disconcertingly came to stand beside her as she pulled out bolts of lace by the score, none of which quite suited.

'Too wide. Good gracious, no, who would buy such a tasteless design?' cried the demanding customer. 'No, no, not so narrow, girl.' And so it continued, with Felicity growing ever more hot and flustered as she lost all her usual skill at charming a customer simply by the 'Dragon's' excessive closeness. She could hear her steady, implacable breathing, feel the fierce scrutiny from her beady black eyes.

When Felicity was almost in tears with frustration, Miss Bridget reached over, and, snatching the latest card of lace from her hand, drew her away from the counter.

'I beg your pardon, madam. Our chief floor walker will attend to you. Mr Reynolds?' She flicked an imperious finger and the obsequious Reynolds bustled forward, at once taking control, his liquid voice oozing with subservient charm.

Felicity, meanwhile, found herself briskly told in no uncertain terms that she should have called the floor walker herself. And for that cardinal sin alone she deserved to be sacked on the spot.

Feeling unjustly treated, Felicity abandoned any further argument with the woman and took her anger to the now familiar office. Without knocking she stormed inside to stand facing Blakeley across the desk. Miss Bridget came scurrying behind, all of a fluster and quite out of breath.

'Do you never knock?' Jarle queried mildly of Felicity. He could almost touch the waves of fury emanating from each woman and flowing over him. He looked at Miss Bridget, who was spluttering flecks of spittle over her thin lips, her normally pallid complexion grown quite purple with rage. 'Never have I seen such insubordination,' she was saying. 'Not in all the years I've been here.' Then he looked back at Felicity.

Her pepper-gold hair seemed to light the whole dismal room, even the dust motes which danced about her. It was piled up on top of her head in some fancy knot or other, very neat and orderly. But last night it had been wild and loose, hanging down her back. He could remember the silky feel of it against his hands as he'd held her close. Staring at her, he began to take in a myriad other tiny details. The intense whiteness around the clear grey of her eyes, the pertness of the stubborn chin and the softness of the round cheeks which he had a sudden desire to caress. Then there was the small, pretty mouth. He remembered with a start the taste of her kiss which had been surprisingly sensual and neither small nor pretty. It had been the kiss of a woman with a seductiveness waiting to be explored.

'Miss Bridget informs me that my presence here is no longer required,' Felicity said, and for a moment he was so absorbed with studying the delightful way her chest rose and fell in little breathy gasps that he quite forgot to answer.

Miss Bridget, however, was less affected by fetching ways and, stepping up to the desk, rapped upon it with one knuckle as if she meant to call him smartly to attention. 'It was your own request, Mr Blakeley, but Miss Travers is quite refusing to go. Never in all my life——'

Mr Blakeley got quietly to his feet, and, smiling benevolently upon her, led the woman gently to the door.

'I am sure you have done your best, Miss Bridget. I shall take care of the matter now.'

Felicity grimaced, feeling like some recalcitrant child waiting to be dealt with by her headmaster. But if Blakeley thought his bullying would succeed where Miss Bridget's had failed then he was mistaken. Drawing in a deep breath, she prepared to counter any argument he might try to be rid of her. She was absolutely determined to stay. Did she not have the right?

Turning upon his heel he quite took that breath away by politely asking, 'Would you care for tea? I'm sure Amy would bring us some. We have a new delivery of Assam.'

'N-no. Thank you.' How could she have Amy wait upon her?

'Then at least be seated.' He brought forward a chair, and, unable to refuse, she perched herself on the very edge of it. 'I'm sorry all this has blown up quite so ferociously. Bee is harmless enough at heart but perhaps a touch over-exuberant.'

What was he saying? Bee? Could he really be speaking of the same woman they called the 'Dragon'?

'However, provision has now been made for you at home in the lodge house. I see no further reason for you to remain here in the circumstances.' And when she would have protested he leaned forward, his voice low and thrumming with sensitivity. 'You have to agree, Felicity, however liberal your views that a job as an eleven shillings a week shop assistant is not one to be coveted.'

'B-but what would I do? Idleness would not suit me,' she told him.

'You don't need to be entirely idle. Women are, I accept, trying out all types of careers now.' He waved a hand vaguely. 'You could try something new, be anything you chose to be, or take up some useful voluntary work as Kate does, I don't know. Something, anything which is more commensurate with your abilities and intelligence.' He meant something, anything which would get her out of his hair, but he sounded so reasonable and his words were so eminently sensible that she found it impossible to disagree. Why, then, did she feel so deflated, so unwanted?

'We still have not solved our disagreement,' she said, almost reluctantly. 'You still have not proved to me that you were innocent of forcing my father into bankruptcy, or explained how I came to be part of the deal.' Her eyes opened wide, challenging him, but they were overbright and he read the uncertainty in them.

Smiling, he gently shook his head. 'And you have not proved my guilt. Let us have done with this vendetta, and with this foolish challenge. Of what purpose is it? I believe you found the answer last night but will not accept it. I did not cause your father's financial problems, Farrel did. As for that marriage contract, I admit it was a mistake. You know as well as I do that no court in the land would uphold it. Not in these modern times.'

She grasped her fingers tightly together in her lap, feeling more dreadfully unhappy than ever before in her entire life. Jarle Blakeley did not want her to marry Farrel, nor did he want her for himself either. 'So I am to meekly go away and do nothing? For the sake of my father's honour?' she said, in a tight voice almost choking with unshed tears. 'Can you not understand that it is impossible for me to do that?'

He came to prop himself on the desk before her, and, gathering her small cold hands in his own large warm ones, tried to make her look up at him, but she refused, keeping her miserable gaze floorwards. 'I do understand. But this obsession you have with your father is making you unhappy.'

Felicity gasped. 'It is not an obsession.'

'Then prove it. Let the past be gone and look to the future, Felicity, for it is there where your happiness lies.'

Sound advice, he thought wryly. He should follow it himself. He stared at her bent head, at the silky gloss of her hair, a thoughtful expression upon his face.

Then she did look at him, a deep, silent gaze, each one holding the other. Neither of them spoke, or even smiled, but a level of understanding of astonishing complexity was transmitted between them.

Moistening her lips with the tip of her small pink tongue she asked, 'What shall I do about—about Gilbert?'

'Nothing. Nothing at all. Make a new life for yourself. Go home, Felicity,' he said softly, watching every movement she made. And one day I may come to you there, said his eyes.

CHAPTER SEVEN

'BOTHERATION,' cried Felicity, as she stuck the needle into her thumb for the fourth time that morning.

She had been right. Idleness did not suit her. Mama had set a scrap of fabric into her hands and a rainbow of silks on a small table by her elbow, and bid her create a charming cushion for her bedroom chair. To be fair, she enjoyed drawing on the design, great fat-petalled poppies and tiny blue-eyed forget-me-nots all curled into a twine of leaves. But from threading her first needle and knotting the first french knot, she was bored. Felicity was privately astonished by the speed with which her interest had waned. Glancing sideways at Kate, contentedly and expertly plying her needle on a cassock cover for the local church, she experienced a pang of intense envy. Why could she not be so content? Was she not like other women?

Perhaps it was because she did not need a cushion cover for her room? Perhaps she too should find a more worthwhile occupation.

'Is there something I can do to help you?' Felicity asked, and Kate looked up, surprised.

'Oh, this is a very simple cross-stitch.' Kate glanced at the discarded linen with its fanciful design. 'You'd find it most tedious.'

The truth of this was so obvious Felicity saw no point in disputing it. She sighed. 'Kate, why do you never find life dull?'

Kate smiled her shy, dark-eyed smile. 'I suppose because I am not clever like you.'

103

Felicity was astonished. She had never considered herself to be clever and she said so now, very firmly. 'If I were clever I should know in what way I have offended your brother, that he should dismiss me so callously from my job when I've done nothing wrong that I can see.' Though she suspected she knew the reason, if she were honest with herself for once. She had flung herself at him like some love-hungry child and thoroughly embarrassed the man. She went hot and cold all over just thinking about it.

To her surprise Kate was chuckling. 'I shouldn't worry too much about Jarle. He does tend to make rash decisions now and then without properly thinking things through, which later he regrets.' Yes, thought Felicity wryly, such as a rash agreement to a marriage. But Kate was looking at her with a quiet seriousness. 'In actual fact, Felicity, I think you've been rather good for him.'

'Good for him?'

Kate nodded. 'He was growing depressed and introspective. His enthusiasm for the shop had quite gone. Now I hope it might return.'

Felicity gave a hard little laugh but a sparkle lurked deep in her eyes. 'You mean that fighting with me has put new zest into him?'

'Something like that,' Kate conceded. 'Though that is putting it rather crudely. He hasn't been himself of late, you see.'

'Why?'

Kate looked sad. 'It hasn't been a happy time in the family since our mother died. I dare say Jarle will tell you about it—when he's ready. Like all proud men, he finds it difficult to talk of matters close to his heart, as if it were a sign of weakness.' She smiled. 'I don't know how I should have coped were it not for the kindness of the vicar and now your dear Mama, of course.'

'I'm sorry,' said Felicity hastily. 'I didn't wish to pry.'

'Oh, you are not at all.' Kate told her then of her family's background and how Jarle's brilliance in business affairs had brought them from the mean back streets of Manchester to owning some of its finest architecture. 'It is not that he is greedy, not like some,' she hasted to say. 'Money to Jarle represents security, for his family as much as himself. But he is still awkward in society.' She gave a rueful smile. 'Perhaps you can rid him of the chip he carries on his shoulder. Convince him, Felicity, that he is as good as the next man and better than most.'

To Felicity, this gave a whole new picture of Jarle Blakeley and she found it difficult to assimilate. Abandoning all pretence of sewing, she came to sit on the floor by Kate's knee. 'Tell me, honestly, Kate. What do you think I should do? I miss working in the shop, even though my job was a menial one. But I had begun to hope...' She flushed, faltering over her words, not wishing to admit that it was more than the shop she missed.

Kate set down her sewing and reaching out, squeezed Felicity's hand. 'Go on. I'm listening.'

Felicity swallowed hard. 'I had hoped that perhaps in time I would be given more interesting work. There are plans on the wall of the office, pictures of the future, and after only a short time working in the shopping hall I can see so many ways of improving it.'

'Why do you not tell Jarle about these ideas?' suggested the gentle Kate.

'Because he would not listen,' protested Felicity, yet guiltily wondering if that were quite fair. They had been too fully occupied scrapping to have any civilised conversation.

'How do you know if you do not try?'

'I suppose I don't. Only with my blaming him for everything...' She paused, then shrugged her slight shoulders. 'It seems I may well be wrong but he has taken offence anyway and there's an end of it.'

'Not necessarily. The very next time he calls, I shall give you the opportunity to speak with him in private and put your ideas to him.'

Felicity's heart gave an odd little jump. 'Oh, dear, do you think that such a good idea? After we've been so much at odds?'

'Perhaps now is as good a time as any to call a truce?' whispered Kate. 'I hate to see you two with daggers drawn all the time.' She shook her head in mock despair. 'You are both so similar in many ways.'

'Similar?' Felicity was outraged. 'We are not at all alike.' But Kate only laughed, a happy sound that became quite infectious.

'Yes, you are. You are both determined, stubborn people, proud and courageous and willing to fight for what you believe is right,' she said, with a surprising firmness. 'Jarle understands your protectiveness towards Lady Travers because he cares for his family too. And, like you, he is creative and enthusiastic, a pioneer of ideas.' Her voice had grown soft as she talked, yet warm with pride. 'He really is a very nice person, and so are you,' she finished decisively, leaving Felicity quite speechless. Kate clearly had no reticence when it came to singing her brother's praises.

'I suppose he has shown a kindness to Mama,' mumbled Felicity, grudgingly. 'But we do not care for charity. I want to work for our keep.'

'You must not look at it in that light,' said Carmella vigorously when Felicity joined her in the garden. She had found her mother hoeing onions, of all things, a large straw hat stuck firmly upon her head and her skirts drawn up above her ankles with strings. 'Jarle Blakeley does not seem at all the kind of person to point the finger and say, I helped this person, or this. He just goes ahead and does what must be done, with no expectation of thanks. Why, take the cotton industry, for example. He was instrumental in getting longer lunch hours for many workers in his father's old mill, so they could breathe fresh air into their lungs at some point in their day. Is that not splendid?'

Felicity raised finely arched brows in surprise at her mother's vehement defence. She'd seen little evidence of his philanthropy. Perhaps it had vanished now that he paid the wages bill.

'And then there is Madame Delphine,' Carmella continued, growing loquacious.

'Madame Delphine?'

'She used to work at the drapery shop. A very clever couturier, I understand. When Jarle took over, he set her up most comfortably in her own establishment then made it possible for her to return to her native country. I'm sure that she did not view it as charity, but was apparently pleased and grateful and that is how you must be, my dear Felicity.'

A cold waft of air brushed Felicity's heart as, haltingly, she agreed. Hadn't Jarle said something about spending too much time on the Continent? 'Does Jarle call upon her?' she could not help but ask.

'I dare say, whenever he can find the opportunity,' agreed Carmella. 'Now, Felicity, Joe and I were discussing where we should site the pond. I think it should go in the rose garden and Joe prefers the edge of the paddock. What do you think, darling?' She leaned upon the hoe, breathing heavily, as she awaited Felicity's decision, which she felt quite unable to give.

Everything seemed suddenly too much. Her mind had suffered enough confusion of late without being asked to see Jarle Blakeley as some kind of ministering angel with white wings. She suspected this latest information had come from Kate who saw him with a prejudiced eye, or else her mother too had been seeing rather much of the vicar.

But who was Madame Delphine? Felicity had not heard the name mentioned before. And why, when the woman's name was associated with Jarle, did she feel so strange? Surely she did not imagine that she was the first girl Jarle Blakeley had kissed? What a baby she was. The woman was clearly his mistress and no concern of hers, thought Felicity, determinedly resolute in her hurt.

'We don't want a pretty-pretty thing with carp in it,' Joe was objecting, rather belligerently. 'We want a pond with a bit of character. For ducks and frogs and suchlike. Nowt to watch otherwise,' he said bluntly.

Felicity liked Uncle Joe. He was a wiry little man with a placid, easy-going sort of nature who always believed in 'speaking his mind'. But he was probably what was termed an 'eccentric' since he tended to do odd things, like collect half-pennies in a bucket and go for long walks on the moors in the pouring rain. But his greatest passion was the garden and his leathery, sun-browned skin, in sharp contrast to his shock of white hair and long beard, reminded Felicity rather of a sprightly gnome.

'Ah, I do see what you mean,' said Carmella with a sudden thoughtfulness. She turned again to Felicity, eyes bright. 'Joe is an ardent naturalist, darling. He knows so much about wild things, you wouldn't believe it. Did you know, for instance, that a newt folds its newly laid eggs in a leaf for safe keeping? Isn't that clever?'

Felicity contrived to disguise her smiles as she expressed suitable incredulity. Evidently a flourishing friendship was in progress between the two. And it was doing Carmella no harm at all. Felicity hadn't seen her look so glowingly beautiful in years. 'You seem quite interested yourself, Mama,' she ventured.

'Oh, indeed, I am finding it absolutely fascinating,' Lady Travers fervently agreed. 'Now, Felicity, you must come fishing with us one morning. It will do you good, bring the bloom back into your cheeks. We set out at dawn, usually.' Carmella bestowed a smile upon Uncle Joe which could only be described as adoring, in her daughter's opinion. 'You wouldn't mind if Felicity came with us, would you, Jo-Jo?'

Felicity almost choked. 'Fishing at dawn? I think not, Mama.' She began to back away, preparatory to making her excuses. Nothing would induce her to play gooseberry, which she quite clearly would be doing if she accepted the invitation. 'Thank you all the same, Joe. I think I will continue with my stroll now.' Even before she had politely made her farewells and half murmured something about seeing them at supper, the pair were striding off in search of spades, possibly to start digging the pond that very moment for all Felicity knew. For some reason she could not imagine, Felicity felt quite choked by their evident happiness in each other.

She walked with an increasing listlessness through the rose walk and on to the path through the sycamore spinney which had recently been cleared, she guessed by Mama and Jo-Jo. Sighing deeply, she found a sheltered spot out of the breeze, and, arranging her skirts with care, seated herself in comfort upon the grass, her back leaning against the warm trunk of a sycamore.

It was a relief, at least, to be able to walk out on a sunny afternoon and not be confined to the shop floor. How dreadful it must be never to see the afternoon sun at all. She tried to imagine what this must be like, and failed. In the winter the assistants scarcely saw daylight, and precious little in the summer, as they were allowed only Sundays off. Diabolical, in her opinion. For all Jarle professed to be making steady improvements, she had seen little sign of it. No wonder he had seen her off the premises. She was more than a thorn in his side. She had become his conscience, stabbing uncomfortably at him, and he did not like that one little bit.

She fluffed out her skirts and, with the gesture, swept Jarle Blakeley from her mind. She would not think of him again. It was a relief, too, not to have to wear the dismal black. This was a favourite dress of embroidered poplin in sky-blue, the fabric for it given to her by Gilbert Farrel. She wondered if she would ever see Gilbert again, and what she would say to him if she did. She had spent hours last evening devising a letter, but had abandoned all her efforts to the waste-paper basket in the end. Yet she could hardly say nothing. They were still engaged to be married. At any moment he could arrive in England to claim her as his bride. The thought brought her no pleasure. She had to admit that marriage with Gilbert had always appeared to her more provident than exciting, yet he was kind enough and would no doubt have made a good and faithful husband. She had once asked for nothing more. But though she refused to believe that Gilbert knowingly sent faulty goods to the Travers Drapery, she knew instinctively that she could never feel quite the same about him. She had changed.

Yet whom could she trust? A rather dull and well-meaning fiancé of long standing? Or Jarle Blakeley, an ambitious entrepreneur who refused to explain his actions? Even the very staff he abused tended to put the blame for their distress on to Miss Bridget, the old 'Dragon', and not on Blakeley at all. It was all most disconcerting.

Felicity stared with unseeing eyes out along the path through the trees to where it joined the open moor. She could understand Uncle Joe's liking to walk on the vast acres of springy turf, scoured clean with wind and rain. She too, even in the short time she had been here, had come to love the wild, open moorland, the sound of the skylark high in the clear northern light. The moor represented freedom. You could turn at will in any direction and walk for miles undisturbed. The choice was infinite and entirely your own. If she had such freedom in life, what would she do with it? What would her choice be?

She stared up through the lattice of branches, hearing again the heartrending loneliness of the curlew's cry, and was surprised to find tears rolling quietly down her round cheeks.

Jarle put off calling at the lodge house for two whole weeks. It was not normally in his nature to play the coward, but he was well aware that that was what he was doing. The odd part of it was that the more he told himself to avoid Miss Felicity Travers, pointing out all her interfering, busybody ways, the more his brain obstinately conjured up pictures of her. After all, he had surely managed to rid himself of any obligation to marry her and provided adequately for both mother and daughter. Yet, sometimes, when he felt neglectful of his sister, Kate's peaceful pale face with its cloud of dark hair would come into his mind but then he would find another face superimposed upon it. Irritated, his guilt would increase, and once again he would postpone the visit.

Finally, he realised, to delay any longer would provoke comment, and that would not be a good idea. The truth was that life in the shop had grown very dull of late, and he was looking forward to seeing Felicity again more than he cared to admit. So the very next Sunday afternoon found him neatly attired in a new grey lounge suit of herringbone worsted with narrow cut trousers. He told himself that he had made no special effort for this call and Kate would probably not even notice. But the very first thing she did was to remark upon his appearance.

'How very smart you are, Jarle. We must have tea in the front parlour if you are to look so grand.'

He blustered and coughed, but since he often called upon his sister in an old Norfolk jacket and tweeds, it was difficult to deny. Kate laughed at him. 'Don't look so sheepish. I'm glad to see you looking after yourself again. You've got far too untidy of late.' She kissed him lightly upon his smooth cheek. 'No prickles either. Whatever next?'

'Minx, stop plaguing me.' He looked about the room. 'All alone?'

'Lady Travers and Felicity have gone for a walk by the river. I think Uncle Joe is fishing down there.'

Jarle grunted non-committally and seated himself in the most comfortable fireside chair as directed, stretching out his long legs and crossing his booted feet upon the hearthrug. Though it was May, a bright fire burned in the grate so he might as well enjoy a little home comfort while he could.

He'd been telling himself all the way here that it was only Kate he'd come to see, and that he wasn't in the least concerned with Felicity Travers. Now he experienced a sensation in the pit of his stomach alarmingly like disappointment. He had to admit that he did enjoy talking with her, although she seemed often in a temper. Kate never allowed such displays of emotion, nor showed any interest in his business activities if truth were told, and he'd begun to toss the idea about of talking over one or two matters with Felicity. Nothing too pertinent, naturally, but it might be interesting to get her views. He knew no other woman whose judgement he'd trust, so it was worth a try. But, darn the woman, never away when she was poking her nose into business which did not concern her, now that he needed her she'd taken herself off for a walk.

Sighing quietly to himself, Jarle prepared to be bored by an endless recital of village affairs.

Tea was brought and brother and sister chatted in friendly enough fashion, but Jarle was rapidly running out of conversation of interest to the quiet Kate, and he was vastly tired of the vicar's titbits of gossip. Privately he considered it would be no bad thing if the vicar took Kate off his hands altogether. Not that he relished a parson in the family, but it would suit Kate down to the ground, and be a whole sight better than spinsterhood, which was the other likely path for her. He stood up suddenly, almost knocking the tiny tea table over in his eagerness to depart.

'Well, dash it, Kate. Can't wait all day just to pay my respects to the Travers family. I'll leave my regards instead.'

'Oh, but they won't be long, I'm sure. Can't you wait a few more moments?' Kate was pink-cheeked with anxiety. 'Have another cup of tea. I know that Felicity wished to speak with you most particular.'

His eyebrows raised a fraction but then fell disastrously. 'Dare say some other imagined staff problem she's discovered. And, no, I've had enough tea to tan my insides for a fortnight, thank you.' Swinging on his heel, he took the two strides to the door, grasped the handle and flung it open to find Felicity herself facing him on the other side.

For a half-moment both stood speechless, and Felicity for one felt her cheeks burn and her stomach jolt most alarmingly. Jarle glowered down at her as if she had performed some misdemeanour just by being there.

'Miss Travers. Lady Travers.' Jarle inclined his head in an abrupt nod of acknowledgement and Felicity's heart sank to her boots. How formal he had grown. She must have infuriated him more than she'd appreciated by her snooping.

Showing none of this behind her gracious smile, Felicity slipped past him into the room, pulling off her hat and gloves and making every effort to appear calm, though her heart was racing. 'Tea, and scones. How delicious. It is really quite chilly out today.'

A fresh pot was sent for and somehow Jarle discovered he did not have to rush off after all, though he declined a refill of his own cup. After some desultory conversation in which the weather, the garden, the state of the fishing, and an explanation by Uncle Joe on how to make the best flies were discussed, the little tea party began to disband. Joe and Carmella had the freshly caught fish to attend to and Kate had some Sunday duties to perform for the vicar. Rack her brain as she might, Felicity could think of no way of avoiding being left alone with Jarle.

They sat facing each other in a silence which was beginning to grow awkward. In the last two weeks she had toyed with various phrases which might prove appropriate when they met again. She felt it only proper to offer some explanation for her unseemly behaviour on that fateful night. But what explanation could she give? Loneliness? Confusion? An over-stimulated imagination? Dismay at the dreadful accusations over Gilbert? Or simply exhaustion? None of these truly served and she could think of no other answer she was prepared to consider. Yet now, with his very physical presence opposite, her mind was a complete blank.

For his part, Jarle had forgotten how prim and proper she was. She sat ramrod-straight, as if poised to perform some duty. If he didn't watch it she would offer him more damned tea soon. 'As a matter of fact I did wish to speak to you,' he said, as if in answer to a question.

She glanced quickly up to meet his gaze and found her thoughts running riot again. He looked so completely mild and harmless sitting in the rosy glow of the fire that, if she did not take care, she would begin to believe the fallacy. 'I cannot think what you might have to say to me,' she said, more tartly than she meant, and saw his lips tighten.

'I can understand your antipathy towards me,' he said, quite gently. 'It must appear as if I'm out to ruin your happiness but that is very far from the case. I wish you to know that I have now carried out a thorough investigation of all my stock of silks, muslins, tea and other products from India. I use several merchants besides Farrel, and their goods appear to be perfectly all right.'

He paused, his brown gaze so full of compassion she felt weak with the power of it. 'On the other hand, goods from Farrel and Co. are very far from perfect. Apart from the items mentioned I found bolts of cloth six yards shorter than they ought to be, weighted containers and fraudulent labelling. Not to mention several tea-chests half empty.'

She was leaning towards him, hands clasped painfully tight upon her lap. 'I cannot believe what I'm hearing,' she said in a small voice.

'I'm afraid it's true, Felicity. I was, in fact, investigating the tea, believing it to have been adulterated, on that first fateful day we met. Probably with used leaf sweepings glazed with gum. It's an old trick. Certainly if a merchant is looking for a fast way to make money there are ample opportunities for cheating within the trade.'

She shook her head, bemused, dumbstruck by what she'd learned. 'But why?' was all she could manage.

'Your father's idea was for Travers Drapery Emporium to be turned into a specialist store, dealing chiefly in foreign products. He envisaged a department for French couture, one stocking goods from the Orient, and, most important of all, one specialising in Indian products. He granted the largest orders to his friend, Gilbert Farrel, who would be bound to prosper with him. It was a good idea and it might well have worked, except that, for some reason best known to himself, Farrel must have got greedy, or impatient, and decided to hurry things up. He knew that your father visited England only occasionally and that much of the ordering was left in the hands of buyers who are far less diligent than a proprietor would be. The large accounts to Farrel and Co. continued to be paid but the shop was no longer getting value for money. But I am certain that some other member of staff must be involved. Your own complaints led me to discover that the cook was selling the meat he was supposed to dish up to Travers's staff for his own profit. I sacked him at once, naturally.'

'I'm glad. I did notice a considerable improvement in the food, as did your hard-pressed employees. But go on with your story.'

Jarle shrugged broad shoulders. 'There is nothing more to tell. The shop began to fail. Farrel, on the other hand, was presumably doing very nicely.'

White-faced, Felicity stared at him. 'Are you saying that Gilbert planned all this?'

Jarle gave a deep sigh. 'Oh, it was all carefully planned.'

'But *why*?' Again the almost heartrending cry. 'Why should he do that to Papa, to me?'

Jarle stood up and walked to the window to stare out at the garden. Clouds had gathered and it was starting to rain. He really ought to be getting back. The week's accounts still awaited his attention but he felt a strange reluctance to leave the closeness of this room. He wished he could answer her question but balked at even trying.

'Tell me about Gilbert Farrel,' he said. 'What is he like? How long have you known him?'

She was thankful that he kept his back to her as she began. 'I suppose I've known him ever since I went out to India. He is a friend of Papa's, or rather was.' She paused before continuing. 'He is ... that is, he is not of my own generation.'

'You mean he is older than you.'

'Yes.' Why was she so reluctant to mention a fact she had long ago come to accept?

'How much older?'

No answer.

Jarle considered, retaining his position by the window. 'As old as your father?'

'Oh, no. He was perhaps ten years younger than Papa,' she protested.

Now it was Jarle's turn to remain silent. He told himself that it was none of his concern if Felicity Travers should have such a desire to please a father that she wished to marry one of his near contemporaries. It was certainly pointless to pursue the matter. 'Why did you choose to marry him?' he asked and closed his eyes in silent self-condemnation.

'Because he asked me, I suppose,' said Felicity rather meekly, and this did bring Jarle Blakeley from his self-imposed exile.

'Good Lord, don't tell me you're such a weak-kneed female you'd marry the first fellow who doffed his cap at you? That's not how you strike me, madam.'

There was a bantering tone in his voice, and, casting a swift, sideways glance up at him, she felt her own lips twitch in response. 'I dare say I've changed a bit. I wasn't always so, so...'

'So much of a rebel?' He sat down opposite her again and she was relieved to see that he was still smiling.

'Mama and Papa thought me homely and rather plain.' She pulled a wry face. 'I dare say they were right. I tended to plumpness as a child and would never have won any prizes at school. So it seemed the only hope for me was a suitable marriage.'

His eyes were roguishly appreciative as he leaned back comfortably in his chair the better to view her. 'Then you have most certainly changed and fined out very nicely, for you are far from plump or plain now,' he said. 'And presumably Gilbert Farrel was considered suitable?'

Felicity stared into the flames reflectively, though she had not missed the small compliment and felt oddly warmed by it. 'At first it seemed that a marriage would be arranged quite quickly. But then it was postponed for some reason. No fault of Gilbert's, despite Mama's comments to the contrary. A monsoon or a riot or something, I forget. Anyway, after that, whenever Mama mentioned it, which she did often, Papa would tell her not to fret. We will fix it for the summer, or the winter or whatever, he'd say. And so a couple of years have gone by in this way.'

'And you are still not married.'

She gave a little shrug. 'I did begin to wonder if perhaps Gilbert had gone cool on the idea, but I confess I was in no hurry to wed either so I never commented upon the delay. But I am still engaged,' she said, most decidedly, and then flushed scarlet as she saw his doubtful look. 'At least, I was, until... Oh, goodness, I cannot think that Gilbert...'

'Then take my advice and cease to think of him,' said Jarle firmly. 'Fill your life with other things.' He was on his feet again, restlessly striding to the door, anxious suddenly to escape the appeal of those grey eyes. 'I must go. I've things to do.' Felicity had followed him and he looked down at her consideringly for a moment then, stretching out a hand, stroked the soft cheek with a gentle caress. 'Forget him, little Felicity. There are many men more worthy of your love. For a person with so much spirit and independent pride, you are vastly lacking in ordinary feminine confidence.'

'I have never found the opportunity to develop any,' she answered, feeling his strength flow through her at his touch. 'Perhaps that is the reason I enjoyed my work at the shop. It made me feel needed...' Having started along this path, she drew a deep breath and bravely blundered on, 'And I should so like to continue.'

He tilted his head to one side to laugh at her, but his hand was up among her curls somewhere, and he had drawn closer. 'What a little schemer you are, and I told you that the job was unsuitable.'

'Then find me another.' Boldly she placed one hand beguilingly against his chest. 'I have so many ideas to improve the shop. The window displays for a start are so dull and solid, no colour or shape to them at all. I could do so much better. And then there are those up-stairs rooms that you never use. They are quite wasted as they are and would make a wonderful tea-room for ladies out shopping.' She stopped for breath and at the expression which was growing in his eyes, not sure whether to be excited or alarmed by it. Her eagerness to return to the shop was not quite so practical as she made it sound and she wondered suddenly if he guessed how she felt.

'Felicity,' he said quietly, almost in wonder. 'You are an endless source of surprise and delight to me.'

A wild, jubilant hope, together with a burning excitement, was born inside her, but not so much at the prospect of getting her own way with regards to the work, but at the thought of seeing Jarle regularly. Perhaps he had missed seeing her too. 'Then I can come back?' But no, his mind, as usual, was entirely upon business.

Jarle frowned, his gaze upon the curl he was twining about his little finger while mentally drawing back from any commitment. 'It seems you and I think on remarkably similar lines, Felicity. I'd intended to chew over a few ideas with you but we ran out of time. I'll call again and we can talk some more,' he finished, rather vaguely. But his eyes sparkled as he smiled down at her and took his hand away, almost reluctantly, leaving her feeling very slightly deflated.

Giving a little head bow he added, 'And now I'd best be on my way before I forget what a gentleman I am and how homely and plain you are.' Upon that enigmatic note, he left her.

CHAPTER EIGHT

LADY TRAVERS looked unusually grave. 'You cannot possibly go out alone,' she told her daughter with a determined firmness. 'It would be most unseemly.'

Felicity offered a patient smile while she stuck a long hat-pin into her straw boater to keep it secure. 'It is but six o'clock on a Saturday afternoon and I am all of two and twenty. What is there for me to do here? Everyone is busily occupied, except me.' Felicity dared not say how much of an outsider she felt for fear of upsetting her mama.

'But it is raining.'

'Then I shall take an umbrella.' Felicity pulled on her raincoat and wound a long scarf about her neck. 'I shall be perfectly all right. Please do not fret, Mama. I have promised Dora and Amy that I will go with them to this meeting and I could not possibly let them down.

'But it could well be dangerous,' Carmella persisted. 'And Jarle may call and find you out.' They had come to enjoy his regular visits but he had not visited for days and she had watched Felicity grow as gloomy as the weather as a result. Had they quarrelled again? There had been a time when Carmella had entertained great hopes that Felicity had put aside all that nonsense about justice for Papa and had become more relaxed. Jarle had become a frequent visitor and the two of them talked incessantly, and with great animation, for hours and hours all about business. It was not a subject which captivated Carmella, nor one she would have chosen for her daughter to engage in with a young man, but at least they were no longer shouting at each other. Then, for

120

some inexplicable reason, the daily calls stopped and Carmella was evidently not the only one to miss them, for Felicity had become increasingly restless ever since. Now she had taken it into her head to attend a suffragette meeting of all things.

'I think it highly unlikely,' retorted Felicity, tucking her umbrella upon her arm. 'And, even if he did, I am quite entitled to go out if I choose to. I am no longer under his dictate, if you recall, since he dispensed with my services.' She was still smarting from the indignity of that act despite a melting of the ice between them.

'I do hope you are not still seeking some silly retribution for the loss of Hollingworth House?' said Carmella anxiously. 'Really, there is no need. Whatever Joshua wanted from life, and God knows sometimes it was hard to tell, it was certainly not a daughter to champion him in his losses.'

Felicity pulled open the front door and shot up her umbrella with vigour. 'I merely requested to visit the shop. *Visit*, that is all. I did not ask again for employment.' Heaven forbid, said her tone, and Carmella gave her a doubtful look.

'And he refused?'

Felicity's small boots clicked down the front steps and her skirts swished angrily as she spun upon her heel to address her mother. 'He point-blank forbade me to set foot inside the door.' Even recollecting this latest encounter brought bright flags of colour into her cheeks. Somehow, finding herself at odds with him yet again had proved surprisingly hurtful.

Carmella clicked her tongue in frustrated agitation. 'What a noddle-head you are sometimes,' she cried, and, almost bouncing upon the top step, flicked her lace handkerchief back and forth as if she swatted flies. 'You always look for the worst in him. Jarle Blakeley is a busy man. You cannot expect him to be always at your beck and call. You have found no proof, have you, that he is guilty of anything other than a normal desire to get on in life? Quite the reverse, in fact. He provides a home for his sister and his uncle, has achieved much in the trade union movement in the past, and now has plans to transform Josh's old shop into a fashionable shopping emporium of august proportions. If he wishes you to stay here and concentrate on domestic issues, what is so wrong in that?'

Felicity stood in the pouring rain beneath her wide umbrella and considered her mother's remark with surprising patience. There had been moments in these last weeks when she'd fooled herself into thinking she and Jarle were growing quite close. But if she overstepped an invisible boundary he would withdraw into some inner shell or stay away for days at a time because she had asked a question which he did not choose to answer, or, as now, made some perfectly simple request. If he did not wish to speak of his past so be it, none the less his whole behaviour was oddly suspicious. She was quite certain that he was hiding something from her. 'There is nothing more to be said on the matter,' she said now with a strained weariness. 'I do not know who to trust any more nor who to believe.'

'I never did trust Gilbert Farrel,' said Carmella, forgetting how hard she had pressed for a marriage between them. 'A self-seeking piece of misfortune if ever there was one. In the circumstances you are far better off without him. As for Mr Blakeley, no matter what you say, Felicity, I believe him to be quite taken with you. And if you would but get this fanciful fixation out of your head you might make a pair of it yet.' She stepped forward as she saw Felicity turn away, though taking care to keep beneath the shelter of the porch. 'He is a most attractive, well-set-up young man who cares about his family as well as his work. If he is a little bluff and plain-speaking at times it is but his honest, hard-working background showing through and nothing to be ashamed of.'

'I am not ashamed of his background,' Felicity quickly retorted, quite mortified by such an idea and coming back to say so. 'And I know there is no sin either in his enthusiasm for business, or bringing in modern ideas, but I could never, never make a—a—pair of it, as you call it, not with Jarle Blakeley.'

'Why ever not?'

Felicity searched her mind frantically for a reason and while she struggled and failed to find one, the rain thoughtfully stopped, so she was able to spend a little time closing up the umbrella and shaking off the raindrops. By then she had her answer.

'I will not be told whom I should marry,' she said proudly, tilting her chin. 'And it will certainly not be a man who feeds his staff tainted meat.'

'Oh, tush, he dismissed his cook, didn't he?'

'Yes.'

'And now daily inspects the kitchens on top of all his other duties?'

Felicity took a step or two away, anxious to be off. She had the oddest feeling that she was losing this ridiculous argument. 'I do not wish to discuss it,' she said, and, to her great surprise, Carmella trotted down the steps to grasp her arm in a firm grip.

'You can be foolishly stubborn at times, Felicity. Is Jarle not permitted one mistake? How very hard you are upon him. We all have to make concessions in life, Felicity. Certainly I had to in the course of my marriage to your father. No one is perfect. Josh certainly was not, kind and generous though he undoubtedly was, to a fault, some might say.' Her blue eyes misted slightly as she looked at her daughter in open appeal. 'Allow for human failings.'

'I do,' said Felicity, crossly. 'You know how I ever tried to please Papa, but he either did not notice or was amused by my efforts.'

'You were his adored daughter who could never grow up in his eyes. Never doubt that he loved you.'

'He did not always show it.'

Carmella gave a sad little smile. 'Josh had old-fashioned views about women, I'm afraid. People are not always what they seem.'

'What are you saying, Mama?' Felicity felt a twist of anxiety at the bleak expression in her mother's face but then it was gone and she wondered if she had imagined it.

'You only know as much about a person as they are prepared to show.' Carmella fell silent again for a long moment. Then, setting the reverie away, she shook her fine head. 'The world is changing, darling, and with it the attitudes of men and women. Jarle Blakeley is not at all like Joshua. You and he can form a proper, modern partnership, and go forward in life on a far more equal footing than I ever had in my marriage for all my efforts. With Jarle's business acumen and your creative thinking and caring qualities, there is nothing that you could not achieve together. It would truly be a proud alliance.'

'A proud alliance?' Felicity repeated the phrase as if in a dream.

'Do not underestimate Jarle Blakeley. He is a gentle, deep-thinking man who means to do all he can to improve this grim world as well as make a firm place in it for himself.' Carmella contemplated the puffy clouds skitting across the sky. 'The union of two proud families. The industry of one linked to the nobility of the other. A fine new partnership for a new century, is it not?' Now she smiled brightly at Felicity who looked quite incapable of stopping this eulogy. 'You do see what I mean, darling?'

Felicity, moved despite herself by her mother's words, could only say in an almost inaudible voice, 'Yes, I do see, Mama. But I'm afraid it is quite, quite impossible. I will not ... cannot ... marry Jarle Blakeley simply because you, or even Papa, ask me to. Apart from any other consideration, it is quite apparent that he does not want me.'

Lady Travers watched her daughter march away feeling very close to despair. She had ever prided herself upon her skills as matchmaker. Often she had succeeded in bringing about an agreeable nuptial arrangement for daughters of her many friends. But her own daughter was proving obdurate far beyond the bounds of natural maidenly modesty. Whatever reason Josh had had for making that incredible agreement, for once he wasn't far wrong. She liked Jarle Blakeley and thought Felicity did too, had she the sense to see it. Carmella gave a deep sigh. But if she was to succeed in this match, which seemed well nigh impossible at this precise moment, then she would need more than mere artifice to bring it about, she would need a helping hand from some other quarter. She did not know from where, nor from whom, only that it was necessary.

It felt good to be out in the open air after almost a week closeted indoors by the rain. Determinedly, Felicity set aside her problems and felt almost light-hearted as she took an omnibus into town, enjoying the jolting swaying of the vehicle and the cheerful banter of its occupants. She had promised Mama she'd take a hansom cab but this was far more fun. A few hours away from Mama, Kate and Uncle Joe would do her good. As would not thinking of Jarle Blakeley for a while. She decided to walk the last few streets to the Free Trade Hall where she had arranged to meet Dora and Amy.

The sky was darkening as late afternoon shoppers with brimming baskets thronged the streets, and Felicity hoped the rain would hold off until after the meeting. Workers were starting to make their weary way home, a muffin man with his tray balanced precariously upon his head was calling 'Muffins and crumpets', and an anxious-faced delivery boy pedalled furiously past on his trusty tricycle causing Felicity to jump out of the way for fear of being run down. All around her were the harmonious sounds of jangling harness, rattling wheels and the piercing whistles of butlers calling for a cab to transport the gentry to the theatre or out to dine for the evening. And, despite the overpowering scent of horses which pervaded the city, she found she loved it all.

She skirted a jet of water from a passing water cart, and, as she reached the stone crossing, smiled at the street sweeper as he swept into action with his long-handled broom, whisking away every speck of the soiled straw that served to muffle the clatter of wheels on cobbles, so that she could cross the stone slabs without splattering her skirts. She tossed him a penny for his trouble and he kissed it before swiftly pocketing it, doffing his cap to her as she swung by, his eyes following the trim shape of her slender figure far longer than was strictly courteous. But she only laughed and did not take offence.

Lights were starting to come on outside the shop windows, casting a warm glow on to the coolness of the spring evening, and she turned up the collar of her Burberry, snug within its fleecy lining. She would spend no more time pining for what she could not have. She was not too sure in any case what exactly she did want, only that it involved a closer contact with Jarle Blakeley than would be good for her, or he was prepared to give. Not even to herself had she fully admitted the effect the man had upon her and how readily she would welcome a less contentious relationship with him. The thought was too shaming and she pushed it from her mind. She would do as Jarle Blakeley himself had suggested and build a new life for herself. What did she care if he did not want her in his sight?

Lifting her chin defiantly, she fell into step behind a group of laughing girls all hurrying in the same direction as herself. Perhaps there would be a good crowd at the meeting, despite the uncertainty of the weather. As she turned the corner into Cross Street she saw Dora and Amy just ahead of her, and, calling out to them, quickened her pace to catch them up.

'Well, if it isn't Miss Hoity-Toity herself,' said Dora, not altogether unkindly. And, arm in arm, the three of them swung along together as if they had been friends for life.

'Have you attended these meetings before?' Felicity asked, curious to learn more.

'Aye. But few working women have the time to attend meetings because they have families and husbands to feed after they finish work, or else, like our girls, they don't dare offend their bosses.'

'You're not saying the girls might be sacked, simply for attending a meeting?' asked Felicity, shocked.

Dora nodded. 'It happens. Most bosses voted for the government, y'see, and they'll not stand for insubordination from their workers. We're supposed to keep quiet and get on with being good shop assistants.'

'Be fair, Dora. No girl has been dismissed by Mr Blakeley for attending a meeting,' put in Amy.

Dora gave a snort of disgust. 'He probably never notices. His head is in some cloud somewhere or else he's off capering across the Continent on some business deal or other.' She stabbed a blunt-tipped finger into her own chest as she turned towards Felicity, the light of battle in her eyes. 'No one takes advantage of *me*. Any way I can take a swipe at the ruling classes I do, so there. While they drive around in their fancy cars my family is near to starving, and I'll not stand by and do nowt about *that*.'

There followed a small, awkward silence in which
Felicity's sick stomach digested yet another reference to
Jarle's frequent trips abroad. It was broken at last by
the gentle Amy. 'This discussion is moving a long way
from women's suffrage. Come on, let's step out or we'll
never get a good seat.'

Trooping into the Free Trade Hall was the longest line
of women Felicity had ever seen. Women of all ages and
classes, their wide-brimmed hats seeming to jostle for
space as the queue stretched far down the pavement and
spilled out across the road. The three girls tacked on to
the end of it and by the time they took their seats near
the back of the hall, with Felicity rammed tight between
Amy and Dora on a hard wooden bench, she felt quite
breathless with the exertion. Yet for all the heat and discomfort there was an air of expectancy, and the buzz of
excited talk grew to a clamorous din. Most of the crowd
was in good humour and some women were singing.
Looking about her, Felicity decided that, like herself,
most women had come out of curiosity and their interest
was passive. But one small and noisy group were beating
on a drum and chanting slogans against the Pankhursts.

'Why do they do that?' she asked Amy, lifting her
voice above the din.

Amy cast an anxious glance in the direction Felicity
indicated. 'It calls itself the "Sick of Suffrage" group
and objects to the way the Women's Social and Political
Union operates. They claim that Mrs Pankhurst is only
interested in her own political ambitions, wanting to
become an important member of the Labour party. They
dispute the need for militancy, claiming that going to
prison clouds the issue and does little good.'

'Do you agree with them?'

Amy shrugged her shoulders. 'I don't know what to
believe. Mebbe they're right that up here in Manchester
we're largely ignored, even though this is where it all
started, except when funds are needed for more spec-

tacular events in London. It creates a sort of resentment but that's where the government is, in London, so it's understandable that more money is needed there. Eeh, don't ask me to judge.'

Further discussion was halted by the appearance on the platform of a small, pretty woman dressed in navy serge, wearing a purple sash over her crisp white blouse. She was smiling and waving at the wild adulation which poured forth from the crowd but as she held up one hand, instant silence fell and the girl began to speak.

'I shall begin by quoting to you the words of Christabel Pankhurst in *Votes for Women*, where she says, "Our hope of winning the vote is based on the belief that spiritual must prevail over material power." I am here today to urge you to hold fast to those principles. I know I am uneducated, but I love my country and I long to see women free.'

Her words were carried clear across the hall, emotional words of great passion and sincerity and Felicity listened to every one. She told of how she had begun in the movement four years since, after fifteen hard years in the cardroom of Woodend Mill, and of going with the Pankhursts to take the fight to London.

'I packed my little wicker basket, put two pounds safely in my purse—it was the only money I possessed—and started my journey to London. When I had paid my fare, I had one pound and a few shillings change.'

Felicity listened with rapt attention to how Annie Kenney had fought poverty and prejudice all her life and how she went straight to the poorest areas of London because she wanted to help others fight also.

'I organised meetings, put questions to the government, took part in demonstrations. We gave women something to dream about, and a hope in the future, however distant that future might be. We must fight on to win it,' she cried, and the hall erupted in loud agreement. Most moving of all was her account of prison life and how frightened she had been on the first occasion, yet had felt compelled to suffer its indignity. Felicity shuddered. The woman deserved respect and admiration, of that there was no doubt, but Felicity could understand the doubts of the opposing group. The whole idea of prison, of hunger strikes, or violence in any form, revolted her.

Nevertheless, Felicity was as carried along by the spiritual quality of the meeting as were her companions. And when the collection plate was passed around for funds to carry the 'fight' forwards, she saw brooches, rings and watches as well as coins in the dish, proving the strength of utter devotion and determination that lay behind the movement. Dropping in more spare change than she could afford, Felicity was quite won over.

'I will fight, you will see. I will do my part too,' she fervently declared, but Amy laughingly shook her head, indicating that she couldn't hear a word.

But Felicity was past caring. Filled as she was with fresh zeal, she knew that if others could sacrifice so much she could at least play her own small part. No more maudlin self-pity for her. She might not be the kind to tie herself to railings and suchlike protests, but she would visit the store, no matter that Jarle Blakeley had refused her access. There was so much to be done. Perhaps Mama was right and she was being stubborn and pigheaded. If she swallowed her pride and offered her assistance free by way of apology for the unjust accusations she had made against him, Jarle would perhaps allow her to help. A new excitement lit within her. There was still time to make amends. Their relationship had grown more friendly these last weeks and if Jarle shied away from her at times, probably it was because he suspected she criticised him. He had his pride too. But if Annie Kenney could come from a carding-room to a political platform, surely one Felicity Travers, daughter of an honest and noble diplomat, could learn a little tact and humility.

Entranced and excited by her decision, Felicity did not at first notice when she became separated from Amy and Dora. Swept out on to the pavement in the crush, she became quickly absorbed in watching a performance of a small playlet, ridiculing the government. She listened to a fife-and-drum band marching up and down the street dressed in their purple, white and green uniforms and sporting huge banners blazing their message for all to see. But then amid the almost festive atmosphere came a discordant note. A piece of slate hurtled through the air and there was the sound of breaking glass.

'They're trying to put a banner on the Town Hall roof,' someone cried out.

'Watch your heads, everyone, more slates are falling.'

Pandemonium broke out as the innocent bystanders desperately tried to retreat but were blocked by the more excitable who pressed forward for a better view. Panic exploded in Felicity's breast. What was she doing here?

'Amy? Dora?' she called out, but there was no answering cry. Pushing as hard as she could, she tried to force her way through the mass of bodies. Any moment now she would be trampled underfoot or arrested and marched off to prison with the militants. She found herself trapped up against a low wall and her head began to swim giddily. She scrambled on top of the wall, desperate to escape the press of the suffocating crowd. Balancing precariously on the wall, she looked out over the heads of the women. Where were her friends? How was she to escape?

'Felicity.' The familiar voice was a balm to her heart and she whirled around towards it, too fast for safety, and, throwing herself completely off balance, pitched forward. The last thing she saw before the crowd swallowed her up was open terror on Jarle's ashen face as he watched her fall.

*   *   *

The sweet innocence of her face softly framed by the honey-gold hair fluffed out across the pillow reminded him even more of a Renoir painting than she had on the day he'd first set eyes on her. A pad of cotton lint had been applied to her forehead but Carmella assured him that there was no serious damage and that she had spent a peaceful night.

'You can take in her breakfast,' she had said, thrusting the tray in his hands before he had the chance to refuse. 'And here is an extra cup and saucer for you to take coffee with her. Millie has made ample. I shall pop in myself later, but in the circumstances I think we can dispense with the proprieties, don't you think?'

And so here he was, gazing down upon her and feeling all manner of strange tugs and odd aches in the middle region of his ribcage. She looked like a child, yet she was not. She was a woman and he had treated her heartlessly, some might say callously. Why had he shied away from her? What was it he was afraid of? To find that he was weak and human like everyone else? Did he not already know that? To find that he needed her? He did not deserve her love, nor want it. Yet he had given his word to look after her and the thought of her marrying Gilbert Farrel was quite intolerable. Jarle recalled another promise he'd made once, and failed to keep. Dared he risk the same thing happening again? Last night had been too close for comfort. Like it or not he might well be obliged to honour his word to Felicity's father. She deserved at least to be kept safe and secure.

He reached out a hand and touched the scrap of lint, stroked aside a soft curl. A smile quirked the corners of his lips as he gazed down at her. Perhaps he could convince her in the end of his good intentions and teach her not to be so meddlesome or so bossy. One thing was certain, life with Felicity Travers would never be dull.

'What . . .?'

Her eyes were open, looking up at him like soft grey clouds washed clean after rain. He smiled at her. 'Feeling better?'

She nodded, which made her wince. 'I think so.'

'You gave us a fright,' he murmured.

'I'm sorry.'

'We'll forgive you if you promise not to do it again.' She smiled meekly at him. 'I'll do my best.'

'Millie evidently believes feeding a bump on the head is essential to recovery for there is enough food here for a houseful of patients.' He indicated the heap of scrambled eggs, buttered toast, grapefruit and huge pot of coffee, his eyes sparkling with humour, and Felicity laughed.

'I can almost hear her saying it.' Struggling to sit up in bed she put her hand instinctively to her head which ached dully.

The merry light vanished at once from his eyes and he gazed at her most seriously. 'You are sure you are all right? I could call the doctor again. We must take no chances with a head injury.' He had half risen from the chair but Felicity put out a hand to stay him.

'I'm fine, really. Perhaps if you could plump up my pillows a little...'

'Of course.' He was on his feet, leaning over her, his hands lifting her gently forward as he plumped and patted pillows and set her back upon them as gently as if she were a precious child. She looked up into his eyes and knew a moment of supreme happiness. 'That better?' he asked, brow creased with anxiety. 'Not much of a nurse, I'm afraid, but I'm instructed to see that you eat at least some of Millie's offering.'

Felicity adopted a suitable expression of obedience as he set the tray across her lap and did her utmost to do justice to the excellent breakfast. She was feeling better every minute, but the unexpected presence of Jarle

Blakeley filling her small bedroom was having a most strange effect upon her throat muscles.

As she ate, and Jarle sipped at his coffee, she cast a surreptitious glance at him and saw how pale he looked. The lines of his jaw were grim and tight-set for all his attempts to sound cheerful. He must truly have been worried about her. Something leapt within her breast, startling her by its intensity. Why should he care what happened to her when she was nothing more than a thorn in his side?

When she had eaten what she could, and Jarle had removed the tray, a thought struck her. 'What were you doing there? Were you attending the meeting also?'

He made a sound in his throat which she did not care to interpret. 'I was looking for you. Carmella told me where you had gone.' He turned his gaze full upon her and his eyes seemed to burn into hers. 'You should not have gone, Felicity. It was a crazy thing to do.' As she was about to protest he silenced her with the blunt tip of one finger against her lips and he leaned closer so that the fan of his breath warmed her cheek. 'I know it seemed merely to be a harmless meeting which you had promised Amy you would attend but these things have a habit of turning nasty. I could not have borne it if anything... If you only knew...'

A white line appeared above his upper lip and Felicity's heart contracted at the sight of the pain in his eyes, then fluttered madly like a wild bird that had scented freedom. Did he perhaps care for her, after all? Did that explain his evident pain and anxiety? 'Knew what, Jarle?' It was the first time she had called him by his name, and she asked her question breathlessly as if she dared not voice it. Taking his hand, she felt it tremble in hers. 'I—I did not mean to make you anxious.'

He seemed to hold his breath for a long moment, as if he were tensing himself to speak. His eyes darkened with an inexplicable anger, but then his attitude changed and he made a conscious effort to relax, stroking the back of her small hand with his thumb. 'The very first moment I met you, you caused me anxiety,' he said, but his eyes were sparkling again and he was smiling. 'Perhaps I should have let you be arrested. It might have been a lesson to you. You have heard what the suffragettes are up to in London, I suppose?' Before she had time to draw breath to answer, he proceeded to tell her with a determined clarity. 'Chaining themselves to railings, damaging property. It takes only one rabble-rouser and these meetings can get swiftly out of a hand. I don't want you mixed up in anything of that nature.'

'You don't want?' She felt suddenly faint at his words.

'Some of these suffragettes go too far. And for what?'

She was bitterly disappointed. For one crazy moment she had thought his concern had been for herself, but it was simply her views on suffrage which were irritating him. 'I am sure they do only what they believe to be right,' she said, rather piously.

He gave a soft little laugh. 'I love it when you sound like a rather fierce goody-two-shoes.'

'I am not.' His careless tone cut through her like a knife. Still smarting from her disappointment, she was quite astonished by the pain about her heart. Her head was throbbing and she had discovered a truth she'd much rather not know at that precise moment. She fervently wished he would stop caressing her cheek, or at least not do so in such an absent-minded manner. Was the man quite without sensitivity? To her horror she felt the trickle of a tear at the corner of her eye.

At once he was all contrition. 'Felicity. What have I said? Is it your head? Does it hurt?' He was stroking the tear away with the tender touch of one finger and more were spurting out as a result. Then his arms were going about her and he was holding her close, murmuring her name. He had meant only to comfort, to soothe her in her overwrought state, but something took a control of him that he had not bargained for and he found his lips moving over her wet cheek and down to the warm moistness of her soft mouth. But there was no softness in the kiss she offered in return and he was astonished by it. Against his better judgement he found himself drawing her tighter into his arms, deepening the kiss. A scalding release of passion and yearning, one to the other, as if each knew instinctively that here was the place to find it.

The sound of the door opening scarcely penetrated the depths of their emotions, but Carmella's bell-like voice certainly did.

'Felicity, darling, look who has arrived. It is dear Gilbert come all the way from India to see you.'

CHAPTER NINE

GILBERT FARREL had not quite known what to expect on his arrival in England but it certainly had not been to find his betrothed in the arms of another man, and this one man in particular. He could feel his blood-pressure rising and pounding against his temples even as he watched them guiltily draw away from each other, their eyes lingering a fraction longer than their hands.

'Oh, dear, I mean... Would anyone like a sherry?' Carmella was in total panic.

'I think it rather early in the day, Lady Travers, for alcohol,' said Gilbert drily, his limpid gaze taking in every nuance of the cosy scene.

'Oh, my, yes, of course.' She searched frantically for her handkerchief, and, having retrieved it from her sleeve, dabbed at her lips, which was a pity for they were quite dry enough. 'So many handsome visitors to your sick-bed, Felicity. I swear you are the luckiest girl.' She gave a little laugh but, since no one else joined in, its hollowness was only too painfully apparent.

Jarle Blakeley pushed back the spindle-legged chair he had pulled close to the bed and, uncoiling his long legs with sinewy grace, got leisurely to his feet. 'I should think a fresh pot of coffee would be most welcomed by Mr Farrel after such a tiresome journey, Lady Travers. And I dare say we could all manage another cup.'

Carmella threw him a look of intense gratitude. 'What a good idea. I shall speak to Millie at once.' Her eyes flickered around the three persons present, Felicity sitting frozen in her bed, paler than Carmella had ever seen her, and the two gentlemen glaring at each other like two pugilists about to fly into action. Darting forward, she snatched up the tray. 'We will leave you to dress, darling,' she informed Felicity, adding several nods and clandestine winks to emphasise the urgency. The prospect of acting as referee with these two combatants was certainly more than she could take on her own. 'We will all wait downstairs.' With these pointed words she ushered the two gentlemen from the room.

She fled at once to the kitchen and took as long as she dared to issue the simple message to Millie, but in less time than she would have liked she found herself compelled to return to the library where she had left the two, still glaring, and ominously silent.

The tension had not eased by the time the coffee arrived, followed swiftly by Felicity, but Carmella was thankful for the diversion of pouring, and handing out cups and saucers.

'How lovely to see you Gilbert,' said Felicity with wonderful aplomb. 'And what a surprise. We had received no word of your imminent arrival.' It was the very slightest reprimand, bravely ventured in the circumstances, but it troubled Gilbert not at all.

'F'licity, old thing. How are you? I say, you're looking jolly pale, and thinner. What the deuce have they been doing with you in this Godforsaken backwater?' He strode across the room, and, enveloping Felicity in his arms, gave her a great bear-hug. Laughing, and pretending to gasp for breath, she pushed him away with a playful pat upon his plump cheek.

'No one can accuse you of being either pale or thin, Gilbert, so I will not ask you how you are, for I can see with my own eyes. Except perhaps that you look a mite tired, which is not be wondered at after your long journey.'

'Have to look after the old tub,' he said, patting the plump curve of his stomach with evident satisfaction.

'You wouldn't want your husband-to-be to fade quite away before we reached the old altar, would you?'

There was the tiniest *frisson* of movement from everyone else in the room, yet no one had apparently moved. Felicity attempted to lift the corners of her lips into a smile but their stiffness rebuffed all efforts, staying obstinately straight and mute.

'Would you care for a wafer biscuit, Gilbert, dear?' asked Carmella, thrusting a plate before his nose. He took two, and, after smoothing down his coat-tails, placed himself neatly in a winged chair set close to the hearth and began to crunch upon them. No one else seemed in the least interested in food.

The awkwardness of the situation was not lost on Gilbert Farrel. He prided himself on being no fool and it would be obvious even to a blind man that something was afoot between the two of 'em. It didn't surprise him in the least to discover that Jarle Blakeley was trying to smarm his way into Felicity's good graces. He'd bought the store over Gilbert's head, hadn't he, so why shouldn't he go for the rest of Joshua's fortune, such as it was? And there was no denying Felicity was a jolly attractive girl. Even if she hadn't owned one of the finest old ruins in England, Gilbert would still have wanted her. He'd wanted her for years, ever since she had been a skinny seventeen-year-old fresh from school. The fact that he was almost twice her age didn't trouble him in the least. He was still very capable of servicing a nice little filly like Felicity, and of enjoying every minute of it. His saliva ducts drooled at the prospect and he began to feel very slightly overheated.

'Well, then, F'licity,' said Gilbert, flicking the crumbs from his coat front with well-manicured fingernails, 'I hope you now have all your Papa's affairs in order. It was deuced boring out there without you, I don't mind saying. A fellow gets lonely, don't you know?' The sooner he got his hands on Hollingworth House, the better. Life wasn't so easy in India as it had once been. Times were changing and he didn't much care for what he saw. He might not have a fortune quite so vast as Blakeley's but he was working on it and he certainly had more than enough to restore the house sufficiently to see him comfortably through a regal retirement, lording it over the local peasants. The idea of playing country squire rather appealed and he puffed out his pigeon chest as fantasies of grateful village maidens coming to beg his favours flitted through his fanciful brain. Maybe Josh hadn't got it so very far wrong. 'Time some knots were tied, eh?'

Felicity sank slowly down upon the sofa and stared at him, her mind reeling. Had she really been ready to marry this man? Despite the coffee, her mouth was dry and her heart was racing. She felt as though she were in shock. She could still feel the pressure of Jarle's lips upon hers, the fever of his embrace. Could it merely have been a momentary madness or was there genuine feeling involved as well? If only she knew. She dared not speak again, for she felt sure only gibberish would come from her lips.

Carmella was valiantly carrying out what must have been one of her finest performances in fatuous small talk ever, and Felicity was filled with gratitude. More than anything right now, she needed time. Time to discover what that kiss had really meant. Time to analyse her own response to it. Time to decide what it was exactly that she wanted. She risked a sideways glance at Jarle where he leaned upon the mantelshelf, one booted foot propped upon the fender. His narrowed eyes were riveted upon Gilbert Farrel until he felt Felicity's gaze, and, turning instinctively, he held it for a long moment and she became suddenly very calm. The expression upon his face had not altered and yet she knew that he smiled at her. He was giving her encouragement, a confidence to speak. Carmella's small talk had faltered and Gilbert

was once more in charge, as Felicity remembered he so
liked to be.

'I rather thought we could marry by special licence,
next week if possible. No need to make a fuss. Wouldn't
be right, not in the circumstances. But nothing to wait
for now, eh? What d'you say, old girl?'

Felicity recalled that she had always hated it when he'd
called her by that preposterous name. But she'd been
too gauche and unsure of herself in those days to object.
She hadn't realised, until she heard Gilbert prattling on
in his schoolboy jargon, how much she had changed in
these last weeks. She glanced again at Jarle, recognised
a slight lift of one brow, and, drawing herself up straight,
turned with a sweetening smile upon the man she had
once been willing to accept as a reliable, homely husband,
and now filled her with revulsion. Yes, revulsion was
not too strong a word. For the slow beat of excitement,
that others might call a pulse but she knew different,
that had started in the pit of her stomach some while
back, told her that she looked for more now in a
husband, much more. And, with luck, she might just
find it.

'I'm afraid things are not quite so clear-cut as they
were, Gilbert,' she said, with a charm she could only
have learned at her mother's knee.

'Indeed?' Gilbert tendered a polite, enquiring gaze.

'You will not, of course, have heard. But when we
arrived in England we discovered that Papa had made
new arrangements for me. Indeed, he seems to have
worked matters out very thoroughly.'

The smile slipped very slightly from Gilbert's florid
face. 'Indeed?' he said again, most unoriginally.

Very swiftly and efficiently, Felicity informed Gilbert
of her father's wish for her to marry Jarle Blakeley, and
the manner in which he had dictated it. 'I must confess
that it came as a surprise, even something of a shock

when I first learned of it. But I have had time to consider the matter since.'

Gilbert's face was turning a particularly unflattering shade of indigo. 'What reason did your father give for this, this...outrageous arrangement?'

Felicity smiled. 'Ah, now, there you've hit upon a mystery. We none of us can guess for certain. However, I know that Papa always wanted what was best for me and I ever strove to be an obedient daughter, as you well know.'

Gilbert was on his feet, sending the copper fire irons clattering in his clumsy haste. 'You don't mean to go through with it? Why, the man is a charlatan.'

Felicity inclined her head with some compassion. 'I knew this would be a shock for you, dear Gilbert. I too thought the worst when I first met Mr Blakeley, particularly in view of Papa's perilous financial state.' She stopped herself from glancing again in Jarle's direction for she knew it would quite unhinge her. She could not, in any case, reconcile herself with the fact that she had defended him at all. Even Carmella was sitting back in her chair open-mouthed. 'But I must say that I've found no evidence of malpractice on *his* part. None whatsoever.' Her slight emphasis on the pronoun caused Gilbert Farrel a moment's pause. But then Felicity too was on her feet and moving towards the door with a smooth grace. 'However, there is no need to make any decisions at present. I am sure you must be quite exhausted from your journey. Millie will have prepared a room for you. Perhaps, Mama, you would call her.'

'Yes, of course.' Ignoring the bell pull, Carmella took the opportunity to flee the room, knowing herself for a coward as she did so.

'I'll not stand for it, F'licity. I'll tell you that straight,' Gilbert was saying.

'Not stand for what, Gilbert?'

'Being jilted. Not the done thing, old girl.'

But Felicity had heard enough. Turning on her heel, she walked briskly to the door from whence she offered her parting shot. Very calmly and quietly she said, 'I am not, and have never been, your old girl, Gilbert. I may, or may not, choose to be so in the future. We shall see. Whatever reasons Papa had for making the arrangement, he was quite wrong to do so. Mr Blakeley and I are agreed upon that. There may be very good reasons for my marrying Mr Blakeley in the end, and I may or may not choose to do so.' She paused, and for a fraction of a second almost lost her nerve. 'On the other hand, he may not wish to consider marriage with me at any price.' She strove to disguise the tremor in her voice.

Gilbert Farrel made a loud unpleasant explosion through his overstretched nose. 'I find that hard to believe. You'd take her like a shot, wouldn't you?' he challenged, facing Jarle with a vindictive narrowing of the eyes.

Jarle returned the offensive stare with a placid indifference in his own and after a long pause said, 'It has been interesting to make your acquaintance, Mr Farrel. Felicity had told me very little about you. Now I can see why. Perhaps you will have noticed that she has become her own woman in these last weeks, something I think which was long overdue. I hold her to nothing, and nor, I think, should you. She may, as she says, choose to marry either one of us. Or neither.' And now he did smile but it offered Gilbert little solace. 'In answer to your question, I would say that any man would be a fool not to feel honoured to be chosen as Felicity's husband. And I would, in fact, be more than happy to abide by her decision on that score. Particularly since you would then be denied the opportunity.'

Smoothly going up to Felicity, he added, 'While Mr Farrel is resting, perhaps you would be so good as to accompany me on a small expedition, Felicity. There is something I wish to show you which I think you might find interesting.' Tucking her arm firmly within his own, he led her smartly from the room.

Since Millie chose that precise moment to put in an appearance, Gilbert Farrel had no alternative but to allow himself to be shepherded upstairs to a darkened room where that good lady assured him that a rest would be as good as a cure, and he'd be right as rain in the morning.

Jarle was proud of Felicity. She had handled Farrel with coolness and panache and in far less headstrong a manner than that earlier Felicity would have done. Gone was the prickly belligerence, the echoes of girlish inferiority, and in its place was a dawning self-assurance, still with some way to go but none the less present. What had brought about such a metamorphosis?

'Am I doing all right?' The meek appeal in the voice at complete variance to the new Felicity she'd so recently exhibited and who still occupied his thoughts made him laugh out loud, but he was at once contrite.

'Don't jerk the wheel, keep your hands relaxed. That's better.' He studied her profile where she sat rigid with concentration behind the steering wheel of his Landaulette. The small pointed chin tilted defiantly, the square jaw held firm, hands and feet moving with a natural co-ordination and complete competence even after one short hour's lesson. The small pink tongue flickered over the pert lips and was held for a moment between sharp white teeth. Jarle watched the action, which was unselfconsciously sensual. He hoped she would not lose that part of her which was the innocent child, the sweet feminine quality he had glimpsed tantalisingly hidden beneath the briskly practical veneer. For wasn't that the part of her which intrigued him the most?

'Now change down for the corner. Slower,' he cautioned. She performed the manoeuvre with skill. It was a quiet road, admittedly, chosen with care. He would not permit her to drive in the city, not yet. But he could envisage a time when she would do so, if only to prove him wrong in his damning opinion of women motorists.

'Why did you let me do this?' she asked him some moments later when they had stopped for a breather.

The grin upon Jarle's face was almost devilish. 'To show dear old Gilbert just what kind of a woman he was wanting to take on and let him decide if he's man enough?'

Felicity's own eyes twinkled with impish good humour. 'That is rather cruel and absolutely untrue. Anyway, you mustn't judge Gilbert too harshly. He is rather a sweetie underneath, you know.'

Jarle leaned close to whisper against her ear. 'He is *boring* and you would be tired of him in no time.'

Felicity caught at the breath in her throat. 'I think I've done enough driving for a first effort. Perhaps you will let me try again another day?'

'Delighted.' He looked down at her seated demurely beside him on the leather seat and he had a sudden longing to repeat the action which had caught him so off guard earlier, in her room. But she climbed down from the automobile and walked around to the passenger seat side and the moment was lost. Jarle shifted himself along the seat to make room for her.

'I should find it most useful to be able to drive,' she was saying, perfectly composed as she smoothed down her skirts, and Jarle watched and listened with fascinated interest. Papa's darling was indeed growing up, no longer needing reassurance, praise or guidance. She had certainly not asked for his on her newly acquired driving skills, apart from that one appeal at first. As she had demonstrated with Farrel and with himself, so with the car. His smile softened, for he guessed the wide vein of pride which ran through her like a rich seam would demand that she always sought perfection, even from herself. But, directed in the proper channels, that wasn't such a bad fault to have.

'This wasn't really what I wanted to show you,' said Jarle. 'Driving the motor car part of the way was a little extra, by way of a treat.'

She smiled her gratitude. 'And I appreciate it. What could possibly be more exciting than this?'

Letting out the clutch, Jarle set the automobile in motion. 'I think you may be surprised.'

He drove her into town, but, instead of taking her to the main front entrance of the shop, made several turns round the back of it and came to a halt outside a large town house, several storeys high.

'Where are we?'

Taking her hand firmly in his, he led her up some steps and through a multitude of rooms, all light, airy and smartly decorated but none of them furnished. 'Is this your new home?' she asked, utterly bewildered, but Jarle only shook his head.

'This is my vision if you like, my dream come to fruition, or at least a part of it. I did try to explain to you once that there were limits to what could be done at Travers Emporium itself, but you refused to listen. I had already purchased this building, so, to teach you a lesson for thinking the worst of me, I decided to keep it a secret until it was complete. Now you can see the results of my endeavours.'

Felicity had the grace to blush. 'Are you saying that this room, all these fine rooms are for your staff?'

Jarle nodded, a boyish smile twitching the corners of his wide lips. 'Isn't that what you wanted, for me to take proper care of them? There are two dormitories, each with two bathrooms. And look at this.' Not relinquishing her hand, he led her at his usual brisk, enthusiastic pace out through a door and along a corridor where he began flinging open more doors. 'These are small flats or apartments which can be occupied by married folk or friends,' he told her. 'Only the new young apprentices will occupy the dormitories. Everyone else in need of accommodation will be offered a flat to share.' He stopped at last from his whirlwind tour to turn her to face him, the boyish enthusiasm melting into anxiety as he examined her face. 'You do like it, don't you, Felicity?'

She gazed at him in astonished delight. 'Jarle Blakeley, you are the most devious man I ever met. Is that why you wouldn't let me come to the shop these last weeks, in case I got wind of it?'

'Partly.' He rubbed one hand over his tousled curls, not wanting to tell her that he'd had a more personal problem to wrestle with. 'But I rather hoped you'd help with the furnishing, though.' He gave her a rueful smile. 'You know my attention to detail on the domestic front. I'd probably forget to put in the beds.'

She burst out laughing and Jarle joined in, pulling her into the curve of one arm with a hug almost of affection. Gently she disengaged herself, freeing herself entirely from his hold, for she did not feel able to cope with such close contact again. Noting the gesture, his face clouded.

'What is it? Haven't I pleased you?'

She looked up into his eyes. 'Is that what you wanted to do?' she asked softly.

'Yes,' he said simply. Then, after a pause spent considering her face, now so charmingly trustful, Jarle came to his decision. One brief meeting with the odious Gilbert Farrel had been sufficient. Besides, he had reason to believe that she would not now be so against an arrangement between them. 'I know the question of marriage between us was not put to you in a particularly tactful fashion. Maybe your father did overstep the mark, or maybe he had reasons best known to himself. Either way, old Redgrove didn't help much by his bumbling. I understood your anger, it was natural enough.

Bit of a shock to have me foisted on you.' Jarle drew in a quick breath but when she would have interrupted he held up one palm to silence her. 'You can have your say in a minute, Felicity. But I really need to get this off my chest.'

'Very well.' She walked to the window seat where she quietly sat down and folded her hands in her lap.

Giving a little nod of acknowledgement, he began to pace the room, hands clasped behind his back as if he didn't quite know what to do with them. 'All that aside, there may well be some sense in it.' He stopped his pacing a moment to give her a shamefaced smile. 'Pardon me for being blunt, but you could say that you are looking for a purpose in life. And I'm not so keen on the way you're finding it at present. All right, I know it's none of my business but I wouldn't like any harm to come to you through this suffragette business, for reasons we don't need to go into now.' But we do, her heart cried. We do. She held her silence, watching him begin his pacing again, counting out his reasons with orderly logic upon his fingers.

'Nor do I care for the idea of your marrying Gilbert Farrel. Apart from the fact that the man is plainly an idiot, I believe him to be a thief. Oh, I know, we've little proof.' Jarle's eyes darkened. 'But we could ask him, eh, and see what he says?' He grinned at her, brown eyes twinkling, and her own lips twitched in response.

'You are very wicked.'

'I'd be interested to hear what he has to say. I don't like him, Felicity, and do not consider him at all suitable for you. Perhaps your father felt the same in the end. However...' Again the slight pause, this time accompanied by a pinkness about the neck and jawline. 'I accept it must be your choice, but, before you make up your mind once and for all whether you are to take him, I wanted you to hear the other side, my side. I'm not very good at this sort of caper but I'll do my best.'

Jarle floundered for a moment. What could he offer her? It would be a lie to say that he loved her, though he had thoroughly enjoyed kissing her, and it seemed to be very much reciprocated. She had already given him her opinion on his fortune and he had no wish to offend her independent spirit.

Felicity was watching the changing expressions upon his face which for a moment lit her heart but then his words gradually squeezed that hope from her body.

'We'd make a good partnership, you and I. See how valuable you would be for the business. You've told me so many of your ideas already, and I know you have others. So have I. We could put your tea rooms in the old staff quarters. We could have a sports department, hosiery, perfumery, hardware, motoring section even, why not?' He lifted his arms and swung them around, punching the air with his fists, eyes shining. 'We can sell anything we damn well like. You can dress the windows in the way you suggested with mannequins and such and we'll light them better, and, oh, I don't know, Felicity, it could be so exciting.' He dropped his voice and turning to her, saw the expression in her face and, totally misinterpreting it, added more calmly, 'I know this is an unconventional marriage and hardly a love match but I'll not force myself upon you, Felicity, if you do not want me. But given the chance I'd be a good husband to you and together we could make this shop into the finest department store Manchester has ever seen. And that would be something of an achievement, wouldn't it? What do you say?'

She gazed up at him with all her love in her eyes and her heart in her boots. Jarle, unfortunately, was not looking at either, he was throwing open the other window and gazing out over the city streets, alive and bursting with commerce, tall factory chimneys stabbing the smoky clouds above like grimy fingers poking the proof of their prosperity.

'There's a whole new world out there, Felicity, just waiting for you and me to taste it. India was the old world, the old Empire. Now we have a new industrial age filled with expansion. The people of Britain will be looking for things to buy and enjoy with their increasing wealth. And we can be the ones to provide those things. So how about it?' He was striding back to her again, restless in his excitement. Capturing her hands between his own, he pulled her to her feet. 'Felicity? You're not going to marry that old fogey, are you? Marry me and build a great future. I need you.'

She might have asked why he needed her. She might have enquired why he disliked Gilbert Farrel quite so much when he had only just met him. She might have asked why, if he was so engrossed in his business, he needed a wife at all and her in particular. And if she'd smiled or used a morsel of her femininity, everything might well have been different. But it was not in her nature, she was afraid of the possible answers so she did none of these things.

As for Jarle, if only he had looked into, instead of avoiding the frank scrutiny of her grey eyes. If only he had considered her reaction to his words instead of becoming carried away by his own enthusiasm. If he had swallowed his pride enough to admit that his interest in business had not fulfilled his needs one bit, that it was she who had breathed new hope into him when she burst upon his life like a ray of golden sunshine and he could no more live without her now than he could stop breathing. Then Jarle might well have discovered a very different reason for his decision from the one he had given himself. But he was a plain-speaking, practical north country businessman with no artifice, too little sensitivity and too much stubborn pride.

So their hands slipped apart again, and their eyes avoided the contact which instinct demanded.

The old Felicity rubbed her damp palms against her skirt and the new one drew herself up to her full five feet two, and answered with all that calm self-assurance so painfully acquired.

'Thank you for your interesting offer. I shall certainly give it my full consideration. But I must also think of Gilbert. You have to remember that we have been engaged for a number of years and I cannot toss him aside without a very good reason.' Wasn't the fact that she didn't love him reason enough? came the betraying thought. 'Later, when Gilbert is rested, we will be better able to talk. He does have a kind side to his nature, and has ever been a good friend to me,' she persisted, overstating her case as was her wont when misery engulfed her. For she knew now with awful certainty that had Jarle given any indication that he cared for her, even a little, she would have accepted his proposal without a moment's hesitation. 'I'm sure Gilbert will be happy to agree to whatever I decide.' In this last she was, unfortunately, entirely wrong.

And, as Jarle drove her back to the lodge house, he had the certain feeling that he had said something wrong but couldn't for the life of him fathom what it was. Worse, he didn't understand why it should trouble him quite so much.

CHAPTER TEN

CARMELLA was in a fluster. 'Perhaps turbot would be suitable. What do you say, Felicity?'

'Whatever you think best, Mama,' said Felicity abstractedly.

Carmella set down her well-worn copy of *Beeton's Book of Household Management* with something very close to exasperation. 'How am I to know what is best? I have never held an engagement party before with two fiancés, one of whom is about to be dispensed with.'

'And does Mrs Beeton have no advice on the subject either?'

'If you are going to simply be facetious we shall get nowhere.'

Felicity flushed, and, looking a little shamefaced, squeezed Carmella's hand with affection. 'I'm sorry. I am feeling a little tense, that is all. Please appreciate the difficulty of my position, Mama. Which man can I trust? What am I to say to Gilbert? For what reason would he perpetrate fraud upon Papa? It makes no sense when he has always expressed such a fondness for me. I have almost made up my mind to take neither of them and risk penury, after all. Can you bear it, Mama?'

Carmella slanted her daughter a sideways glance. 'Are you suggesting that your only criterion for choosing one of these gentlemen is the question of money?'

'No, of course not.' Felicity was shocked by the very suggestion.

'But it sounds very like.'

'You can be sure Blakeley is not going to die for love of me,' said Felicity crossly. 'His offer is a most practical, businesslike proposition. I wonder he doesn't ask me to sign upon some dotted line.'

'Then marry Gilbert,' said Carmella with mendacious indifference.

Felicity's heart plummeted softly. 'Do you think that I should?'

'He is certainly well placed, and you were happy enough with him at one time,' she said airily, covertly noting her daughter's reaction to the suggestion.

'But that was before...'

A pause. 'Before what?'

Felicity sank into gloom. Before she had seen Jarle Blakeley? Before she had seriously begun to contemplate agreeing to her father's outrageous plan? Before she had come to love him? Would marriage with Jarle, painful though it might be knowing that he did not love her, be any worse than marriage with Gilbert whom she cared for not at all? Waking or sleeping, Jarle's face was in the forefront of her mind, like a devil to torment her. How could she ever live without him? 'Before I knew the extent of our problems,' she finished, rather irritably, and Carmella smiled knowledgeably.

Closing her *Beeton* with a snap, she got to her feet. 'Yes, I think the turbot will do very well. Millie can dress it with a little lobster and shrimp sauce. And we shall conclude with Indian trifle and almond macaroons.' Satisfied, Carmella strode to the door where she paused to look back at her daughter. 'In the end it is just as easy to select a husband as a fish for dinner. You choose the one you are most fond of.'

With a wry smile she left Felicity to her gloomy contemplation on the wisdom of having a dinner party at all. Mama made it sound all too simple but how could it be? If it were, she would not feel so utterly wretched and confused. But what of loyalty? Duty? Whom did she owe that to? Certainly none to Blakeley. But to Gilbert? Papa? And what of Mama? She gave a heavy sigh. No, a decision was not going to be easy. There was also the question of how well Jarle and Gilbert would behave towards each other at dinner. The atmosphere between them on that first occasion had not been particularly conducive to good relations. Well, at least the vicar had been invited, to try to even the numbers, so if necessary she could always seek ecclesiastical intervention.

In the event the dinner party proved to be a surprising success. There was one difficult moment as they all filed in. Carmella led the way with the vicar, a suitably neutral choice, but one which left Kate and herself in something of a quandary. However, in the blink of an eye, Jarle captured Felicity's hand and tucked it possessively upon his arm. Casting an anguished apology in the direction of Gilbert's snort of disgust, Felicity had no option but to allow Jarle to escort her in to dinner.

He pulled out a chair for her and as she took it his fingers brushed accidentally against her bare arm, at least she assumed it was accidentally, and she could only hope he did not sense the quiver of response which shot down her spine as a result. Before seating himself next to her, he managed to press his lips close to her ear in that daring manner he had which set her heart thumping as he whispered softly, 'Think carefully, Felicity. But for pity's sake, don't make a mistake.' And, smoothly taking his seat, ignoring the shafts of fury directed across the table at him from Gilbert's pale blue eyes, he smilingly congratulated Carmella on the fineness of her linen and the intricacy of her floral display.

'Such a gentleman,' she said later as the three ladies retired to the library for coffee, and the relative merits of their dinner guests could be discussed undisturbed for at least as long as it took for the gentlemen to smoke one Havana cigar each.

Felicity sat in an agony of doubts and confusion. All through dinner she had been intensely aware of Jarle's presence by her side. He seemed to anticipate her every need and charmingly offered her the sauce, the cruet, a little cream for her trifle, seconds before Gilbert had thought of it. If she hadn't been in such a torment of emotion she would have found the whole scenario rather funny. She was sure that Jarle leaned ever closer to her on purpose, and, as he held fast to every dish while she served her own plate, she was blushingly aware of his gaze searching her face yet she forbade herself to meet it. She knew that she would be quite lost if she did.

'And I had never realised what a wit the dear vicar is, my dear,' Carmella was saying to Kate. 'He made such delightful fun of his own efforts at learning how to write a sermon, I was quite enchanted.'

Kate's cheeks burned and she bit her bottom lip anxiously. 'I am so glad you liked him, Lady Travers.'

'For goodness' sake, Kate, I do wish you'd stop calling me by that long-winded title. Carmella will do excellently well.' She reached for a second macaroon and bit into it with still-perfect teeth. 'I was so sorry that Jo-Jo wasn't able to join us, but he has gone on some expedition or other.'

Kate gave a little giggle. 'Uncle Joe always manages to find some excuse to miss a dinner party.'

Carmella glanced at Felicity's face, gone paler during their sojourn in England, and at that moment deep in thought. The girl tried to carry the world upon her shoulders with never a thought for herself. Well, she'd relieve her of one burden. Clearing her throat, Carmella set down her coffee-cup, brushed the non-existent crumbs from her lap and turned a smiling face towards both girls. 'The reason I mention it is that Jo-Jo and I have a bit of news we wish to impart but, as you say, dinner parties are not his forte so he has opted to leave it to me to tell you.'

'What news?' asked Kate, since Felicity seemed not to hear.

Carmella wriggled in her seat, rather like a child who could not sit still for excitement. 'Well, my dears, Jo-Jo has done me the honour of asking me to be his wife, and I have accepted.'

The clock ticking stolidly in the corner was the only sound for the full length of one of its meticulously measured minutes. Then it was as if Felicity and Kate came from a trance as both cried out together, 'He has *what*?'

Carmella chortled with delight. 'I thought that would stir you. Yes, it is quite true. We believe we are not quite in our dotage yet and can give each other considerable happiness and companionship, and even a little romance.' She blushed suddenly like a young girl. 'Why not? Love is not the sole province of the young. Jo-Jo is an absolute darling and has opened up a whole new world for me. We shall, naturally, wait until next year, when it is quite proper for me to consider a wedding.' She glanced anxiously at her daughter. 'I do hope, Felicity, that you will not interpret this as disloyalty to your dear Papa. We had some happy times together once but that was long since.'

Felicity flew across the room and enveloped her mother in a delighted hug. 'I am pleased for you, Mama. I hope you will both be very happy. You are years and years away from your dotage, you old rascal, and deserve not to spend them alone.'

Kate next offered her congratulations and there were a few tears and much laughter before she too confessed that marriage was not entirely out of the question for herself. 'John is hoping for a larger parish so that he can afford to take a wife,' she said. 'Of course, I have told him that money is of no importance.'

'Very proper,' agreed Carmella firmly.

'But he is quite determined,' said Kate dolefully. 'He says the bishop is aware of his wishes so I can only hope that we will not have too long to wait.'

'You must make sure that is the case,' agreed Carmella. 'A woman can grow morbid waiting too long for matrimony.' This last comment, Felicity knew, was directed at herself.

Sighing deeply, she planted a kiss upon Carmella's soft cheek. 'Have patience, Mama, do.'

'Have you decided what you are to do, Felicity?' asked Kate tentatively, not wishing to seem as if she were prying, but Felicity only shook her head.

'I shall do what seems right when the time comes,' she said vaguely, not knowing exactly how that would come about. 'For the moment I am quite determined to refuse both of them,' she said very stoutly and got to her feet. 'Perhaps, Mama, you would be good enough to ask Gilbert to meet me in the garden by the old cherry arbour. There are one or two matters I would like to clear with him.'

'Yes, of course,' said that good lady. 'You won't be too hasty, will you?' she flustered, but Felicity only smiled.

'I have given the matter great thought. But since the discussion will involve some pertinent and personal questions I would prefer it if we were alone,' she said, and Carmella regretfully withdrew, refraining from voicing her own private thoughts. The decision must be made by Felicity alone, she knew that, but she sometimes wondered if she had been quite fair to her in shielding her quite so carefully from realities. Perhaps a less sheltered life would have helped her now in this time of decision. Carmella hovered at the door. 'Felicity...' she began, but then stopped, swallowed deeply and, spinning on her heel, fled from the room. After all these years, she was still the coward, pushing unpleasant truths away. She hated herself for this damaging flaw but knew with a sure desperation she could do nothing about it. It was already too late.

* * *

Gilbert stumbled down the dark path, alternately calling her name and grumbling as a bramble tripped him or a stone slid beneath the polished soles of his boots. He found Felicity seated in the small summer house which Joe had recently built for Carmella in place of the rickety arbour. It was a simple rustic structure and not in Gilbert's style at all. Dusting the wooden seat with his red silk handkerchief, he forced himself to sit upon the wooden bench.

'There is a certain matter I wish to discuss with you,' said Felicity, coming straight to the point. As soon as she had heard his foot upon the path the nervous fluttering had begun, but, now that he was here, she felt perfectly calm, anxious to have the interview done with.

'I shall be happy to discuss whatever you wish,' said Gilbert, patting her hand with a show of affection. 'May I first say how very charming you look this evening. White taffeta makes you look as pretty as a water-lily. I'm sure you'll make an equally charming bride.'

Felicity could not repress a slight shudder. She had no wish to be likened to a lily, water or otherwise, which held associations of funerals and death, nor was she ready to commit herself to marriage at this early stage in the conversation, if at all. In truth, her response to his touch had told her a good deal and a certainty had formed within her that, no matter what he had to say, marriage with Gilbert Farrel was quite out of the question. She had changed these last weeks in more ways than she cared to consider.

'Is it true that you supply Travers Emporium with silks? And the new delicatessen department with tea?'

Gilbert reeled with surprise. The last thing he had expected was to discuss business. 'Why, yes. That is correct. Why do you ask? Surely you're not dabbling in business? Not the done thing, don't you know, for a gel?'

Had he always sounded quite so fatuous, when she had once thought him witty? 'There is no reason why I should not "dabble" in business as you put it, if I choose to,' she crisply informed him, and, realising his blunder, he tried at once to rectify it.

'No, no, of course not. No reason at all, if it amuses you. Mind you, it's not the sort of thing I should want you messing with once we are married.' He'd keep her occupied pushing perambulators, he thought, rather bluntly. That should quell the meddler in her. 'Province of the husband to deal with the common chore of earning a living, eh?'

'You had no objection to my working in India, at the mission,' Felicity reminded him.

'Ah, the mission.' He nodded his head sagely. 'That was different.'

'Why?' she asked, genuinely interested, but he only laughed.

'Come, come, F'licity, old girl. Should've thought that was obvious. Not besmirching your pretty hands with money on that occasion, were you? You cannot compare doing your bit for the natives with running a store.'

Felicity stared at the round smiling face, so oddly boyish in so mature a man, and marvelled that his paternalism had not grated upon her before this. She started to disagree with him but thought better of it. They were not here to discuss the emancipation of women, fascinating subject though it was. Her one consideration was to discover his part in her father's problems and all qualms at asking the vital question were now quite gone.

'Were you aware that your firm persistently cheated my father?' she asked, and leaned back against the knobbly wooden back rest, slightly breathless, to await his reaction. She expected shock, outrage, denial or a complete assertion of ignorance. He did none of those things. Instead he merely turned pale eyes impassively towards her and smiled.

'What kind of a question is that?'

'Exactly what it sounds,' she persisted.

'Sounds to me very like a lack of trust. However, it is rather vague. There are many different kinds of cheating, after all. If you cheat a man at cards or his wife cheats on him with his best friend then that is reprehensible and not to be tolerated.' Gilbert smoothed the bristly hairs on his new moustache before continuing. 'Business, however, is very different and a form of cheating is considered acceptable practice, par for the course, as it were. The secret in business matters is to be one step ahead of the other fellow. If this involves a little stretching of the truth then so be it.'

Felicity was aghast. 'Stretching of the truth? You call a deliberate flaw in a length of fine silk *acceptable practice*?'

There was the very slightest pause. 'You have proof that it was deliberate?'

'No,' Felicity conceded. 'But what of the tea? That was not genuine either, and there are other instances of wrongly labelled goods, short measures, weighted containers. Do you consider those to be acceptable, also?'

'One has to be tough in business, Felicity, if one is to survive.' He puffed out his pigeon chest with self-importance. 'As a girl, you couldn't possibly understand the full implications of it all. As I said before, these little peccadilloes are not for a pretty woman to bother her head about.'

Felicity had heard enough and was on her feet in a trice. 'You may call them merely peccadilloes but I call it thieving, and I could not possibly consider marriage with a man who carried out such atrocities. I am sorry, Gilbert, that our long friendship should end in this way, but I can no longer consider myself engaged to you.'

Gilbert too was on his feet, and shock was evident now, to such a degree that his florid face actually wobbled with distress. He must have done nothing but

eat since I left, to grow so fat, Felicity thought incon-
sequentially. 'You cannot mean that, old girl.'

'I am not your old girl.'

'F'licity?' he groaned, stroking his fingers up her arm
beneath her lacy shawl so that she was forced to hold
her breath rather than show how it made her squirm.
'You and I are old friends. I mean to be a good husband
to you. I mean to look after you and your poor Mama,
to restore Hollingworth House to its former glory and
all that. We could build a pleasant little life for ourselves
here in England. India is not what it was, old thing. Got
to move on.'

'Then you must do so without me,' said Felicity, attempting to remove herself from his grip but failing as
his fingers curled about her arm. 'In any case,
Hollingworth House no longer enters into it.'

Gilbert's gaze was blank. He was enjoying the feel of
her plump little arm beneath his probing fingers and his
eyes were moving over the rest of her with renewed ap-
preciation as his other hand reached out to grip her waist
and pull her closer. Desire was slow to rise in him, but
now it quite dazed him with its urgency. 'Come on,
F'licity, let's kiss and make up. Lover's tiff, what?' His
lips were parted in anticipation, oblivious to the fact that
she was less than eager to receive his kisses, when her
words finally penetrated and he stopped. 'What was that
about Hollingworth House?'

Felicity pushed with the flat of her hand against his
chest, trying to heave herself off him. 'It has nothing
more to do with me,' she gasped, wondering why she
had always thought Gilbert weak. He held her like a vice.

'Explain.'

The one word, issued in a clipped voice, made her
jump. 'There's little to explain. Hollingworth House belongs to Jarle Blakeley now, not me. He bought it from
Papa along with the shop.' She felt him begin to shake,
but not with the dawning of the passion she had

anxiously noted a moment before. This was pure rage. Hot blood rushed to his face before draining away, leaving it so white it was almost blue. Even in this moment of supreme danger to herself, Felicity experienced the unwelcome thought that, however upset he had been to lose her as a wife, he was a thousand times more distressed to lose Hollingworth House. 'Please let me go, Gilbert, your fingers are hurting my arm.'

Flecks of saliva flew from his tongue which flickered and curled with venom. 'He can't do that to me. Not after I kept quiet.' He gripped Felicity still more tightly, shaking her slightly and making her cry out involuntarily. 'I did hold my tongue, just as he asked me to. I promised him I would. Damn the man. Your father has cheated *me*, Felicity, do you hear?'

With not a clue what he was talking about, Felicity had the wit to stay calm, guessing panic would only send him more off his head. 'I told you, the situation has changed. It is not Papa's fault. Nor Blakeley's either, for that matter. It was a simple business proposition. Now do try not to get upset, Gilbert, and let me go, there's a dear,' she wheedled, but he didn't seem to be listening.

'I'll make Blakeley pay for this,' he yelled, and he looked down at her as if suddenly aware he still held her. What had he been about to do? Oh, yes. The possibility of revenge on Blakeley through Felicity was enticing. 'And you are the gilt on the gingerbread, eh? I'll not be made a fool of, not even by your father, Felicity. We'll tarnish the gilt a bit, eh? For old times' sake.' His mouth was hovering perilously close, and, as despair closed over her, she prepared herself to lose the battle of avoiding his kiss. Her anxiety turning to a desperate concern lest that alone might not satisfy him, she found him suddenly wrenched away and she fell back upon the bench.

There was a loud crack, a grunt, and the next moment she was staring at Gilbert's flaccid body spread-eagled upon the path, a look of complete surprise on his puffy face.

'It's all right, I haven't killed him. Though for a moment I dearly longed to.'

'Oh, Jarle.' Then she was in his arms and she did nothing to avoid this kiss. Quite the opposite, as she wrapped her arms tightly about Jarle's neck and prayed that he would never let her go. But he did, all too soon, and there was a question in his eyes as he smiled down at her.

'Does that kiss indicate that you have made up your mind?'

Shyness flooded through Felicity and she stepped back away from him, fighting for composure. 'I—I could never marry Gilbert. He as good as admitted he deliberately set out on a course of fraud and seemed unperturbed by it.' She still felt shocked by Farrel's attitude and glanced nervously down at his comatose figure. 'Shouldn't we call a doctor?'

Jarle's gaze, however, was riveted upon Felicity, for he knew the moment of decision had come and he felt surprisingly light-hearted about it. 'And what of me?' he asked quietly. 'Have you considered my proposal?'

An owl hooted in the depths of the woods behind them and a night breeze ruffled Felicity's hair, bringing more curling tendrils into disarray about her flushed cheeks. A ripple of longing coursed through Jarle with such an intensity that he shuddered with the shock of it. His relief that she was not to marry Gilbert was almost overwhelming and he wondered at it. She was slanting a shy smile up at him, tilting her chin and almost pouting those soft lips. He could not see the pounding of her heart but he felt a strange tightness in his own chest as he waited for her answer.

'If your offer still stands, Mr Blakeley, I should be honoured to accept it,' she said and for a moment the awesomeness of their decision struck them both dumb.

Then Jarle pressed his lips together and said very seriously, 'Right. Let's get on with it, then.' And taking her hand he marched her back into the house.

They were married almost at once in the local village church and Kate's vicar officiated. It was a very quiet wedding, as was only fitting, but Carmella made as much fuss as she was allowed by inviting most of the small parish to share in the wedding breakfast with them. Which was just as well for Millie had, of course, excelled herself and they would have been eating roast ham and game pie for weeks otherwise.

Felicity wore a gown of cream charmeuse with a fitted over-bodice of Limerick lace finishing with a tiny frill around the low-cut neckline. Her slender waist was shown to smooth perfection and the ruched skirt was caught up into a fullness at the back to form a slight train. She chose a simple wreath of flowers for her hair in place of a hat and when Jarle first set eyes on her he caught his breath in surprised pleasure.

Today nothing was to mar their pleasure. They laughed, they danced, they ate, and, when the day was done and the guests had departed, Carmella came to her daughter's room to which she had gone to change and await her new husband.

'You looked so beautiful today I was proud of you,' she said, smiling broadly.

'Soon it will be your turn,' teased Felicity with shining eyes, thinking nothing could spoil this unexpected happiness she had found. Jarle had been all she could have wished for in an attentive lover, though he had never repeated that kiss she had so welcomed in place of Gilbert's. Tonight, however, she felt sure their love could finally be expressed in the sharing bond of that most intimate of unions.

'All in good time.' A frown appeared at Carmella's brow and Felicity, ever conscious of her mother's moods, noticed it at once.

'Something is troubling you, Mama. What is it?'

Carmella sighed and gathered her daughter's hands between her own. 'Oh, I don't know, youth, I think. When you are young you believe everything will be beautiful and stay wonderful for ever and ever. But life can be cruel sometimes.'

'I do not know what you are talking about,' laughed Felicity, going to hang up her wedding dress and making a private vow to keep it forever.

Carmella cleared the discomfort which blocked her throat and went to sit on the window seat so that she could say what must be said without looking directly into Felicity's eyes. 'I dare say I should have spoken to you years ago, but I never got around to it. The fact is——'

'Mama,' interrupted Felicity with warm humour in her voice. 'I do know what to expect. I am not quite a ninny.'

'I'm sure you are not,' flustered Carmella, quite put-off her stroke but inwardly relieved that she did not have to go through all that tiresome business. Carmella fidgeted on her seat. 'A woman must devote herself to her husband and always see the best in him. Remember that, Felicity, but a man, well, he often has rather a different way of looking at things . . . at the relationship. A man is more independent.' Making a sudden decision, she got to her feet and came over to Felicity who was by now sitting in the wide bed with the white linen sheets turned neatly down before her. Carmella felt the prick of tears at the back of her eyes as she looked at her daughter, once so young and protected, now a grown woman awaiting fulfilment, and the choking in her throat made it almost impossible for her to continue. 'Oh, dear,' she mourned, mopping at her eyes with her lace handkerchief. 'I am behaving as all bad mamas behave at their daughters' wedding. And I only want you to be happy. I know this marriage began in a somewhat unorthodox way but you are so lucky to have such a gentleman for a husband.'

'Mama, do not take on so,' laughed Felicity and then more softly, 'Is it all reminding you of your own wedding, with Papa?'

'I dare say that is it,' Carmella sniffed. 'There is no reason why you and Jarle should not enjoy many happy years together as man and wife. I am sure he will be the most devoted and loyal of husbands,' she finished with a pleased sigh. Almost at once she heard a step upon the stair. 'Oh, my, here he is. Now do be happy and smiling for him, and remember what I have told you.' After fluffing out Felicity's curls and straightening the lace unnecessarily upon her nightgown she popped a kiss upon the hot little cheek and left her daughter to puzzle over the fact that Carmella had in fact told her very little.

But the presence of her new husband smiling down at her from beside her bed soon sent all other thoughts out of her head. He was still fully dressed in his smart grey morning suit, and all her new-found confidence evaporated at sight of him and her limbs felt weak as water. It was all very well to pretend to Mama that she knew what was what, but her experience of men before she had met Jarle Blakeley had been confined to a little hand-holding from Gilbert. To her dismay, she felt her cheeks begin to burn as the thought that there would be far more than such niceties this night flickered across her mind.

'There is no need to be alarmed, Felicity,' Jarle gently informed her, and taking her hand sat beside her on top of the counterpane. 'I would never dream of hurting you.'

'I know you would not,' said Felicity in a small voice.

She looked so vulnerable and incredibly young sitting upright in that great white bed that Jarle could scarce contemplate the fact that she was the same Felicity who had tossed her leaflet on 'Votes for Women' so carelessly across his office on that first fateful day. He still asked himself how it was that he had found himself here, in this incredible situation. He stroked her velvet-soft cheek with his thumb and heard her breathy little sigh, now so familiar to him. He did not love her, did he, so why was he here? His fingers slid down the line of her throat and smoothed the silky softness with a lightness of touch that had sent other women wild. But it was not deliberate on his part, he was not even thinking of those other women. He had no wish to love her nor for that matter to have her love him. He did not need the responsibility. But they were married and he was a man. Jarle saw how her eyelids drooped and how she swayed slightly towards him. She smelled of rose petals and clean soap and the pink and white icing on Millie's home-made wedding cake.

She was his wife. He had considered waiting a while before claiming his conjugal rights, or whatever the phrase was. But, by the look of her, that might not prove necessary.

Felicity was rubbing her cheek against his hand. He could almost hear her purr like a soft kitten and his hand trailed its softness over the firm swell of her breasts hidden beneath the lacy gown, and lingered there for the fraction of a moment. His own heart began to pound. What was the matter with him? Was it what he wanted too? He found his own desire mounting, a need to hold her in his arms so strong he could barely contain it. She was looking at him now, a mute appeal in her wide grey eyes. She wanted him to make love to her. The sensual woman he had first discovered in her was very much in evidence this night. He leaned towards her and his eyes were fixed on the rose-pink softness of her parted lips.

But perhaps she wanted more than that, more than he could give? Damnation, what was he thinking of? These kind of complications were not part of the bargain. He had never meant to love her. Jarle pulled his hands away from the creamy smoothness of her shoulders where somehow her nightgown had slipped to reveal a hint of the full young breasts which could be displayed to still further advantage were he to make the necessary explorations.

And, as Felicity looked trustingly up at him, he seemed to be glaring at her with a brooding, dark look that despite the shivers of excitement it lit within her seemed desperately serious. Then Jarle got up from the bed and strode away and Felicity's heart gave a little jump of disappointment. Surely he would not leave her like this? If he rejected her now, how would she endure it?

CHAPTER ELEVEN

PANIC gripped Felicity and she was beset by sudden nerves. Would all her hopes be ruined? But seconds later Jarle was striding towards her and she was looking blushingly away. His lithe, powerful body in all its hard masculinity seemed to glisten in the lamplight and she was soon gazing up at him mesmerised as he pulled the sheets aside and climbed in beside her.

'Felicity?' He reached out an exploratory finger to stroke her cheek, her small straight nose, and onwards to wonderingly trace a sensual touch, light as a butterfly wing, over the lips, the small pointed chin and down the arching curve of her neck. When he stopped again she thought she would die from the tide of unfamiliar sensations he was awakening in her. Would he not touch her again? Was she at fault in some way?

'I—I'm afraid I'm grossly ignorant. What would you have me do?' she stuttered, and, to her unbounded astonishment, he let out a sudden shout of laughter and pulled her into his arms.

'Felicity, you are a treasure, a delightful, unpredictable treasure. Sweet, innocent Felicity, don't ever change, I beg you. I think it is the child in you that fascinates me the most.'

But as his lips made their claim upon hers it was not the child in her he kissed, nor the child which responded. If tutor she needed in the art of expressing her love, she found him that night in Jarle's tender guidance. That first time was a gentle coupling which none the less brought a joyous release to both parties.

'Now you are my mine,' he murmured, and she saw his teeth gleam as he smiled at her in the half light.

'You speak as if I were a possession,' she said, rather breathlessly, but he only laughed softly against her ear, and, as she lay curled in the curve of his arm, she thought how simple it all was and wondered at her nervousness. She told herself she was now content but deep within her was a core of disappointment, of unfulfilment. What could be wrong? Had she expected too much? Certainly not a declaration of undying love. What, then? She snuggled closer, pressing her small body against the hardness of the male one beside her and felt him stir. When Jarle took her this time, it was with less curb upon his passion and he delighted in the dawning desire and knowledge which he awakened in her. She clung to his shoulders, to his head, desperately arching her body to meet his, and, in the moment of climax, crying out his name as the only way she knew to express her love for him. Later she wept in his arms, the deep ache within her at last assuaged. And later still, when he slept, one arm flung across her, she did not mind that sleep was a long time in coming, for she could replay that moment of ecstasy over and over in her mind.

In the morning, when he woke her with a kiss, she blushed to find herself clad in no more than a single sheet. But as she would have clung on to its fragile protection, Jarle laughingly flung it aside.

'Too late, my sweet. We'll have no Victorian modesty here.' He smoothed his lips over her flat stomach and the swell of her breasts before claiming her lips in a kiss that brought her vividly awake and gasping for more delights, which Jarle was only too happy to provide.

Within the sweet protective curl of Jarle's body Felicity slept again and did not wake until the sun was streaming through her bedroom window, telling Felicity that the day was well advanced.

Her morning tea-tray stood untouched on her dressing-table and the place beside her was empty. Remembering the ecstasy of the previous night, she pushed aside a stab of disappointment that he should abandon her so soon and was wondering where he was when there came a knock on the door.

But it was only Millie who strode across the room towards her.

'Mr Blakeley asked me to inform you, when you was up and dressed he said, and not a moment before,' Millie announced, 'that he'd gone into work as usual and how he hoped you wouldn't mind, in the circumstances.' Millie was not too sure what circumstances he meant but assumed that it would make sense to Felicity. For her own part she could understand a gentleman like Jarle Blakeley rushing back to his work, wedding or no. His sort were never likely to sit about and twiddle their thumbs all day making pretty speeches and such.

'Thank you, Millie,' said Felicity, feeling the disappointment bite more keenly. She sipped thoughtfully at her orange juice as Millie fussed about the room. She had promised herself no self-pity and had entered this marriage with her eyes wide open so had no reason to expect romantic overtures nor his undivided attention. When Felicity had first met Jarle Blakeley she had made accusations against him which had proved to be totally unfounded. If he did not love her, was it surprising? After last night it was difficult to imagine he had no feelings for her, though she was well aware that men were different in this respect from women. But the past was behind her now and the future in her own hands. Could she not teach him to love her? She would do all in her power to make herself irresistible to him by night and indispensable by day. This was the first day of her marriage, and, if she had nothing else, she had hope.

'I had thought to go in myself, as a matter of fact,' Felicity said airily, as she bounced out of bed.

Millie was taken aback. This was not at all the normal run of things. 'Into the shop?' she cried, astounded.

'Yes, indeed. There is much work to be done if we are to have the improvements put into effect before Christmas and I am anxious to do all I can to help.' Nothing could dampen her high spirits this morning, not even Millie's disapproving frown. Felicity began to unfasten the ribbons on her lacy *peignoir*. 'I think I shall wear the grey twill suit, Millie, if you wouldn't mind brushing it down for me.'

'Aye, right you are,' said the bewildered Millie, not too sure she liked this unconventional way of doing things. Women of her own class barely took an hour off for their wedding, but the gentry were different. She shook her head, mystified, as she brushed and shook the immaculate suit. Mind you, the Travers family had always had a way of doing things different. Look at Sir Joshua, back and forth between India and England as if it were no distance. And Lady Travers, getting herself affianced to that Joe. Still, he was harmless enough, she supposed, and had certainly brought the smiles back to Carmella's face, which she hadn't seen for many a long year. Millie's own face took on a perceptive, interested look as she helped Felicity to dress. The little miss had some plan buzzing in her head, Millie could tell. But if Felicity wasn't for saying, she wasn't for probing.

'There you are, proper smart you look, too. Will you wear the blue straw?'

'No, Millie, a simple grey turban, I think.' Felicity smiled at her life-long servant and friend. 'I don't expect this to be an easy day so I want an unfussy hat.'

'Very good, miss. Ooh, there I go.' Millie grinned good-naturedly. 'I should say ma'am, eh?'

Felicity smiled for a moment without speaking. 'Don't ever change, Millie. Right now I need all the love and support I can get.'

'Eeh, you've always had that, love.'

'I know.' Wrapping her arms about the scrawny neck, Felicity hugged the wiry body close, then laughed, brushing the tears from her own eyes. 'What a pair of softies we are.'

Millie looked at her with assessing eyes. 'Everything all right, love?' and Felicity nodded, too choked to manage any words. 'That's all right, then. All a bit much, eh, finding yourself suddenly a married lady? Well, if things aren't quite as they should be at the beginning, it wouldn't be the first time,' she added shrewdly. 'These matters have a way of sorting themselves out, in time. Anyway, least said, soonest mended.'

'Everything, Millie, is just fine. I'm simply being foolishly emotional. I am also ravenous so one of your famous breakfasts is most definitely called for.'

'No sooner said than done,' chortled Millie, thinking, That's more like it. If Miss Felicity had a good appetite, on this morning in particular, maybe things weren't so bad, after all.

And everything was fine, thought Felicity, humming softly as she finished her toilette. It was simply that she sought perfection. Perhaps she was too greedy, but, loving Jarle as she did, she couldn't help herself. She wanted his complete love, not merely the physical part, and from the rosy tint of that first magical morning she could see no obstacles to achieving that desire. They were, none the less, gathering.

Felicity arrived at the shop just as it was opening for the afternoon trade. But this time, as she walked through, it was with serene confidence, though only too aware of the curiosity in the swivelling eyes which followed her progress. This time as she entered the office, she experienced an altogether different emotion, for no longer was she here to spy and snoop. But, recalling the unexpected passion she had displayed in his arms last night, she did wonder how she would ever face him. Consequently she was not too disappointed to find the room empty. Amy came rushing in.

'Oh, Felicity, I mean, Mrs Blakeley. We weren't expecting you.'

Felicity laughed, drawing off her gloves as if she meant to get down to business at once. 'You were right the first time. Felicity will do very well. You and I are still friends, I hope.'

'I'd like to think so,' said Amy, sounding doubtful.

'Where is Mr...?' Felicity stopped and swallowed before continuing, 'Have you seen my husband?'

'Mr Blakeley has gone out on business, madam,' said Amy, keenly aware of Felicity's new role, which had caused quite a stir among the staff.

'Oh.' Felicity looked about her, rather at a loss. How to begin? Where to begin? 'Then perhaps you could help me, Amy. I would like to familiarise myself with the entire premises so that I can be of more use to my husband in any decisions he needs to make.'

'I beg your pardon, madam?'

'I wish to have the opportunity to crystallise my ideas, Amy, so that we can discuss the improvements more intelligently,' she explained to the bemused Amy.

'Mr Blakeley generally makes up his own mind, madam,' ventured Amy. 'I wouldn't like to risk interfering.'

Felicity tried, unsuccessfully, to restore first-name terms but was forced to abandon the attempt. It proved difficult enough to persuade Amy to show her the full layout of the shop. She kept saying that she hoped Mr Blakeley would not disapprove, or mind her showing Felicity this or that. It began, very soon, to grate upon Felicity's nerves.

'Are you happy working here, Amy?' Felicity asked, after they had traversed one or two empty rooms on the top storey.

'We all like our new quarters, madam,' she said with a new eagerness. 'Goodness, yes, I share with two other girls and we can bathe any night of the week and no being kept awake by hundreds of snores.'

Felicity chuckled softly, remembering well those snorts and snuffles, and cast a teasing look at Amy. 'Shall you marry your young man now, do you think, and take on one of the other flats?'

Amy's eyes widened. 'Eeh, how did you guess? I hadn't thought. Would that be allowed now?'

'Most certainly it would. You shall be allowed one evening off a week,' Felicity laughed, 'for courting purposes. Lots of things are going to change here, Amy. You see if they don't. We shall fill this place with warmth and light, banish the dullness and the dreary displays. We shall use imagination and flair and make this the kind of department store women will flock to.' Her eyes were shining and Amy listened, enthralled. 'A shop, Amy, is far more than mere fittings and stock. It should have a heart, a policy which proves that it cares for its customers. Mr Blakeley has had to cope alone up until now, on top of all his other business interests, but with me beside him he will find it so much easier.'

'I am delighted to hear it,' said an amused voice from the door and Felicity whirled to face him in a fluster of confusion.

'Jarle. I—I didn't know you were back.'

'Evidently.' His brown eyes were warm and sparkling, seeming to swiftly encompass her entire person before making a move towards her.

Amy glanced from one to the other of them, made her excuses and beat a hasty retreat. She knew when not to play gooseberry.

'Did you sleep well?' Jarle mildly enquired, bringing a rush of betraying colour to Felicity's cheeks.

'I believe so,' she said, rather primly, and he laughed.

'Well, if you are to work beside me,' he continued, his eyes still teasing, 'we must find you a desk. Would you like mine?'

Felicity gasped, appalled. 'No, of course not.'

'But you would have taken it gladly once,' he reminded her, a touch of seriousness behind the jesting.

'We are all entitled to make one mistake in our lives,' she said.

'Only one?'

Felicity was flushed with confusion, not sure how much of his attitude was serious and how much mere banter. 'I hope I have learned my lesson not to jump to conclusions,' she said quietly and was relieved when he came to take both her hands between his own. She thought he might be going to kiss them, but, no, such gestures were not Jarle's way. He squeezed them reassuringly in the warmth of his own.

'We shall put all that behind us now, eh?' And she nodded, more than ready to agree. 'But I confess I'm glad to see a softening in the somewhat entrenched attitude you took and I shall remember what you said about mistakes.'

'Why?' she asked, puzzled and just a little piqued.

'It may well prove necessary to remind you of it one day.' Then, before she could press the point further, he offered his arm and said, 'Now, partner. Shall we begin?'

A small kneehole desk was procured for Felicity and placed in the small room which adjoined Jarle's office. Besides this, there was a cupboard in the wall, a chair and a set of bookshelves.

'Bit bare and functional at present,' said Jarle. 'But I'm sure you can liven it up with curtains and a rug or two. Take a look in the shop later. Meanwhile there is work to be done.'

'Work?' Felicity had been trying out the small leather chair which swivelled most delightfully when she moved. She tidied the neat row of pens in the stand, set the blotter square and opened and closed a few drawers. Now she looked at Jarle in alarm. 'What would you have me do? I know nothing of retailing.'

Jarle burst out laughing at her panic, then, seeing her mortified expression, changed it to a smile of encouragement. 'It's not so very difficult. Imagination and common sense is all that is really required. Oh, and the ability for hard work, of course.'

'Naturally,' Felicity agreed, anxious to take in every word he said.

'In fact, you pretty much summed it up yourself rather well to Amy just now. I'll tell you what.' Jarle leaned his fists upon the desk and as he bent towards her she quivered at the warmth of his breath caressing her cheek. 'We'll start with the nasty part, take our medicine first as my old mother used to say, then we'll get down to the pleasure of discussing these plans I know you've already studied, and start tossing some ideas about.'

Felicity felt her confidence return in a surge at his un-hesitating acceptance that she should be a part of his plans, part of his life. 'Right you are,' she said, stealing his favourite phrase, and he grinned at her before swinging on his heel and striding back into his own office. Seconds later Felicity was scurrying after him.

'What exactly did you mean by medicine? Which nasty part are you talking about?'

Jarle gave her a rueful smile as he lowered himself into his wide leather chair and picked up the small hand bell to summon Amy. 'Why, Miss Bridget, of course, who else? Before we do anything we must first speak with her.'

Felicity blenched. 'Miss Bridget will never accept me.'

'You are my wife, she must,' said Jarle. 'Though I accept she has shown little sign of listening to a word I have said since I took over. I suspect she was left very much in charge until then.'

'Why do you not dismiss her? The girls are terrified of her.'

Jarle gave a soft laugh that sounded ominous to Felicity's finely tuned ears. 'I assure you, I am not. She's good at her job for one thing and I appreciate efficiency.' Jarle looked Felicity full in the eye. 'I think Miss Bridget may well be the accomplice we seek but without definite proof I can do nothing.'

'Accomplice?' Felicity was thinking rapidly. 'I suppose Gilbert would need someone on the spot to cover up his tracks and report the success or otherwise of his plotting.'

'Exactly. So tread carefully with her, Felicity—with all of them. I would not have you involved.'

'But I am involved,' Felicity protested. 'He was my father.'

Jarle gave an impatient little sigh. 'We are not concerned with your father now, Felicity, we are concerned about the store itself, and its future. If I have somewhat neglected domestic detail these last months, it is chiefly because my major consideration has been to make this business profitable again. I'm winning, slowly, but we still have a long way to go. All our plans and improvements will be money wasted if it is bled of its profits by some unknown source. And if someone is lining his or her pockets from all this, they will not take kindly to meddlesome interference from you, so for once curb your natural curiosity.'

Felicity ruefully had to admit the sense of this yet felt bound to add more fervently, 'Yet, I cannot ignore the effect all this had upon poor Papa.'

Jarle looked as if he were about to say more but then changed his mind and lifting up the small hand-bell gave it an excessively vigorous clatter. Delightful companion though she was, he thought, she could be as stubborn as a mule at times. She could force his hand in the end and that would be a pity for he had no wish to hurt her unduly.

'I believe you sent for me.' Miss Bridget's black-eyed glare managed to convey the impression that such a thing was unheard of.

'Ah, Miss Bridget, yes, indeed.' Jarle leaned back in his chair and smiled up at his chief shop assistant with seeming benevolence. 'You will be aware that change is in the air? Travers Drapery is about to becomes Travers New Department Store.'

Miss Bridget's lips tightened. 'I'm aware there have been some changes we might not have expected.' She flicked a glance in Felicity's direction where she sat quietly in the corner.

Felicity at once got to her feet and came round the desk to Miss Bridget's side. 'I can understand any surprise you may have felt at learning of my marriage with Mr Blakeley. And to find me here, in a position of some authority.' Felicity paused to offer a smile but met with a wooden blankness. 'Perhaps it did seem rather sudden, but as you may recall this shop once belonged to my father and by marrying its new proprietor I was merely carrying out his last wishes. Of course, my own feelings on the subject needed time to be reconciled, so I can understand how—that is, why...' she slithered to a halt. Why was she going over all this to Miss Bridget, who was not at all interested?

'I'm sure it's none of my concern,' said Miss Bridget, looking down her nose, and Felicity cringed, her confidence immediately going on the slide. The woman had not even the manners to offer her good wishes.

There was a short, awkward silence.

'What my wife is saying,' put in Jarle, getting to his feet and coming to stand beside Felicity, 'is that in future she will be an equal partner in this business.' He smiled at the woman, though it did not quite reach his eyes. 'I am sure you will be only too ready to co-operate. For my part I'm delighted she has agreed to help for there is an awesome body of work to be done if the changes I envisage are to be implemented by Christmas.'

'I have always striven to please,' said Miss Bridget, in a tone which said the opposite.

'There will be a number of changes, naturally,' Jarle continued, as if she had not spoken. 'Which we will inform you of in due course. In the meantime we accept your kind felicitations and ask only for your loyalty to Travers Department Store in the future.'

Since Miss Bridget had not offered any felicitations, Felicity was highly amused to see the woman's usual aplomb fall into disarray.

'Will there be anything more?' she asked through frigid lips.

'Not at present,' said Jarle, returning his attention to a sheaf of papers he held in his hand. But, just as Miss Bridget reached the door, he continued blandly, 'Oh, there was one other matter I've been meaning to mention. I believe we've discussed it before. And that is the question of the fine system.'

Miss Bridget quailed slightly beneath the cold on-slaught of Jarle's gaze. 'I don't think I quite understand.'

'It is perfectly simple,' said Jarle, pleasantly enough. 'I confess that I had thought the thing abolished but Fel... I learn that that is not so. Do you know why that should be?' The ice in his tone brought the shivers to Felicity's innocent heart but Miss Bridget was made of sterner stuff. With narrowed eyes she faced her employer.

'There is nothing wrong with such a system. Most of the large stores operate one very like it, certainly all the ones I have worked in, and they have been of the very highest calibre.' Not like this one, her posture said as she looked down her own sharp nose.

'I cannot say that I am greatly interested in what other stores choose to do, Miss Bridget. It is this store which concerns me and we will have no such system here.'

Miss Bridget's colour began, very slowly, to change. 'You will never keep these girls in line without it,' she said sharply.

'I'm sure you meant it for the best,' put in Felicity. 'But I believe we will get more loyalty and better service from staff who are not constantly in fear of losing their pay, or indeed their jobs.'

'Excellently put,' agreed Jarle, striding round the desk to fling open the office door. 'I think the matter should now be perfectly clear. Is that not so, Miss Bridget?'

He inclined his head with a polite dismissive nod and the woman had no alternative but to acknowledge that it was but as she made to leave, Felicity stepped quickly forward. 'By the way, what happens to the fines the girls pay?'

'What happens to them?' Miss Bridget stuttered, her composure now in ribbons.

'Yes.' Felicity met the older woman's frantic gaze with a direct grey-eyed stare. 'What happens to the money?'

Miss Bridget drew herself to her usual ramrod straightness. 'If you think I have misappropriated——'

'I have said nothing of the sort, Miss Bridget,' said Felicity quietly. 'I would simply like to know where it is.'

'In a box, under my bed, but I...' she unwillingly began, and Felicity nodded.

'As I thought. Then perhaps you should return it.'

Miss Bridget almost gaped. 'But I c-couldn't begin to know——'

'Perhaps I can offer a solution,' put in Jarle quietly, but smiling at Felicity added, 'If you agree, it could be paid in to some children's benevolent society. I am certain they will find some good use for it.'

Felicity beamed her approval. 'An excellent idea. See to it at once, Miss Bridget.'

Stone-faced and grey with controlled anger, Miss Bridget stalked from the room to do as she was bid. But

Jarle watched her go with a touch of misgiving. If they had unwittingly stirred up more hatred in her cold spinster heart, the store, and, more important, Felicity, might be in even greater danger.

Over the following days, Jarle and Felicity gave no further thought to Miss Bridget. They were both thoroughly engrossed in their new plans for the store by day, and their developing relationship by night.

'I think we should abolish the shopping-through system,' suggested Felicity one evening as they sat on in the office discussing the day's business after the shop had closed. 'Customers should be allowed to enjoy the freedom to browse and look about them and not be accosted the moment they enter the shop and then handed from counter to counter.'

'Do you not think they like being treated with deference?' asked Jarle. 'It is the way it has always been done.'

'And they will still be treated so,' returned Felicity with equal firmness. 'But if we wish this store to appeal to a wider variety of persons in the future then we should drop these outmoded methods. Many customers find the constant calling of a floor walker to attend them intimidating. We must move with the times, must we not?'

Jarle's eyes lit with enthusiasm that was so often present these days. 'You're absolutely right, Felicity. Travers Store shall be one of the new variety which offers the kind of freedom needed to explore its delights to the full. People could spend all day here. Shop, take lunch, meet their friends, write letters, why not?' he persisted when he saw Felicity smile.

'Why not?' she agreed.

'And we could offer credit to our more affluent customers,' said Jarle thoughtfully. 'In which they can choose what they wish and pay on a monthly account.'

'Would we not lose money by that?' asked Felicity, slightly shocked, but Jarle shook his head.

'We shall charge them interest for the privilege. It will help finance the stock for the poorer clientele.'

'Privilege?'

'Of not paying cash.'

Felicity found this philosophy beyond her grasp and laughingly said so. Smiling at her, Jarle thought, not for the first time, how pretty she was and how much more charming now that she was relaxed and not forever seeking problems. He had always enjoyed the thrust and challenge of business but had never expected to find the same pleasure in a marriage. Now he was not so sure. Felicity's ideas were not only imaginative but close to the needs of the people who would use the store, an astuteness which he could only admire.

But his pleasure in his new wife was not confined to a business level alone, satisfying though that was. Each night in his arms she grew more passionate, opening to him without coyness or restraint. She was a constant source of surprise and delight to him and he found himself looking forward to each new day, and night, with her. He glanced now at his fob watch, then smiled at her in a manner which brought hot blood coursing through her weakened limbs.

'It is late. I think it time we went home, don't you, Felicity?'

As for Felicity, she was becoming more and more hopeful that the marriage would prosper. It seemed incredible to her now that she had ever been at odds with Jarle or thought him unsuitable as a husband. She could hardly bear to be out of his sight and felt a deep relief that she had not been coerced into marrying Gilbert Farrel. Now, as she climbed into Jarle's automobile to be driven home, the familiar breathless core of excitement burst into life within her at yet another night to be spent in his arms. How lucky she was to have such a gentle but ardent lover for a husband. The bad times were over, and things could only get better, she was sure of it.

CHAPTER TWELVE

GILBERT FARREL impatiently paced up and down the dusty court, feeling more peeved with every turn. He was not accustomed to lurking in back alleys and if that girl didn't hurry she'd get more than the sharp edge of his tongue which was already due to her.

He glanced at his fob watch. Quarter after seven o'clock. She'd agreed seven precisely. He'd wait five minutes more then he'd be forced to make alternative arrangements. A door banged and he heard the clatter of boots on cobbles. She was hurrying towards him, face pale and shiny with sweat, red hair flying.

'You're late,' he greeted her but Dora only grimaced.

'That old dragon made me count everything twice. Took me twice as long to finish the unpacking. Now, with comin' to see you, I'll probably get no supper.'

'You get well enough paid for your trouble,' he said unsympathetically, pulling her into the shadow of a doorway.

'Aye, where is it?' Tilting her face up at him she gave a little swagger as if to show she wasn't afraid of him, Mr High and Mighty, but one glance at his face made her reconsider and she softened her tone a little as she continued. 'You owe me three months' back pay.' She held out a small, rather grubby palm.

Gilbert stared at it for a moment as if he'd never seen a hand before, then, taking it, he twisted her arm about her back, whilst he pushed his face close to hers. 'You've been talking to someone, haven't you, Dora?'

'I haven't. I swear.'

'Some of our little tricks have been discovered,' he said, and her eyes widened. 'I don't like that, not one little bit.' He gave her arm another squeeze and Dora bit hard on her lower lip so that her cry was no more than a whimper. 'Fortunately they haven't learned how I really made my money, and you won't tell them, will you, Dora? Not if you know what's good for you.' He slid a small leather pouch into her hand and she grasped it greedily. 'That'll ensure your silence for now.'

'You know I don't blab,' Dora responded, pushing the pouch down the front of her blouse. 'It in't no business o' mine how you made your fortune, is it?' With few scruples and many mouths in her family to be fed, she'd come to depend on this regular income, usually sent as a banker's draft. She had her own post office account building up nicely. Good feeling that was. And just for counting things out wrong, making out there were more than there actually were, or mixing up bad stuff with good so no one'd know the difference. Easy. One day she'd have enough to be out of this place for good. Somewhere new and exciting, like America, where a person could spread her wings a bit.

He released her arm and she rubbed it gingerly, wondering if it could be broken. 'It's been a good game, eh, Dora? Pity in a way that it's over.' He leaned back against the wall, studying her, wondering if she could be of any further use to him.

Dora gaped with disappointment. It was life or death to her brothers and sisters, not a game. And she'd moved them to a better house, wanting to get her mother out of the damp sewer they'd lived in so long. But the rent was more. How would she ever pay it now? 'If it's over I wants to know about that bonus you promised me.' She poked her shiny face up at him. It was worth a try, she thought.

He laughed, at least she thought it was a laugh, somewhere deep in his throat. 'And what bonus was that?'

'You said as when you got what you wanted, you'd
see I was all right, a bit extra to put by for a rainy day,
like. So if you've got it, where's my share, then?' She
sounded truculent in her desperation.

He stared down at her, brow creased in thought. He
could well afford to retire. He'd always intended to, and
give up this and his other little enterprises in exchange
for luxurious comfort and respectability. One way or
another he'd been determined to amass a fortune and
make himself the equal of such men as Sir Joshua Travers
who took money for granted. As a result he and Carmella
had welcomed him as a suitor for their gentle daughter,
which had fitted in very nicely with Gilbert's plans to
establish himself into the old aristocratic circles with the
benefit of new money.

They had always assumed that that money came from
honest trading. But then Josh had done a little probing,
in that over-protective way he had where his family were
concerned, and had turned a bit sniffy about some of
Gilbert's activities. Not that any of them were quite
outside the law and who was Josh Travers to make
judgements, in any case? But the wedding had been called
off, and, despite Gilbert using every ploy at his disposal,
it seemed he had failed to change the old man's mind.

And Jarle Blakeley had won.

Gilbert had gained some satisfaction from playing his
old tricks on Joshua himself after he'd taken it into his
head to buy this store, but it wasn't enough. Gilbert
wanted more. 'There might be one more little thing you
can do for me, Dora, my sweet.'

Her eyes narrowed keenly, instantly suspicious of the
false endearment. 'What's that?' She was anxious to be
gone but unwilling to lose the opportunity of earning
another sovereign or two.

Gilbert smiled. 'I seem to have lost out on part of my
plans,' he told her, thinking of Felicity. 'But it may not
be too late to win over the rest. It will doubtless involve

a little artifice, at which you are more than adept, in order to bring someone down a peg or two.' He meant to have Hollingworth House, if he could but think of a way, and no jumped-up guttersnipe nor do-gooding aristocrat would stop him.

'No one'll get hurt, will they?' Dora asked. She drew the line at violence. No one could call Dora naïve, and, though she didn't trust this one as far as she could throw him, she was ready to take his money for silly little cheats that folks should be more wary of. But she knew what it felt like to be pummelled to within half a breath of your life, as did her mam, and she didn't want to be involved in any of that stuff. 'So long as that's understood, I'm yer girl,' she said.

He nodded. 'Good. I want you to keep your ear to the ground. Everything they do, everywhere they go, I need to know of it. Understand? Report to me here same time next week and don't be late. I'm depending on you, Dora.'

'You can trust me,' she scoffed, not realising that he hadn't given her any proper assurance.

The next few weeks were the busiest Felicity could ever remember. When she and Jarle were not poring over plans together they were training shop assistants in the new systems, superintending displays and seeing commercial travellers to order goods for the autumn season.

Jarle instructed builders and carpenters on the alterations they required but constantly asked Felicity for her opinion and often left the finer details of colour and design entirely to her.

'Ring up Mason and Hargreaves,' he told her one morning. 'Ask them where the devil those designs are that they promised us a week ago.'

'Ring them up? Me?' Felicity asked in an uncertain voice and Jarle raised his brows at her.

'Why not? Are you not a modern woman?'

'But what should I say?'

'Whatever needs to be said to elicit the information you require and get the job done,' said Jarle succinctly, then, as she still sat staring uncertainly at the telephone, urged her, 'Go on, pick it up. It doesn't bite.'

Mr Mason of Mason and Hargreaves was evidently not accustomed to having his business efficiency questioned by young ladies and said as much. When he learned who she was he treated her as a doting but dim wife and asked to deal with her husband. This did nothing to endear himself to Felicity, and, irritated by this blatant prejudice, she half offered the telephone to Jarle. But smiling, he only shook his head, then, pressing a kiss to her ear, whispered very loudly, 'Tell the pottering fool your husband has every faith in you and so should he.' Possibly Mr Mason heard this, for he certainly proceeded to describe his plans at some length and Felicity listened in growing despair. When he began to speak of cupids and fountains she quite lost her patience.

'I do not want it to look like some temple from a Greek legend, nor a palace of the French Renaissance, a fashion which has prevailed too long in my opinion. I wish Travers New Department Store to be English. Is that so very difficult to achieve? Yes, pray do call in with some new designs which we will discuss at some length. Thank you for your time. Good morning.' Felicity set the earpiece of the telephone back upon its hook and looked up to meet Jarle's admiring gaze.

'Good for you. That's telling him.'

Towards the end of July, the shop was to be closed for two weeks while new electric lighting was installed along with the electric lifts and two escalators. This latter was causing much excitement among the staff, who were, in any case, highly wrought up in anticipation of their annual holiday. Little trade would be lost for those two weeks since the mills and factories in town would also be closed and the trains packed with tired, excited workers off on a week or two's holiday to the seaside. There would be no such luxury for Jarle and Felicity, however. They had more than enough to do for weeks to come and Felicity was happy to accept that. Though a part of her regretted the loss of a honeymoon alone with Jarle, being with him was all she asked.

As each day passed in a welter of activity and decisions, and each night in the vibrant warmth of his arms, she fell ever more deeply in love with her husband.

Sometimes she would catch him watching her, a thoughtful expression upon his face, as if he didn't quite know what to make of her, or of their life together. She took this as a hopeful sign until one day in July when her world tumbled about her ears and she knew nothing would ever be quite the same again.

Preparing for the closure, Felicity went to Jarle one morning to tell him that the builders wished to discuss the new plasterwork which would be required for the restaurant on the third floor.

Jarle had been working at his desk and, laying down his pen upon the blotter, he left it with some reluctance to follow Felicity upstairs.

'I shall be glad when we are rid of this mess,' he remarked as they skirted piles of rubble and ducked beneath ladders. 'The sooner we get back to normal, the better.'

As the discussions with the plasterers progressed, it became apparent that the architect's designs had been left behind in the office. Felicity volunteered to run down and get them.

'Though I shall be heartily pleased when the lifts are installed,' she called back cheerfully as she set a brisk pace down the polished treads of the stairs. By the time she reached the small office again she was quite flushed and out of breath but quickly began to rifle through the books and ledgers on the shelves, searching for the required document. For all he was a brilliant businessman

Jarle was still incredibly untidy, she thought with fond amusement, picking her way through political tracts, books on industrial relations and endless sheafs of statistics. Meeting a blank, she turned her attention to the desk, smiling wryly to herself as she remembered the last time she had searched Jarle's office.

'Ah, there it is.' She found the folded drawing half under the blotter but, as she pulled it out, it brought with it another sheet of paper. The words 'Dearest Jarle' caught Felicity's eye and her heart gave a loud thud in her breast. With a growing sense of dread she was quite unable to prevent herself from reading the whole thing, if only because it was so irresistibly short.

> How lovely to hear from you. We are both fine and making good progress. You sound depressed. No, I do not think you should reveal our secret to Felicity unless it becomes absolutely necessary to your happiness. In which case you know you would have my full support, as ever. And don't let H.H. worry you either. You paid a fair price for the shop at least. Think of H.H. as a gift and accept it graciously as I have learned to accept gifts from you. Come and see us soon, you rascal. D.

Felicity read it swiftly through again.

H.H. could only be Hollingworth House and the implication was that it had been given to Jarle as a gift. Felicity could not imagine any circumstances in which her father would willingly do such a thing, even if her mama was correct in her assertion that he hated the house. But if what the letter said was true then it seemed that Jarle had not, in fact, paid for Hollingworth House, not bought her home at all.

But it was the other matter mentioned in the letter which now caused her most concern. For 'D', whoever she was, thought it best if Felicity did not learn of 'our secret', whatever that might be. Her heart thudded with fresh pain as Felicity realised she'd assumed the writer to be a woman. But what woman would write so intimately to Jarle? D. D for Diana, for Dorothy or Daisy or... and then it blazed upon her mind, scorching her heart to shrivelled ashes. *D for Delphine*. Of course. Felicity held the proof in her own trembling hands, not only that Jarle had once kept the couturier as a mistress, which was not unusual, but that for some reason he was anxious for Felicity not to hear of it. The only logical reason could be that the relationship between them was still very much alive. What else could be meant by their determination to keep it from his new wife?

It took her a long time to climb the stairs back to the third floor and Jarle gave her a penetrating look as, handing him the paper, she avoided contact with his eyes.

How she got through that day was a mystery to Felicity. Her misery threatened to choke her, and, leaving her dinner scarcely touched, she begged a headache and escaped to her room. She lay upon the bed for a long time before summoning the energy to slip out of her clothes and between the sheets, face down upon the pillows where she could thoroughly explore her pain as if she were probing a sore tooth.

She had been fooling herself all along. Jarle did not and never would love her. Since in his constant trips to the Continent he had failed to persuade his French mistress to return, marrying Felicity was a convenient way of keeping his bed filled. If she was also of use at the store, so much the better.

When Jarle came to their room later that evening, she feigned sleep, hoping he would creep away. But she reckoned without his stubborn persistence.

'Felicity? Are you unwell?' Had she not just learned how little he cared for her she would have thought there was genuine concern in his voice. 'Should I call a doctor?'

Her sudden illness puzzled and worried Jarle, but then he believed women were prone to strange ills. Could this be one of those occasions? He was ignorant in such matters but Felicity had never struck him as the swooning sort.

'It is merely a headache,' came the muffled reply from the depths of the pillows.

'Then I shall bathe it for you.' Jarle strode from the room and returned with a cloth damped with witchhazel and carrying a bottle of eau-de-cologne, which he understood ladies used. With well-meaning masculine clumsiness, he set about applying both to her forehead and wrists. Felicity would have preferred to remain unmoved by these ministrations and did indeed struggle to keep her eyes firmly closed so that she did not look into his. But the soothing rhythm of his touch and the caressing massage he applied to her neck and shoulders soon had her stirring with fresh desire. Her betraying body unfurled beneath his touch, turning towards him like a flower to the sun. And when his lips started to torment her with tender kisses, lightly brushing her eyes, her cheeks, her ears, she thought she would go wild with the sensations he evoked in her.

'Are you feeling better, sweet Felicity?' Jarle murmured at last, drawing back the sheet.

Their lovemaking that night was, on Felicity's part at least, more wildly passionate than ever before. It was as if she needed to combat the awful pain which threatened to destroy her. She wanted to banish the pictures which tortured her mind of her husband in the arms of another woman. She heard his gasp, revelled in the fierce strength with which he took her and heard his cry of triumph as they reached a climax almost as one. Later, when Jarle slept, Felicity stroked his lips with the tip of one finger. She pushed back the dark curls from his brow and the tears ran unchecked down her cheeks. But not from happiness this time, but as a poignant farewell.

Felicity managed to avoid Jarle for most of the following day, and when he spoke to her she was coolly non-committal. When he asked her to supervise the setting of new window displays she declined, declared she had some matters to attend to at home, and walked from the building, acutely aware that his gaze followed her every step.

Not trusting herself in his company, she left a note informing him she had gone to visit her mama and would stay overnight.

The next night she again pleaded a headache and when Jarle came to her bed she gave such a convincing imitation of sleep that he did indeed leave her in peace. Far from bringing her solace, this only made her cry all the more into her pillow.

On the fourth day of this miserable regime, Jarle's patience finally snapped.

Felicity had found it exceptionally hard to concentrate, so had abandoned her paperwork and driven out to Simpsons. But even here, at a task she enjoyed, choosing the autumn range of furnishing fabrics, she was so riddled with bleak indecision that she felt quite unable to choose between one pattern and the next. In the end she offered her apologies, promised to call again when she was feeling less tired, and left, despondent with defeat.

Returning to the shop she gained some satisfaction from seeing how much brighter and more inviting it looked. The assistants smiled more and customers wandered about, remarking upon the colourful displays, the fine selection of goods and buying, Felicity guessed, far more than they had intended.

So she was almost smiling as she entered her office but was taken aback to find Jarle standing by her small desk, the expression in his eyes, even the set of his square shoulders, rigid with anger.

'You look well pleased with yourself.'

'J-Jarle,' she stammered. 'I—I wasn't expecting you.'
She could hear her heart pounding.

'Do I need an appointment to see my own wife?' he
snapped. 'You certainly seem to be damned busy these
days.'

'No, of course not. And please don't swear.'

'Don't play your high and mighty goody-two-shoes
act with me, I've had enough of it. Think yourself too
good to share your bed with a boy from Canal Street,
is that it?'

Felicity was shocked by the suggestion and stammered
in her anxiety to dismiss the very idea she could be so
prejudiced. 'N-no, that isn't true.' Fighting to get her
emotions under control she occupied her trembling
fingers with unpinning her hat. 'Please do not start all
that again. You know it is nonsense,' she said, as
reasonably as she could.

'Or is it that now you have your darling Papa's
precious store in your grasp you have no further use for
me, except to have the benefit of my fortune to furnish
it.'

Felicity whirled to face him. 'How can you say that?'

Jarle got up unsteadily from the chair and came round
the desk to face her. 'Because you believe you need no
one but yourself.'

I need you, she wanted to cry, gazing at him in anguish,
but bit down hard on her tongue in case it should betray
her. 'Have you been drinking?' she asked, for he sounded
very slightly unwell.

Her question brought an explosion of fury. 'Don't
lecture me, madam.' Then reaching out, Jarle grasped
her slender shoulders, pulling her closer. 'Felicity, tell
me what I have done to offend you. We were getting
along so well.'

'In bed?' she said, in a tight, bleak voice. 'That is
important to you, isn't it?'

Jarle looked perplexed but finally nodded as his face froze into icy wariness. 'Was it not so important for you?'

How could she answer such a question? She pressed her lips firmly together and tilted her chin in proud defiance while Jarle's fingers tightened on her arm and his gaze held hers, as if he could force her to admit it by his sheer strength of will. 'And what of our marriage? Is that not important either?' he asked, and she quailed beneath the contempt of his fury yet forced herself to remember the letter and all that it implied. He had used her because she was available and amenable, as he would any other possession.

She shook herself free of him. 'Do we have one?' Her voice sounded cold, more distant than she'd intended, and her heart thumped as she felt him flinch.

'I told you once that I have no wish to force myself upon you, Felicity.' His eyes came back to meet hers and now it was her turn to flinch at the grim expression in the dark depths of those beloved eyes. 'Until now you have given every impression of being satisfied with the arrangement. For some reason best known to yourself you have decided to call an end to it, but I am still your husband, still a man.'

'And you have a man's needs,' she taunted, deliberately hurting herself as much as him. 'Then visit your mistress. Isn't that what is done in a marriage of convenience such as ours?'

Jarle's brows creased with a puzzlement so convincing that she almost believed it genuine. 'What mistress? What new fantasy is this?'

It is no fantasy. I have the evidence, she wanted to cry but she only shrugged herself free of him and said, 'Isn't it always the case?'

'Sometimes,' he agreed, so oddly quiet that she dared not turn to look at him, however much she might long to see his expression.

'It is no concern of mine. You must satisfy your needs where you will. I care not what you do,' she said airily, inwardly shaking at having to speak such untruths.

'I see.' His voice was low and hard as ice, freezing the silence which stretched between them. 'Why did you marry me, Felicity? Was it simply because your papa told you to?'

She whirled to face him, unable to resist the strong denial. 'No.'

'But didn't you always obey your father, like the good dutiful daughter you are, or pretended to be? And he protected you, too much, some might say, from the realities of life.'

Her cheeks flamed. 'That's not true. My father encouraged me. It was his idea, for instance, that I help at the mission,' she told him hotly.

'And so you did.'

'Yes.' She paused, confused, realising what she had implied. 'But I enjoyed it. I wanted to be there. There was always so much going on.'

'You did it to please him?'

'No. I did it because I enjoyed it.'

'If you enjoyed India so much, if it was all so damned wonderful, why did you not stay?' Jarle demanded.

'You know why,' she said, her voice soft with pain. 'Papa left instructions with Mr Redgrove for us to return on his death, because of his financial situation.'

'And so you did.'

'Yes.' Again she felt vaguely irritated that he had trapped her into admitting unquestioning compliance but she none the less felt helpless to stop the direction of his argument. 'We had no choice. We could not stay in India.'

'There is always a choice in life, Felicity,' he said, his voice surprisingly thick with emotion, or was it brandy? 'It depends whether you are strong enough to make it.

Presumably Papa likewise had a large say in when, or even if, you married good old Gilbert?'

Felicity stayed silent.

'And when he changed his mind and instructed you to marry me, ever the obedient and dutiful daughter, once having satisfied yourself you owed no further allegiance to Gilbert Farrel and that I was not the fraudulent rogue you'd first imagined, you felt well able to carry out his wishes, did you not? But once having done so,' Jarle continued remorselessly, 'you felt no further loyalty towards me, your husband. You had spent it all on your blessed father.'

Felicity was appalled by the swing the argument had taken, and tears burned her eyelids.

'That is not true,' she said, faint with shock.

'Then why? Tell me, for I would like to know. Why did you agree to marry me, Felicity? What possible reason could you have?'

Jarle had her by the shoulders again, his fingers burning their presence upon her arms. She wanted to fall against him, to cry out her love for him, to speak the truth that scorched the tip of her tongue and seared her heart. But how could she? He had not married her for love. Ever the practical businessman, he presumably had no time for such fanciful emotions. A French mistress, apparently safely married to a compliant husband abroad, and a doting, obedient wife at home. What could be better? Felicity determined not to give him the satisfaction of letting him see how he hurt her. She would keep her pride at least. 'I married you because it seemed the right thing to do,' was all she said.

He flung her from him as if with loathing and she stumbled against the corner of the desk, clinging on to it for support, recoiling from the glittering anger in his buckskin-brown eyes.

'Because that way you could get your scheming little hands on the shop and on my money to pay for its expansion. No doubt in some strange way you are taking revenge on me for your father's tyranny.'

'My father was not a tyrant,' Felicity burst out furiously.

'You have yourself admitted as much. Everything he instructed you to do, you did it.'

'Suggested, suggested, *not* instructed,' cried Felicity, near to tears.

'He instructed you to work at the mission and you did; to marry Gilbert and you agreed; to come to England and leave everything you loved, and you came. And he instructed you to marry me and you did. What is that if not tyranny? You say it was because it was the right thing to do. Right for whom? Because you wanted to? No.' His voice grew dangerously soft and she quivered at the depth of anger in it. 'Because *I* wanted you to? No. Because *he* wanted it, your darling papa who was the shining idol of your life. But he is dead, Felicity, dead, dead, dead. And I am alive.' Driven at last by despair and a longing he could not, would not identify, Jarle barbed his words with a cruelty he could no longer restrain.

He saw her rock upon her heels as if he had struck her, her pale face turning to grey ash, and he remembered its once golden glow. He saw her fingers scrabbling upon the polished surface of the desk and how she strained for breath with lungs squeezed dry of life and he knew a piercing, heartbreaking agony. His arms went around her and he was holding the shuddering body close, murmuring her name over and over.

'I never meant to hurt you, Felicity. Forgive me. Dammit, why do I always say the wrong thing?'

Holding her tightly in his arms, he buried his face in the sweet-smelling softness of her hair and knew a respite from his pain he would never have believed possible. 'Felicity,' he murmured again, his mouth moving over that tiny ear and down to the small hollows in her neck. Never had he felt this aching torment, never such a need for a woman before. And he knew that, however he might deny it, his destiny was inextricably linked with hers. He felt her body arch naturally into his and he strained her closer. For a second they were as one again, but then she was pushing him away, the tears sliding over her round, flushed cheeks.

'I know you have a mistress, I know it. I found the letter on your desk when you sent me down for the drawings. There is little point in pretending, for I even know her name.'

'Don't say it,' said Jarle quickly, pressing his fingers to her lips. 'Oh, Felicity. What can I do with you now?' Then he closed his eyes, as if against a great pain. When he opened them again all the anger had died and with a *frisson* of shock she saw only compassion written there. It was not what she wanted to see. Turning on her heel, she ran from the room.

CHAPTER THIRTEEN

WHEN Jarle left the shop he went straight round to his solicitors in John Dalton Street. Mr Redgrove swept aside all other matters he had on hand, left three people waiting in the dusty passage, and ushered him into his office at once.

'Sorry I didn't call first to make an appointment,' Jarle muttered, flinging himself into a high-backed chair, not listening to Mr Redgrove's assurances that it was of no consequence. Almost at once he was on his feet again and pacing the threadbare carpet. 'She has accused me of keeping a mistress. And as a result has banned me from her bed. What do you make of that, Redgrove? What am I supposed to do now?'

Mr Redgrove hovered nervously, unable to seat himself while his client stalked back and forth. 'I can understand your anger, sir.'

'Anger? I'm not angry.' Jarle stopped his pacing and looked at Redgrove in surprise. 'No, dammit, I'm not. I should be. I have every right to be.' He gave a short laugh, knowing his feelings were too complex to be described merely as anger. 'But she found Delphine's letter. What the hell am I to do about it? Yet again I am cast as the villain and all for the supposed sullying of her father's honour.'

Mr Redgrove tut-tutted and shifted the chair a little, thus managing to persuade Jarle to sit, if not to relax. 'Have you explained fully to the young lady how this—er—delicate situation came about in the first place?' he quietly asked. 'It may well make a difference to her attitude.'

Jarle shot from his seat and gave Mr Redgrove such a quelling look that he instantly regretted the question. 'No, I have not. Do you think I'm quite a rogue? That's the very thing I've been trying to avoid.' Then, drawing a deep sigh, he sank back into the chair again and shook his head in sad despair. 'I take your point, Redgrove. I dare say she will have to be told but she is so determined her dear papa has been wronged by all and sundry that anything I say to the contrary will only sound like petty quibbling, particularly if I use it to get myself off this potentially lethal hook.'

'I do see that.' Redgrove nodded his head solemnly, then blew upon a large handkerchief, making his pinched nose turn red. He was ever a victim of summer colds. 'And Sir Joshua was not an unlikeable man, for all his— eccentricities,' he said.

Jarle smiled at the euphemism. 'I seem to be plagued by eccentrics on all sides.'

'Perhaps you underestimate Miss Felicity. She seemed a most sensible, practical sort of female person, not given to swooning and the like,' he said, recalling that it had been the mother who succumbed to such afflictions while the daughter took everything with stoical grace.

'She has had shocks enough recently,' murmured Jarle. 'I wanted things to be more settled between us before ... Besides, I promised Sir Joshua to keep it from them both until they were at least accustomed to their new life here. Later, I thought, if the right moment presented itself ...'

Redgrove grunted in sympathy then cleared his throat. 'But it may well prove to be necessary for your own future happiness if Miss Felicity holds you at fault.'

Jarle looked bleak. 'Yes, I do see that. Dammit, Redgrove, what am I to do?'

'May I enquire if she knows of that other matter?'

A long silence ensued, during which Jarle clamped his large fists together, leaning forward with elbows on knees, head bowed. He thought about the hopelessness he'd once felt about his life, and how much easier it had been to fight it since knowing Felicity. 'No,' he said at last. 'Nor will she.'

'If I may say so, Mr Blakeley, do you think that wise? Your attitude is a trifle short-sighted. She is your wife, after all, your helpmeet through life, and with quite a sweet charm if I remember.' Redgrove's pale eyes glazed for a moment in memory. 'She could well be a source of great strength to you.'

Jarle ground his teeth together so that the solicitor winced. 'If there were any hope of it being a true marriage... As it is...' He paused, his thoughts whirling. He recalled that last time they had made love, the total lack of inhibition of Felicity's passion. And these first weeks of his marriage had startled him by the depth of harmony they had achieved. For all his earlier reluctance to enter matrimony he had no wish to see it end in this way. Just as he was learning to value her, fate had played a cruel trick upon them both. The prospect of risking her scorn, her disgust even, was more than he could contemplate. No matter what it cost him, he would not do it. Some things were best left undisclosed. 'It is too soon,' he said firmly, his mind made up. 'There must be some other way.' Too much stood between them, like a huge, ghostly fortress that could not be scaled.

An uneasy silence fell between the two men as each was lost in private thought.

At length, mindful of his other clients waiting, the solicitor cleared his throat. 'Is there anything particular I can do for you, Mr Blakeley?' Redgrove was saying and Jarle dragged his mind back to listen. 'You have only to say.'

'Yes.' Now he was the businessman again, on his feet, all personal needs set aside. He spoke in his usual crisp, authoritative tone and Redgrove frantically scribbled notes. 'Adjoining the store there is a retail milliner's, a barber's shop, a public house and a private residence.

Buy them for me, will you, Redgrove? I have no doubt Felicity will need the extra space to fit her grandiose plans.'

'Are these buildings for sale?' asked Mr Redgrove in some surprise, but Jarle, his errand complete, merely shrugged as he reached for the door-handle.

'Everything is for sale, at a price, which in this instance is not important. Good day to you.'

Once Jarle had left the store, Felicity cleared a corner of an adjoining stock-room and spent an uncomfortable night on a truckle bed. But the next day, on the pretext that she wished to be near at hand during the building works, she had the room fully cleared and cleaned out, and a more comfortable bed installed. With a pitcher and bowl set upon a chest of drawers, a rag rug on the floor and a few clothes hanging in the wall cupboard she felt herself adequately accommodated if in more spartan circumstances than most of the staff now that they had moved to their new quarters. But at least she was free from the endless torture of sharing a bed with Jarle. She could deal with her aching loneliness better here, for she could keep her mind fully occupied with the task in hand.

She placed a sepia photograph of her father upon the chest of drawers. It had been taken before his last visit to England, and, looking at it more closely, she could see how the shadows of tiredness and anxiety marred his normally handsome features. He must have felt so cut off and alone in his determination not to worry his wife and daughter with his financial problems, she thought.

'I have truly not let you down, Papa,' she murmured. 'I may have failed in my marriage but I am resolved not to fail you. I'll make of this store exactly as you would have wished.' Remembering another photograph that still stood in Jarle's office, she could not resist going to fetch it, gazing at the happy family group and at the young man with the wide smile at centre back. As she set it alongside that of her father she looked down at them both, the tears standing proud in her eyes, before splashing her face with cold water and climbing into her empty bed.

For a while Felicity coped with the arrangement tolerably well. She rose early, breakfasted in the staff canteen and was making her morning tour of the shop the moment it opened. Where appropriate she stopped to offer encouragement or praise for a particularly eye-catching display or good sales figures, believing fervently that this would be far more beneficial than Miss Bridget's scold and punish methods. But the self-imposed regime was hard.

Jarle moved about his own business chores with a face set cold as stone. They spoke only on essential matters and if their glances should briefly touch Felicity met only an ice-cold indifference, or worse, the dreaded sympathy that seemed to confirm all her worst fears. She could just about tolerate his indifference but she had no wish for him to feel sorry for her. She did not want to feel sorry for herself. Yet each night as she lay down in her cold, hostile bed, she yearned for the warm strength of his presence and had to grip tightly to the mattress in case her traitorous body should weaken and run to him as all her instincts cried out to do.

Once she did so, only to find Jarle's town house empty save for one or two servants and Jessie, who told Felicity that he was at a political meeting. The loyal Jessie added, with a note of slight disapproval, that Mr Jarle spent most evenings there these days, when he was not at the store. Felicity thanked her and left quickly, asking Jessie not to mention her visit. She did not go again.

Now, as she spent the rest of the morning as she usually did, seeing people, dealing with orders, checking the unpacking and movement of stock and answering the thousand and one queries from the decorators, her one desire was to work so hard that sleep would overtake her pain. Yet she knew it would not.

And as usual at lunchtime Amy brought her a sandwich and cup of tea since she could never persuade Felicity to come up to the dining-room at this time

'See you take a rest after lunch,' Amy scolded. 'You'll be ill if you go on at this rate.' But Felicity barely raised her head to listen.

'I've far too much to do. Thank you, Amy.'

'I'm surprised Mr Blakeley allows it. I don't know what he can be thinking of,' she finished, close to over-stepping the boundary of propriety.

'I answer for my own actions,' said Felicity. 'Thank you, Amy. That will be all.'

But Amy proved stubborn for once. 'Well, it's no way to be carrying on, you being so recently married and all.' She shook her head and a few tendrils of fair hair escaped her neat bun, softening the firm severity of her young face. 'You told me once to call you Felicity so I'm going to speak my mind and you can like it or no, but I shall say it anyway. The way you're treating your new husband is the surest way to losing him. When I marry my Arthur,' she said, suddenly turning pink-cheeked, 'you'll not find me spending more time here than I have to, and I enjoy my work, so there.'

There was a moment's silence before Felicity answered, and if Amy had hoped to provoke action by her comments then she was disappointed.

'I dare say,' said Felicity with studied calm, reaching for a sandwich. 'But the two cases are not comparable.'

Amy backed to the door, wondering whether she should feel insulted by this confusing statement or simply more worried than ever. 'Anyway, I'm off to my monthly suffrage meeting this evening,' she said, giving a little laugh. 'So I suppose my Arthur will feel a bit neglected for once.'

Amy was almost out of the door when Felicity said, rather quietly, 'I'd like to come with you. What time does it start?'

Amy gaped. 'Come with me, ma'am?'

Felicity smiled. 'It was Felicity a moment ago. Why shouldn't I? You've just said I need to get out and about more.'

'Aye, but I didn't mean . . . I'm not sure it would be proper for you and me to . . . And you're a married lady now.' Amy was kicking herself for having mentioned it. She knew well enough what Mr Blakeley would have to say upon the matter.

'So is Mrs Pethick-Lawrence but she is a suffragette,' Felicity persisted. 'Will Dora be going?'

Amy shook her head, frowning slightly. 'I haven't seen Dora for ages. She's keeping herself to herself a bit lately. It's only a little local meeting, no famous speakers, not like the last one,' she gabbled, hoping to put Felicity off.

'Then there shouldn't be any problems, should there? Now I really must get on, Amy. I'll see you later.'

And, knowing when she was beaten, Amy withdrew. Standing outside the closed office door she gave serious thought to the situation. Felicity was not behaving as a young, happy wife should. Something was amiss between them two, and with young Dora, sneaking about and asking a lot of tomfool questions about where Mr and Mrs Blakeley went of an evening and what they did. As if she knew, or cared. None of her business, nor Dora's neither and she'd told her so. Silly girl probably had a penny crush on Mr Blakeley, and couldn't get used to the idea of him being married. She'd seen it happen before.

Shaking her head in despair at the foibles of human nature, Amy bustled off to get her own lunch. But Mr Blakeley wouldn't like Felicity attending another suffrage meeting. Still, it was only a small affair and they'd be safe enough, so what did it matter? He need never know.

The pair of them set off just as the clock chimed a quarter after seven. It would take only a matter of minutes to reach the hall but they stepped out briskly, arm in arm, Felicity glad of something to take her mind off her own problems and Amy glad of her company.

But in the shadows of an alley behind the store stood two figures, and if Felicity had seen their faces in the lamplight or heard the chink of coin that passed between them, she might have remembered Jarle's warning to stay clear of such gatherings.

The meeting, as Amy had implied, was poorly attended, consisting of a few stalwart members who tried to spread themselves about the half-empty hall to give it an appearance of fullness.

Dora, surprisingly, did not put in an appearance and Amy repeated her concern over her friend's behaviour of late but there was little time to go into details as the speaker took up her stance and began to address the straggly audience. But on this occasion Felicity took in little of the woman's words, her thoughts elsewhere. At the end of their terrible quarrel it had almost been as if he were offering a way to heal the rift between them. Yet this quarrel had been filled with bitterness, quite unlike their earlier sparring between adversaries weighing each other up. Jarle had said some terrible things that she could surely never forgive or forget.

'We women are said to be strong, yet with men we are weak as babes,' the speaker, an ample-bosomed lady in tweeds, was saying. 'When will we learn to be our own people, to make our own decisions? First we are the obedient daughters to our fathers' bidding, then wives to our husbands. If we have problems as children we expect our fathers to solve them for us. We look upon them as extraordinary beings. But not because they are men, but because we are children,' she thundered, and thumped the table with her plump fist, making everyone in the hall jump, except Felicity who sat riveted. 'But we cannot go through life as children. We must learn to solve our own problems, to view our husbands as equals not as father substitutes, to gain their respect as we offer them our own. Do this, ladies, and you will find your voice. And people will listen to it.'

The woman sat down to a flutter of polite applause. Tea was being poured from the big brown enamel teapot even as the chairwoman tendered her thanks. But Felicity paid no heed. She drank her tea without tasting it and barely responded as Amy touched her cold hand in concern.

'You all right? You're frozen and it's baking hot in here.'

'I'm just tired. I think I'd like to go home.' Felicity got to her feet, anxious suddenly to leave the stuffy hall.

It was then that they heard the commotion, and from the back of hall streamed a horde of women.

'Quick,' cried Amy. 'Let's get out the back way.' But it was too late, for with the intruders came the more pervasive force of the local constabulary.

Women ran in every direction while others stood about, bewildered, wondering what was happening. The constables blew their whistles and wielded their truncheons in what to Felicity seemed an unnaturally harsh manner.

'What on earth is happening?' she cried, clinging to Amy's arm as they struggled through the confusion, but her friend only shook her head, as bewildered as everyone else.

'There's been windows broken at the police station, and a small fire started,' shouted one woman. 'And we're being blamed.'

Everything happened so quickly after that. Amy was wrenched from Felicity's grasp, the lights went out, and screams rent the air as the crowd seemed to heave and Felicity was swept along with it.

Bile rose in her throat. She was terribly afraid. She thought she glimpsed a familiar face out in the packed street but then it fused into the shadows and she was being pushed into a vehicle packed with women. The doors were slammed shut, moonlight shining through iron bars, and she knew at once where she was. It was the Black Maria. She had been arrested and was being transported, along with the other women, to the prison cells.

The trial, if that was what it could be called, took little over ten minutes the following morning. After an uncomfortable night in the police station cell, Felicity stood with the other women in the dock and listened in a daze to the charges brought against them.

'For disturbing the peace and obstructing the police in the course of their duty, fined ten shillings or seven days' imprisonment,' intoned the magistrate.

No witnesses were called, no statement asked for. No proof was offered or asked for that the suffragettes had indeed been the ones to perpetrate any crime of disturbance. All the women refused to pay the fines, opting steadfastly for prison, to prove their cause. Felicity could not, in all conscience, set herself apart as being any different.

They were taken, again in the Black Maria, to the women's section of Strangeways prison. Though, from the singing and cheering which occupied them

throughout the journey, Felicity felt they must be off to
a fair at the very least. But the festive atmosphere soon
died the instant they arrived. Lined up along a corridor
by silent wardresses, they waited as one by one they were
questioned. Name, age, address, place of birth, previous convictions. Felicity gave her simplest name and
Travers Drapery as her address. She made no mention
of the lodge house, or her mama, Jarle or her married
name. She could spare them that at least. The wardress
noted the details without comment.

This was followed by a most undignified medical
examination and the handing over of all her posses-
sions: purse, handkerchiefs, even the combs from her
hair.

'How shall I keep it tidy since you have taken everything from me?' Felicity was moved to protest, but was
simply marshalled into line with the rest by way of reply.
Clad in prison uniform, she found depression begin to
fold in upon her as she followed her fellow prisoners
along a dark corridor, out across a yard, and into another
section of the building. The sound of clanging doors
and the grinding of locks and bolts punctuated the route,
each one piercing fear deeper into her heart. What was
she doing here? Would Jarle pay her fine? Did she want
him to?

A wardress handed her a yellow badge to attach to a
button on the bodice of her prison dress. It was a number
nine, the same as that upon the cell door through which
she was now being pushed. The door closed behind her
with a resounding clang, and, blinking in the dim light,
she looked about her.

There were two plank beds illuminated by a single
electric light bulb and a small trace of daylight filtering
through a window covered with grating set high in the
far wall. Upon one bed sat a girl, and, as she lifted her
head to look at her new cellmate, Felicity knew deep
shame. Exhausted and emaciated, grey skin stretched

tight upon her cheekbones, hair lank and brown, the girl sat dully incurious, her thin arms wrapped around her slightly swollen belly. What right had Felicity to complain in comparison with this poor creature?

Over the next hour, Felicity learned the sad facts of the child's life. Her name was Lucy. Little more than fifteen, she had no home, no parents and now, since her employer had thrown her out after taking his pleasure of her, no job either.

'No more crying,' Felicity told her. 'I can find you a job, and accommodation to go with it.' The girl's disbelief finally turned to gratitude when she in turn learned Felicity's story. From that moment on they were fast friends. But Felicity could not help but wonder how many such girls there were in the city.

Each morning they were woken by the rattle of keys, the bang of doors, and the approaching heavy footsteps of the large wardress, and yet another weary, sleepless night could be abandoned and the chores of the day begun. They scrubbed out their cell, swept the long corridors and did a dozen other menial tasks. Felicity hated cleaning out her tin drinking mug with soap and brick dust. It had to be polished brightly but no water was permitted for this purpose. She hated the dank atmosphere of the cell and the sweet-sour smell of the place. Most of all she hated the food which consisted chiefly of bread and thin gruel with the occasional addition of potatoes. But Felicity could eat little.

'I'm beginning to long for some plain old mutton stew, tainted or not,' groaned Felicity by the fourth day of this regime as they sat endlessly knitting stockings as usual, but young Lucy only smiled; unused as she was to the riches of regular meals, it mattered not to her. 'I do wish I knew where Amy was,' Felicity kept repeating, missing her friend dreadfully. She tried not to think about Jarle. It did not surprise her that he had not come to offer to pay her fine. She was well aware of his feelings about her involvement with the suffragette movement. Besides, she couldn't possibly have accepted it, so what did it matter?

'They say as some of the suffragettes are on a hunger strike,' Lucy told her. 'And they're wanting everyone to join in.'

But Felicity's mind was on other things as she started to turn the heel on the long stocking. 'But a visit would have been nice,' she murmured, half to herself, and then to Lucy, 'The trouble with this tedious job is that it gives you far too much time to think.'

As the Black Maria drove its cargo away into the darkness, a figure had stepped out from the shadows, a wry smile upon his fleshy face.

The very next morning this same figure presented himself at the office of Travers Drapery and demanded that Mr Jarle Blakeley be sent for, forthwith.

'I have a matter of great import to put to him,' said Gilbert Farrel, with his usual pomposity.

Since Jarle was not in the building, nor was Mrs Blakeley, nor Amy for that matter, and the place in some consternation over these absences, it took some little time before the two adversaries stood face to face. Unable to disguise his smirk of satisfaction, Gilbert Farrel opened the proceedings.

'Have you not mislaid your wife?' he asked, his full, moist lips curling grotesquely.

Not for the world would Jarle own to this toad of a man the state of his marriage. 'I was forced to stay at Hollingworth House last night. What is it you are prattling about, man?'

'Ah, so you are unaware of Felicity's current abode?'

Jarle hung on to his temper with every vestige of willpower. 'And?' he prompted.

'And I am. She is presently staying under His Majesty's pleasure at Strangeways prison. I was sure you would wish to be speedily informed of that fact.' The reaction to this simple statement was even more satisfactory than Gilbert had hoped for. Jarle Blakeley looked positively ill. Every vestige of colour drained from his face but he stood as silent and still as a deer pole-axed with terror. Gilbert moved in for the kill.

'Of course, I am sure you can pay her fine and get her released, though, knowing Felicity's stubborn streak, she may well refuse it. Don't these suffragettes go on hunger strikes and such? In Holloway they've started force-feeding them. Pushing a tube down into their stomach and pouring milk down. Can you imagine?' Gilbert smoothed a finger over his moustache, his plump upper lip curling in distaste. 'However, that is very much by the way, I dare say. The point is, I am sure the last thing you want at this crucial point in your expansion plans is bad publicity. Hence the reason for my visit.'

'What are you saying?' Jarle found his voice at last, one filled with venom and Gilbert quavered very slightly before it.

'I understand that Felicity has given a false name, sensitive to your feelings, perhaps. On the other hand, she could be concerned for her mother's health. Carmella has been below par for some years.' He tutted with un-convincing sympathy. 'It would certainly do Lady Travers no good at all to learn of her daughter's latest madcap escapade.'

Jarle was gathering his wits, the shock beginning to fade slightly. Furious as he was with Felicity, and con-cerned for her well-being, he determined not to let this loathsome creature best him. 'Spit it out, man, or must I wring it from your thick neck with my bare hands?' He half moved towards him and Gilbert flinched.

'Only I know of her true identity, having by chance seen her packed into the Black Maria on my way home after a late supper. I cannot tell you how alarmed I felt at seeing her so roughly treated.' He hurried on as he

saw Jarle's face darken. 'But I would not dream of re-
lating this information to another soul.' He paused, offering a mirthless smile. 'As I am sure that is what you
would wish.'

'I do wish it,' said Jarle, his heart beating slow and
hard in the depths of his chest. Watching Gilbert with
narrowed eyes, he knew the toad was very far from done.

Gilbert began to pace the office in a careless manner.
'You are, I know, a most generous man. And an exceedingly rich one. You would not wish any harm to
come to Felicity.'

'Harm? What harm? You are trying my patience to
the limit; take care, Farrel,' growled Jarle and Gilbert
began to feel a prickle of uncertainty and the first flush
of nerves. Always, in his previous encounters of this
kind, his quarry had been anxious, terrified of the resulting publicity or possible consequences of whatever
misdemeanour had been brought to Gilbert's attention.
They would frequently volunteer large cash sums without
being prompted. This man was different. But then
Gilbert was not after cash. He stopped his idle pacing,
and, draping himself into a leather armchair, gave his
full attention to his would-be victim.

'I had an arrangement with Sir Joshua that
Hollingworth House, the family stately home, was to be
mine.'

'If you married Felicity, which you did not,' Jarle reminded him. 'I did.'

'Then you are a fortunate man to have so delightful
a treasure. Surely you would not begrudge me second
prize?' The smiled vanished and the thick lips quivered.
'Hand Hollingworth House over to me, as is my just
dessert, and I will see that Felicity is returned to your
bed this very evening, safe and well, her reputation and
health unscathed and her identity unexposed with the
resulting benefit to your business interests. Otherwise, I
cannot be answerable for what may happen.'

There was a long, appalling silence. So long, that Gilbert began, very slightly, to sweat. He already knew Jarle's habit of turning over a case thoroughly in his head before replying to a question but either the man was slow-witted or, unthinkably, oblivious to Felicity's plight.

At last he spoke. 'I would be obliged, Farrel, if you would take yourself off my premises, and never set foot in them again. If you know what's good for you.'

'But——' Gilbert began, but got no further, for, as Jarle made a movement towards him, Gilbert jittered away so violently that his heel caught in the rug and he sprawled ignominiously backwards upon it. Never had he felt such a complete fool, for Blakeley had merely been reaching for the door, which he now held wide.

'Get up, you snivelling coward. For your future reference, Hollingworth House no longer belongs to me. I bought the shop from Sir Joshua in exchange for settling his extensive debts. The house he gave to me to deal with as I wished, since he had no funds left and no wish for it to fall into the wrong hands. In my capacity as a Councillor I handed it over to the city and a trust has been formed for its upkeep as, I think, Sir Joshua would have wished. It will be used for some suitable charitable purpose for the benefit of the poor.'

Gilbert Farrel was completely dumbstruck. This spelled doom to his dreams, the death of all his carefully nurtured plans. Yet he saw how it had come about as a result of a friendship long since turned sour. But then, he thought, there are other fine houses in England, and other marriageable daughters, and if they were not so taking as Felicity, at least they would be appetisingly rich.

Getting to his feet, he dusted down his stylish grey silk coat with a careless flick. 'Then I shall bid you good day and leave you to control your errant wife as best you may. You have my condolences, sir.' Whereupon he

strode from the room and from the shop, his mind
already picking out other more likely locations. Perhaps
Cheshire? Or Gloucestershire?

Left alone, Jarle wasted no time in summoning Dora,
who soon broke down in tears and revealed the whole
sordid tale. She told how she had been working for Farrel
for years, nibbling away at the fragile profits.

'But nowt as serious as this,' she wailed. 'I never meant
anyone to get hurt.'

So it had been Dora all along and he'd done Miss
Bridget a disservice. Fortunately she need never know
of his suspicions. 'Stop blubbering, Dora, and tell me
how she came to be arrested. Are you saying Felicity was
hurt? Was there a riot?'

Dora's heart softened at the sight of anxiety in his
grey face. Eeh, he must be proper taken with Miss Felicity
for all their seeming coldness towards each other, she
thought. There was no understanding the middle classes.
'Not much of one, don't worry. I was asked to create a
disturbance after the meeting. He didn't say why but I
was to bring the S.O.S.'

'The who?'

'A group of women who've formed a society called
"Sick of Suffrage". They operate here in Manchester.'

Jarle gave a mocking laugh. 'Perhaps I should join.
But go on, Dora.' He made her sit and mop up her flow
of tears and tell her tale in an orderly fashion, though
he had to suffer an extended family history first.

'I didn't know anyone in the S.O.S. so I asked some
of the shop girls to help. We only meant to throw a few
stones, but it got out of hand and a fire got started
somehow.'

'And are some of these shop girls in prison too?' Jarle
asked.

'Very likely,' Dora agreed, going off into fresh par-
oxysms of noisy misery. 'I didn't know it had owt to do
with Miss Felicity. He promised me no one would get

hurt. But he lied, didn't he? And now I've lost me job and all.' She put her head in her apron and sobbed.

Jarle gritted his teeth so fiercely together that his jaw ached. 'He used you, Dora, as he uses everyone to his own ends. But he'll not be back. There are no pickings left for him here. Now wipe your tears, there's work to be done. Ask Miss Bridget to come and see me, will you?'

Dora was on her feet in an instant. 'I will, sir. And I'm so sorry. I wish as how I could undo it all.'

Smiling gently, Jarle led her to the door. 'We'll say no more about it. Your job is safe this time, Dora. But let's have more loyalty in future, eh? This shop is going up in the world and if you're a sensible girl you can go up with it.'

She looked up at him with wide shining eyes, overflowing with tears and instant love. 'Oh, I will, sir. You can count on me, sir. Thank you, sir,' and she ran from the room, her allegiance to him secure to her dying day.

Jarle softly closed the door behind her. He walked through to Felicity's makeshift bedroom and stared down at the two photographs beside the single bed. Should he pay her fine? Would she be hurt if he did not, or protest if he did? And what effect would seven days in prison for the sake of her beliefs have upon her? He tapped his fingers thoughtfully together, then began to pull the sheets from the bed preparatory to having it returned to the sick bay. It might do her no harm at all and be worth the risk.

Perhaps if Jarle had known exactly what Felicity was facing he would have had second thoughts upon the subject.

CHAPTER FOURTEEN

ON THE fifth night Lucy started to be sick. Fearful for the girl's poor state of health and for the child she carried, Felicity beat upon the cell door for help. None came and the vomiting continued. Throughout that long wretched night Felicity did all she could to easy Lucy's ordeal and returned again and again to hammer upon the door. Shortly before dawn Lucy rid herself of her burden and fell into a comatose state, her skeletal ribcage barely moving. In a last desperate bid to gain attention Felicity smashed the tiny window of the cell with her tin mug and screamed for help. This time it worked. Moments later came the heavy tread of footsteps, the jangle of keys in the lock and the door was flung back.

'Lucy has lost her baby,' was as much as Felicity could manage before the two wardresses gathered up the unconscious girl and the poor scrap of humanity that had been her child and carried them off.

Seconds later, they were back for Felicity and bore her off to a small dank cell with neither light nor bed. Handcuffing her wrists together, they left her propped against the wall.

'That'll teach you to make a noise at night,' said one.

'But I did it for Lucy, and her baby,' protested Felicity, horrified by this new state.

'We'll decide what's best for them.' And, on this unyielding note, they left her.

Throughout that unspeakably awful day, Felicity consoled herself with the knowledge that at least Lucy would be having proper care. No one could be so inhumane as to deny it.

Felicity found that she could walk two strides in each direction, which she made herself do from time to time. There was no illumination in the cell apart from the small chink of daylight seeping through a grating high in the wall, this time without the benefit of glass. She was glad of it as a means to tell the passing of time, if nothing else. When darkness fell outside, she curled up on the floor and tried to sleep.

She was brought a dish of watery gruel and a slice of dry bread but Felicity could not eat it. The last thing on her mind was food. She asked about Lucy but the wardress did not even speak to her.

'Tomorrow is the seventh day,' she kept repeating to herself, as a child held a comforter in the dark. 'As soon as I am released, I shall make it my business to find out about Lucy, and about Amy.'

But at the end of that endless seventh day came only a second dish of gruel. She felt sick with disappointment.

'When am I to be released?' she begged.

'You've been given two days longer as a punishment,' the wardress informed her, as if it were a source of immense satisfaction to her, and the most comfort she would allow was to take off the handcuffs before clanging the door shut for a second night in the punishment cell.

On the ninth day when Felicity was finally allowed out by the chief wardress, the sun shone and she was forced to cover her eyes with her hands for long moments before she dared open them. When she did so, it was to find Miss Bridget gazing upon her.

'Good afternoon, Mrs Blakeley. I trust you are well,' she said, a hint of the schoolmarm reprimand still in her tone.

Felicity looked slowly about her at the empty street. Miss Bridget was quite alone and the disappointment she felt on that score was keen. 'Quite well, I believe,' she said calmly, and the chief wardress, seemingly satisfied with this answer, bobbed her beribboned cap and withdrew back into her cosy office for a fresh pot of tea.

'I have fetched a cab for you, Mrs Blakeley. I should think the walk would prove too much for you at present.'

'Thank you, Miss Bridget. I am truly grateful,' Felicity said feelingly, as her dazzled eyes focused upon the hansom cab patiently waiting at the kerb.

She swayed with giddiness at her first attempt to move and would have fallen to the ground had not Miss Bridget caught her in her strong arms and almost carried her to the cab. With the help of the driver she was soon installed and they were bowling gently down the long street.

'Where is Amy?'

'She came out two days ago,' Miss Bridget informed her casually. 'None the worse for her experience, if a mite wiser.'

'There was a girl...' Felicity's mind whirled with questions but exhaustion was robbing her of the will to speak them. With supreme effort she tried again. 'Lucy. What happened to Lucy?'

Miss Bridget's eyes softened slightly as she turned her stick-like body towards Felicity. 'Was that the girl whose cell you shared?'

Felicity nodded. 'She lost her baby.'

'And her life,' said Miss Bridget bluntly, though with some compassion. 'An old story, I'm afraid.'

'She was only a child.' It had been no more than Felicity had expected, and she had hardly known the girl, but she wept for her all the same. In those five long days and nights a bond had been formed and a promise made.

'You look thinner. You've not been on one of them hunger strikes, have you?' Miss Bridget asked, disapproval strong in her voice, and Felicity assured her that hunger seemed to be a necessary part of prison life though not willingly intended on her part.

Miss Bridget sniffed her general disdain of the subject and continued decisively. 'I have taken some of my best beef tea to your mother, with instructions to give you a small cupful three times a day until you are quite yourself again. Too much would be a mistake at first, but it has excellent sustaining and restorative properties.'

Felicity glanced at her in astonishment. 'That is most kind. Thank you.'

Miss Bridget's flat cheeks flushed slightly pink, and she plucked the fingers of her gloves with great concentration as she spoke her next words. 'Perhaps you will see your way to giving me a further chance, Mrs Blakeley. I was over-hasty in my judgement of your improvements to the shop. I beg your pardon, to the department store, as it will soon be. Mr Blakeley has informed us all that sales are well up, a fact which I had noted for myself as a matter of fact.'

'Thank you again, Miss Bridget,' murmured Felicity, quite overcome, whereupon the elderly woman turned to her with something very close to animation upon her worn face.

'And wait till you see the new tea-rooms all done in blue and gold as you planned. And the art gallery is bound to be the finest in Manchester, if not the whole of the North of England.'

'I can see it is already causing some excitement,' said Felicity, with a gentle laugh, as she rested her head wearily back upon the cushions.

It was not until they were almost at the lodge house before she dared ask the question uppermost in her mind. 'Does Mr Blakeley know that I—that I am free?'

'So far as I am aware,' said Miss Bridget airily. 'Though I must say I haven't seen him for days. He's been spending a good deal of time at Hollingworth

House now, when not occupied on some Council business or other.' She tutted and clicked her tongue. 'As if he hadn't enough to do without going back into politicking. He is a very busy man, you know.'

'I do know,' said Felicity glumly and turned her face to the window.

She had forgotten how much she had missed the warmth of her mother's companionship and was glad to see Kate again and even talk fishing endlessly with Uncle Joe.

They tiptoed constantly into her room, bringing the beef tea and other treats, making her feel like an invalid and studiously avoiding any mention of Jarle, as though he were not her husband, as though he did not even exist. At length she could stand no more and she declared her intention of getting up.

'Oh, my, do you think that is for the best?' Carmella flustered, flapping her hands about as she was wont to do when filled with indecision.

'Yes, I do,' said Felicity, most firmly.

'Very well, then,' Carmella capitulated, tucking Felicity back into bed even as she said it. 'You may come down this evening and enjoy a pleasant dinner. Shall you like that?'

Felicity smiled and hugged her mother. 'I should like it very much. You are happy, aren't you, Mama?' she asked and Carmella, looking unusually serious, replied,

'Yes, my darling. I am happier now than I have been for many a long year.'

When she had gone Felicity ruminated on this puzzling statement for a long while before slipping into another doze. A quiet dinner with Mama, Kate and Uncle Joe would be delightful.

But there was a fourth member waiting at table when she arrived, rather late, as she'd felt almost too despondent and lethargic to attend. If it hadn't been for

Millie chivvying her she might very well have changed her mind. Now her heart gave a painful thud as Jarle half rose as she hurried in to the dining-room, an apology forming on her lips. It died on the instant and her hand automatically flew to tucking stray tendrils of hair in place and smoothing her skirt, her natural feminine vanity making her wish she'd chosen to wear something far more attractive than a plain blue linen suit.

'Ah, Felicity, at last.' Getting gracefully to her feet, Carmella took her daughter's hand and led her to a seat beside her husband. 'You have missed only the soup, darling, and Millie shall bring yours upon the instant.' When this was accomplished, Carmella turned to her with a smile and continued, 'I am so glad that you are looking more yourself. We have all been most concerned about you.'

Felicity covertly cast a glance in Jarle's direction to see if he showed any sign of agreeing with this statement. He sat impassive as ever, quietly awaiting his main course. Much irritated, Felicity sounded decidedly snappy as she replied.

'I really think you are making far too much of it. There were girls in that place in a far worse state than I.' Perhaps from pique over Jarle's apparent unconcern or rebellion at her mother's over-fussing, Felicity related Lucy's tale to them, without any attempt to soften the impact of it. 'I'm sure she was only there because she had nowhere else to go, no one to care for her. It is quite appalling that the female sex is so little thought of in this city, in this country,' she said, warming to her theme.

'Felicity, darling,' interrupted Carmella gently. 'I believe we already heard this sorry tale from Amy, though not so graphically, I'll admit.' Felicity flushed at the implied criticism.

'But something should be done to help such people,' Felicity cried.

'I agree.' Jarle had spoken for the first time that evening, and, at the sound of his voice so close beside her, the very timbre of it beloved to her, Felicity felt quite unable to meet his eyes which she was well aware were directed upon her. 'Which is why I made over Hollingworth House to the city for some suitable charity purpose. If you wish, it could become a home for destitute girls. Or whatever you will, Felicity, you have only to say the word.'

Now she did look at him. Very nearly stared openmouthed. While she was busy reorganising her thoughts about him, Jarle explained how this had come about, much as he had done earlier in the week to Gilbert Farrel. Felicity's reaction, however, was quite different. 'Then you are not to open it as an hotel, after all?'

'I am permitted to change my mind, am I not?' he asked, then, as she said nothing more, added, 'I thought you would be pleased.'

Felicity stared at him for an instant before answering. 'I think you are a most devious man. It is a great pity that you did not tell me all this earlier. I believe it quite wrong for a husband and wife to have secrets from each other,' she said, not sparing him the frostiness of her glare. It was a hurtful remark to make but not only had he kept this magnanimous gesture quiet and left her so long thinking ill of him, but he had not visited her in prison or come to collect her when she was released. Worse, he had married her without love, and, instead of succumbing to her charms, had merely been concerned how best to tell her about his mistress. And, as if all that were not enough, he had criticised, nay, ridiculed, the great love she still held for her father. Turning deliberately from him, she gave her full attention to her soup.

Carmella looked anxiously from one to the other, then into the ensuing silence said very brightly, 'Jarle has been telling us of your exciting plans. I'm sure a honeymoon cruise will be the very thing to bring some colour back into your cheeks, Felicity. How wonderful. As I said the other evening, you have been working far too hard of late. Why did you not tell me you were going away?' she scolded. 'Fancy keeping such thrilling news from your mama.'

Felicity stared at her, the soup spoon frozen halfway to her mouth, then, turning her head to look at her husband, was astounded to see him actually wink at her.

'We decided only recently, did we not, Felicity, that we were both in need of a break? We have accomplished a good deal, both at Hollingworth House and at the shop. The rest can proceed without us for a while. I decided it was time I paid some attention to my new wife before she despairs of me.' Slipping his arm around her shoulders, he gave Felicity an affectionate squeeze and there were little breathy sighs and 'Oh's and 'Ah's about the table. 'I believe it is long past time we got better acquainted, don't you think?'

Felicity set down the spoon very carefully upon her plate, her gaze riveted by the unmistakably wicked glitter in Jarle's eyes. It told her without question that when he spoke of a honeymoon that was exactly what he meant. Whether she wanted him or not, he intended to return to her bed, and, presumably, like many a wife before she would be obliged to turn a blind eye to his 'indiscretions'.

They were five days out from Liverpool, having stopped at Brest and Biarritz. Felicity was a good sailor, so not even a fair swell in the Bay of Biscay had troubled her. Their next port of call would be Lisbon some time the next day, and from there they would travel the short distance to Mont Estoril on the Portuguese Riviera where

Jarle had booked hotel accommodation for them. They had occupied separate cabins, and throughout the voyage he had behaved with perfect decorum, which was something of a relief since it afforded her the opportunity to sort out her thoughts and decide how she felt about his behaviour and whether she could forgive him. This, however, proved less easy than she would have wished. It was far more pleasant to laze on a deck-chair and enjoy the sunshine, or watch the energetic play deck games with noisy hilarity. Jarle spent a good deal of time about his own business, or pleasures, walking the decks or swimming in the pool. He did not say and she did not ask. But sometimes he would sit beside her and they would chat in friendly enough fashion as they had been wont to do in the weeks before their marriage at the lodge house. If she had a choice between taking Jarle with a mistress, or not at all, how could she possibly banish him from her life?

'Cruises are the up and coming way to spend a holiday,' he told her. 'And this ship is twenty-nine thousand tons with a speed of at least twenty knots. Not quite as much as the *Mauretania* and the *Lusitania* but impressive, eh?'

'Indeed,' Felicity said, gravely digesting this information, and she saw him glance at her and laugh.

'All right, I'm sorry for boring you. I assume everyone to be as fascinated by statistics as myself,' and she smiled at him, her grey eyes twinkling.

'I like to listen to you talk.'

'Do you?' he asked, moving perceptibly closer, one hand straying along her arm where it rested on the chair arm. Gently she removed it.

'Will you tell me why you so studiously ignored the fact that I was in prison?' She had never meant to say these words but they just popped out.

'I was only trying to behave in the way I thought you wanted.' He gave a wry smile. 'Left to my own devices

I would have stormed up to that prison and forced them to release you.'

'Would you?' she asked, rather breathlessly.

'But you've made so much of a thing about your independence, and the rights of women, that I thought you wouldn't thank me for it.'

'I suppose I can't have the best of both worlds,' said Felicity, with a sad little sigh. 'Campaigning for women's rights and wanting to be nurtured all at the same time, can I? Hardly seems fair.'

Jarle's smile now was merrily wicked, and once more he smoothed her arm with the back of his hand. 'Oh, I don't know. It may be possible. Under certain conditions.'

And once more she moved her arm away. 'I don't think we should rush things, do you?' she said softly. 'If this marriage is to have any chance of developing it must be on its own terms. Now, you were telling me about the ship.'

But Jarle swung himself into an upright position on the side of his deck-chair so that he could lean over her as he talked. 'Are you saying that it might have a chance?'

She stared up at him, and felt her whole body melt at the expression in his dark eyes. After five days at sea he looked tanned and fit, and more relaxed than she had ever seen him. He was dressed in swimming shorts and a light, open shirt, doing nothing to conceal the power and breadth of his bronzed chest. With his knees against her arm she had a sudden and outrageous longing to smooth her hand over the length of his bare thigh and she turned her face away in case he could read her thoughts. 'I don't know,' she murmured.

'Felicity, we started badly, you and I. And the other night I said some unforgivable things I'd just as soon you forgot.'

She sat up in her chair and hugged her knees. 'We have both said a lot of things we've later regretted. But perhaps there was more truth in your words than I cared to acknowledge. I am no longer a child who must constantly be seeking support and advice from an omnipotent father figure. I am a woman, and it is time I behaved as one. I believe I once said that everyone was entitled to one mistake. You forgave me for accusing you of fraud and vowed to remind me of that remark one day. It is surprising that you have not already done so, but I have not forgotten.' She smiled at him, and, as she heard him catch his breath, was unaware of the secrets she had revealed in that look. Secrets she had vowed never to reveal, but that could not be prevented from brimming forth from her frank grey eyes. Taking her hand in his, he gallantly raised it to his lips and kissed it.

'Tonight, I shall wine and dine my delightful new wife and we shall dance till the dawn creeps over the horizon. Perhaps this can be a new beginning for us, Felicity. We shall see.' His voice was low and heavy with meaning and the yearning she felt for him gripped her heart as fresh hope was born within her. Could it be that he cared for her after all, just a little?

'We shall see,' she repeated and they both smiled into each other's eyes as gently as any young lovers who had just made a most remarkable discovery.

She chose to wear her wedding dress, which was as creamy and beautiful as it had been that day in June when she had happily believed all her problems to be solved and that a new life had opened for her. She had been sure that love would come, then. But the shop, and to a certain extent the ghost of her father, had haunted them ever since. And now this other, infinitely more disturbing problem had come between them. If she was to be permitted a second chance, she meant to make the most of it. She loved Jarle Blakeley. She loved him with all her heart and soul and being and Felicity knew that, no matter what it cost her in terms of pain and pride, she could not stand blithely by while some other woman stole him from her. If there was any way she could think of to make him love her too, then she would do it.

She took particular care with her hair, brushing it till it shone like the gloss on satin, coiling and patting it into place on top of her head. She tucked a pink rose among the golden curls, and, after pulling on long satin elbow gloves, and fluffing out her skirts, she knew that she was as ready as she would ever be, despite the fluttering of sick nerves in her stomach. Gazing at her own reflection in the mirror, she moistened her dry lips with the tip of a pink tongue.

'You are your own person,' she told her reflection. 'Make your own decisions and choose your own path in life. If you love him, you must tell him so, as only a woman can.' She stared at the round, childlike cheeks flushed pink as the rose in her hair. She gazed into the clear grey eyes and they gazed unblinkingly back. Then, taking a deep breath, she whirled away from the mirror and left the room, her decision made.

Jarle was waiting for her in the main stateroom. Aware of the open admiration in his gaze, she allowed him to lead her to a quiet corner, away from the crowds, where two white Chippendale chairs were set at a table. A bottle of champagne was cooling on ice and a waiter hovered, ready to pour.

'You look very beautiful,' he whispered against her ear as he held out the chair for her and she thought she would faint on the spot with happiness.

The evening passed in a whirl of such delights. The champagne brought a sparkle to her eyes, the meal of fillets of veal, roast goose and creamed vegetables, followed by a bewildering choice of sweets and cheeses, was a joy to the palate. And the beauty of the room,

gilded in silver and gold leaf as finely as any hotel, even
to the enormous flower displays on the grand piano, were
all and more than she had imagined.

And when he led her to the music-room where a small
orchestra played and a chandelier with crystal pendants
reflecting the prismatic radiance of hundreds of electric
light bulbs hung from a ceiling of white and gold she
felt almost overwhelmed by the wonder of it all.

'I have travelled on a number of ships,' she told him,
'but this one is the most beautiful I have seen.'

'I'm glad you like it,' he said softly, and then his arms
were holding her close and they were dancing a slow
waltz, their hearts beating as one, quite out of rhythm
with the music. Not once did he allow any other young
man to dance with her, though several made the attempt. Even the captain was politely refused, much to
Felicity's gasping distress.

'You cannot treat the captain so rudely,' she protested, as Jarle led her possessively on to the dance-floor.

'Why not? You are my wife, remember, not his.' His
cheek came down against her hair as they danced and
as they moved together across the floor she reflected on
that small, innocuous sentence. She was his wife, but
not his love. That might still be as much as he wanted
from her. But she would never know if she did not attempt to find out. Swallowing the lump of nervous
emotion that rose in her throat, she moved her head
slightly and met his fiercely burning gaze.

'I never forget,' she said quietly, 'that I am still your
wife, that we are married.'

The music stopped and so did they as he continued
to look down at her for a long aching moment. When
she was almost sure he would not speak, he murmured,
'Neither do I, Felicity. Though certain matters have been
lacking in attention recently, wouldn't you say?'

Her heart was beating so slow and heavy in her breast
she could scarcely breathe let alone speak, yet she must

do so. 'I fear this room is too hot. Would you mind if I retired?'

He led her from the floor without speaking. Collecting her wrap, he followed her along the ship's corridors and saw how resolutely she walked ahead of him. Had she indeed meant what he thought? Jarle recalled the look in her eyes that afternoon, remembered the soft pliance of her body within his arms as they danced. Was he ready for such a commitment? For he guessed that if he went to her now there would be no turning back. At the door of her cabin she stopped and turned to face him. He handed her the wrap.

'Goodnight, sweet Felicity,' he said, and cupping her face between his hands he kissed her. It was a disappointingly chaste kiss though it still served to set her heart racing. 'Sleep well,' he murmured and the next moment was striding away down the long corridor, and Felicity was fumbling frantically with the doorknob, desperate to get inside her cabin before the tears fell.

But she would not let them fall. Her throat felt hot and tight with the effort and her whole body trembled as she slid out of her dress and hung it in the fitted wardrobe. A solid ball of pain was lodged somewhere deep inside her and she could do nothing to ease it. She tugged the combs and pins from her hair and tossed them on to the small table where they fell with a clatter. She set the pink rose in a tooth glass of water and shook out her long honey-gold hair so that it fell in rippling waves down her back. But she did not have the patience to brush it. Avoiding the sight of the accusing mirror, she pulled on her lacy nightgown and was about to fling herself into bed when she heard the tiniest sound, no more than a scratching at her door.

She knew, of course, what, or rather who made the sound and an involuntary whimper escaped her lips. She must let him in. Even if Jarle could never love her as she loved him, she knew with an unshakeable certainty that she could not live without him. She must take him as he was, or not at all. She opened the door and stood back for him to enter.

He was leaning against the doorpost. 'I wondered if we should discuss this problem we have a little more,' he said, giving her a wry smile that softened the angular lines of his face.

'Why is your nose crooked?' she asked, the question having popped unexpectedly into her head. He looked surprised, as well he might, and touched it with one finger.

'Broken as a boy in some fight or other,' he said carelessly but with a touch of unease. 'Sign of a rough childhood, I expect.'

Felicity sat down on the edge of the bed to regard him with a thoughtful frown. 'You have told me very little about your history.'

He did not answer. He was looking at how the lamplight dappled her hair in little glowing patches. And the small face framed within the curls was turned up to him with a beguiling trust that enchanted him. The rosebud lips, moist and glossy, were softly inviting, almost begging to be kissed. And those eyes... Jarle had known many women but for all his thirty-two years he stood before this one as gauche and green as a young schoolboy. And then she smiled. It was a smile of radiance, of confidence, of maturity, and of invitation. She moved further on to the bed so that he could come and sit beside her.

'Perhaps one day, soon, I shall tell you,' he murmured, mesmerised by the appeal in her eyes but still not daring to touch her.

'I want to know everything about you,' she said, and lay back against the pillows, her eyes never leaving his, her fingertips starting to lightly stroke the strength of his bare, muscled arm beneath the silk robe he wore.

'Felicity Blakeley, what are you about?' he teased.

'It is really quite simple,' she said very seriously, gazing up at him with glowing eyes. 'No more looking back, only forwards. Isn't that what you once told me? Whatever your faults, or mine, Jarle, we are married. You are my husband and I would have it no other way.'

Jarle gazed down at her, intrigued. Just when he thought he had come to know her, she surprised him yet again. 'Do you not wish to hear about this mistress you accuse me of having?'

She shook her head very firmly. 'Not at all.'

'I have had mistresses, Felicity, but——'

'Hush,' she murmured, stopping his words with soft fingers. 'Not tonight.'

'Then you believe me?' A light flickered in his eyes and she was afraid to quench it.

'If you wish it,' she answered, and smiled at him with all the enticing desire she possessed. And, as Jarle's lips came down upon hers, all her problems and misgivings melted away in the heat of the hunger that raged through her. She could learn to be the kind of wife he wanted. She must. That night Felicity made a private vow never to speak of it again, believing she now knew all there was to know about her new husband. But as the ship sailed inexorably closer to Lisbon, high in a hillside villa waited a figure who knew much more.

CHAPTER FIFTEEN

THOSE first few days were close to idyllic. Mont Estoril was a short half-hour by train from Lisbon and here Felicity and Jarle settled in one of the Riviera's finest hotels. It was run on English lines and so language was no problem, much to Felicity's relief. She and Jarle occupied a suite of rooms overlooking the quiet bay. Every morning she would wake to the dazzlingly bright sunlight, the balmy sea breezes wafting through the open windows, and she would stretch and curl against Jarle and perhaps wake him from his slumber and they would make love again, more intensely and sweetly on each occasion.

Then they would breakfast on the balcony, marvelling at the blue of the Atlantic rivalled only by the cloudless sky, breathing in the fresh morning scents of eucalyptus, orange trees, and the myriad variety of palms which filled the hotel grounds. Later they would stroll together along the shore road as far as the Boca da Inferno, so called for its wildness on stormy days. Or they might swim, or simply lie on the hot sands fringed by the brightly painted, delightfully picturesque villas of the Lisboan aristocracy. Accustomed to the heat of India, Felicity revelled in the sun, and was soon the golden girl she had been on that first day they met when she had inadvertently pelted him with flour.

'I shall never be entirely fashionable,' she mourned, watching the strolling promenaders with their sensible parasols. 'So if that is the kind of woman you like, you will have to look elsewhere.'

'Are you fishing for compliments, Mrs Blakeley? For, if I remember correctly, do you not have a weakness for fashionable hats?' he teased, as they sipped their orange juice at breakfast. 'You are very much the kind of woman I like.' Then, slipping down her *peignoir*, he kissed one bare golden shoulder. 'All I ask from a wife is complete and utter obedience.'

'What nonsense,' she cried. 'Am I not to have a mind of my own?'

'Most certainly, so long as it listens well to mine.'

Felicity knew he was teasing but a cloud of uncertainty gathered about her heart. 'I do hope you are not entirely serious, Jarle,' she said and he had the grace to look shamefaced. Moving his chair closer, he took her hand in his.

'I am clumsily trying to make a point, yes.'

'And what is that?' Her tone was very faintly defensive.

'It is that I would prefer you to call an end to your suffragette activities.' He held up one hand as she would have interrupted. 'I know they are important to you, but there are other ways you can continue the fight for what you believe is right for women. You must understand that I cannot tolerate the prospect of your being harmed in any way. You must see now how easily these riots occur, often when least expected. What if you had been injured?'

'But I was not,' Felicity protested. 'And I feel I must do something, Jarle. This is a most important time for women, a time which could well determine how women progress for the rest of the century.' She leaned forwards in her seat, her whole expression begging him to understand.

'Women will be granted the vote soon, I am sure of it,' Jarle said. 'And when they have it they will want someone to speak for them in Parliament.'

'You mean a leader?'

'I mean a woman Member of Parliament. It will come, Felicity—why should it not be you?'

Felicity flushed with pleasure at this expression of his faith in her. 'I should enjoy the challenge,' she confessed.

'I did not break my nose as a child,' he said unexpectedly, and she stared. 'I've not liked to tell you about it,' he whispered. 'Because it is my burden.'

She faced him squarely. 'Why? Are we not friends? More than friends? I would find it no burden to share your troubles.'

Lifting her hand, he rubbed it softly back and forth across his lips. It was almost an absent-minded gesture as his eyes seemed fixed on some distant point, far out to the empty sea. Felicity dared scarce draw breath, though her heart raced from his touch. 'It is time you knew,' he said. 'It will explain to you many things, not least my abhorrence for violence and rioting in particular.'

'Mama and Kate have told me much of your family background; it is not important.'

'It is to me.'

'I'm sorry, I did not mean——'

Jarle took a deep breath. 'I know. It is only that while I became obsessed with politics and the rights of others my own mother was sick, and I never *knew*.'

'If she did not tell you, how could you be expected to know?' said Felicity. 'I expect she deliberately hid it from you.' She might have added, As you have hidden this pain from me.

Jarle nodded. 'She was proud.'

'As is her son.'

Jarle gave a bitter little smile. 'Pride is sometimes hard to live with. She was tired and old, her time had come. But that is not the whole of it. There is more, much more that I have to bear.' He paused for a long moment and Felicity kept the silence with him, not wishing to risk the sensitive process of unburdening which had so painfully begun. 'On the day she died she cleaned her windows because that was the day she always cleaned her windows, no matter that she was crippled with pain. Young Tom helped her, because he always helped her, and I attended my political meeting because it was the day I always went. An ordinary day among a host of ordinary days.'

He stared at her, and she saw how the anger burned in the brown eyes, overriding the pain. 'But this particular meeting became ugly. People were demonstrating, a riot broke out. That is when my nose got broken. And when Tommy came running for me . . . to tell me . . .' Jarle could not go on. The pain scorched his chest, seared a hot knife through his heart. 'He never saw the horse. The noisy crowd had panicked and it bolted. Dear God, Felicity, it broke him as if he were a wooden doll that had fallen from a child's cart and I was too busy with my own concerns to even notice. I have carried the guilt of it to this day.'

'Oh, Jarle.'

'It is something I am learning to live with.' Jarle gave her the ghost of a smile. 'In many ways you have already made my burden easier, yet in others there is still room for improvement. I asked you to give me your word never to risk becoming involved in a demonstration or riot. Now you see the reason, I would like to think you would keep it in future.'

Felicity was filled with contrition. 'I promise that I shall never do anything to hurt you,' she said. 'My days of attending political demonstrations are over. Now put it from your mind. You were not to blame.'

But Jarle was not done. 'I brought you here, Felicity, in order to tell you of this. There were reasons why I could not tell you before. But now the time has come for you to meet someone very special to me. She is looking forward to meeting you.'

'She?' Felicity's heart gave a little skip.

'The person who has cared for little Tommy ever since his accident.' He stood up, briskly urging her to dress. 'Put on a wrap, for Dee lives at Cintra, a cooler, more mountainous area, and I would not have you catch a chill.'

Felicity did as she was bid, but her mind was troubled and her heart began to thump, for surely she had heard that name before.

They drove in an open carriage up into the hills, a wild region of jagged peaks and breathtaking views. Occasionally they glimpsed women in vivid reds and greens, beating their clothes clean in a fast-running stream and the women would stop their work to smile and wave at the young couple sitting so close together in the carriage.

'You can just see Lisbon over there,' remarked Jarle, one arm snug about her waist. 'We must try to fit in a visit before we go home, if only to view the fine park named after our King Edward.'

Home. She did not want to think of it. She had wanted this idyllic honeymoon never to end. Leaning against him, she resolutely closed her mind to speculating on the purpose of this drive, determined to enjoy the bitter-sweet quality of her love for him.

They came at last to a neat white villa almost buried in mimosa, orange and lemon trees and bougainvillaea. The brilliance of the colours against the stark white walls made Felicity catch her breath as she stepped down on to the cobbled drive.

'What a beautiful place. Does . . . does your friend live here?'

Jarle laughed as if she had said something funny. 'She is not my *friend*.' The emphasis on the last word caused Felicity to glance at him in incredulity, the taste of bile souring her throat. How could he behave with such blatant disregard for her feelings? Surely he did not intend to actually introduce her to his mistress? The pain was almost unbearable as he led her to the polished front door. 'Her name is Delphine Philippe, but most people call her simply Dee. She is a very special person and I would not have you prejudiced against her simply because she is perhaps a trifle unconventional.'

The sun faded from the sky. The earth stopped revolving and every bird paused in its song as these words fell upon Felicity's unwilling ears. 'Madame Delphine,' she whispered. 'I thought she lived in Paris?' Safely out of the way.

'She does,' Jarle agreed. 'Except in the summer, when she lives here.'

'She must be very rich, then,' said Felicity almost pettishly as Jarle beat upon the door once more. She saw how his eyes sparkled with anticipated pleasure, how his whole body seemed poised with eagerness. He can hardly wait to see her, she thought, a wave of sickness washing over her.

'Dee, where are you?' he shouted and pounded on the door yet again. Felicity did not want the door ever to open. She did not wish to look upon her husband's beautiful young mistress, as she was quite sure she would be. And he said he had brought her here deliberately. Was it some kind of twisted revenge for the accusations she had first made against him? Or was it simply that he intended to reveal to her the manner in which their future marriage was to be conducted? She clasped her hands tightly together and prayed for strength.

Then from behind came a delighted squeal and, as they both turned towards it, a hurtling figure in startling peacock-blue flung herself into Jarle's outstretched arms. It was some moments, during which there was much hugging and kissing, before the two pulled apart, still laughing, and still with arms entwined. Felicity prepared herself for the worst and looked into her rival's face.

She was not young. She was not even beautiful, though undoubtedly she might have been pretty once. She was

all of five and forty, decidedly plump and with masses
of wild white hair which flew about her shoulders like
curling crinkled snakes. She wore a bright green pina-
fore which clashed appallingly with the peacock-blue
gown, and a pair of well-used gardening gloves much
spotted with holes.

'Can this be Felicity?' Madame Delphine gazed at her
for a second, moist-eyed, before taking her completely
by surprise and kissing her on both cheeks. She smelled
of chrysanthemums and fresh air. 'I have so longed to
meet you.'

While Felicity searched her mind frantically for some
suitable response, Jarle caught her completely off guard
yet again by saying, 'Felicity, allow me to introduce to
you my notorious sister, Dee.'

'Your sister?' She swayed slightly, not believing she
had heard correctly. The relief was so great that she was
sure she would faint clean away. But why had he not
told her this before? She looked questioningly up at him.

'That's right. I warned you I had a large family scat-
tered about the globe. Dee is the eldest of our brood
and quite the wickedest, I'm afraid.'

'But I thought . . .' Felicity could scarce find the words
to express her feelings, particularly as Jarle was smiling
so proudly upon them both.

'That she was French? Many people think so until they
meet her,' he said quietly, his eyes gently teasing.

'My late husband was French, bless his sweet memory,
but I'm a simple Lancashire lass like all the rest,' Dee
chortled, and, gathering Jarle to her in another warm
hug, said, 'What are you doing standing about here like
lemons? Come inside and I'll put the kettle on.' The offer
sounded so incongruous in the heat of that Portuguese
summer day that all of them, Felicity included, burst
out laughing.

They settled for ice-cold lemon tea, which was most refreshing, but Felicity was soon to learn that there were more surprises in store.

They had been talking small talk, about the climate and how this riviera was becoming increasingly fashionable with the rich. Jarle had told his sister about the progress they were making in the shop, and Felicity had described her wedding and the dress she had worn for it in great detail. And, as they talked, she had come to like more and more this warm-hearted woman who wore such outlandish colours and whose whole face lit up from within whenever she laughed, which she did frequently.

Then, leaning forward in his seat, brows drawing together in puckered anxiety, Jarle suddenly asked, 'How is he?' and the colour and laughter seemed to seep away from the room, leaving it still and quiet and overstuffy.

'He is well, Jarle,' said Dee very quietly. 'Much improved, I think. Monsieur Capot is pleased with him.'

'Is there any sign that . . . ?' Jarle's eager words were calmly interrupted.

'No, Jarle. He said it would be cruel to pretend Tommy could make a complete recovery.' Then, turning to Felicity, she said, 'I dare say Jarle has told you of the tragic accident our young brother Tommy suffered beneath the hooves of a runaway horse? It broke his back, and he will spend the rest of his life in a wheelchair.'

Delphine spoke the words simply, without any call for sympathy, yet Felicity expressed it as sensitively as she could, remembering as she did so how Jarle had felt so responsible for this tragedy that he had kept it from her as if it were some great crime. Strangely it brought a warm glow to her heart that he had finally unburdened himself to her, and she could understand now his fear of crowds, and the dangers of riot. Perhaps he had thought she might hate him because of it. She must teach him otherwise.

'Tommy has been working with a very clever physio-therapist in Paris, who can do wonderful things by massaging and exercising weak muscles,' Dee explained. 'It seemed at one time that Tommy would stay flat on his back, but now he can sit up and turn his head and use his hands and arms. He has a future that is at least tolerable.'

'I'm so glad,' said Felicity.

'He longs to see you,' said Dee, but then, smiling up at her brother, added, 'But most of all he waits with impatience for his hero to call. Besides, there are things which Felicity and I need to discuss.'

Jarle was on his feet in an instant. 'I shall go to him at once. I have presents in the carriage,' he said, but Dee laughingly shook her head.

'Fetch those later. Put the boy out of his agony.'

Jarle strode to the door, but, instead of wrenching it open, he stopped, then came back to stand by Felicity, looking down into her eyes.

'You have learned much about me this day,' he said softly.

'Long past time,' she said. 'I too look forward to meeting Tommy. Perhaps he will be allowed to visit us in England.'

Jarle took her hand in his and rubbed it gently with his thumb. 'I should like that very much, when he is strong enough. Thank you. But, Felicity, there is another matter which needs to be aired. If I was reticent in revealing it, you must find it in your heart to forgive me.'

'What more dark secrets have you kept from me?' she laughed, but Jarle did not join in.

'The circumstances were difficult. Now Dee has expressed a wish to tell you herself. I hope you will be generous.' Placing a cool kiss on her forehead, he left her, and Felicity turned startled, questioning eyes in Dee's direction.

'Good heavens, *madame*. What can it be?'

Not meeting the younger woman's gaze, Delphine offered more lemon tea, which was refused. She poured one for herself, then, sighing softly, leaned back in her chair and left it untouched. 'It is difficult to know how to begin,' she said, and in that moment real fear touched Felicity's heart. She knew with an awful certainty that the news she was about to hear was not good and then Dee's first words brought her whirling mind swiftly to attention for it was the last thing she had expected to hear.

'I first met your father about ten years ago on board ship. He was visiting England, to see you probably, since you were in school there at that time. I had joined the ship at Lisbon. Recently widowed, I too was returning home to visit my family.'

'I—I did not realise that you knew my father,' stammered Felicity.

Madame Delphine sat pleating the peacock-blue satin between nervous fingers as she spoke in the smallest of voices and Felicity wondered if she had dreamed the words in her head.

'I was your father's mistress,' she said, in her quiet, matter-of-fact way. 'Oh, it didn't happen right away. On that first journey we talked. He was concerned about how he should spend his eventual retirement with so little of the family fortune left, and I was a young widow of thirty-four, stung with shock at losing a beloved husband. But we kept in touch after that. Later, we became lovers, but always with the utmost discretion.' She lifted her shoulders in a helpless little gesture and her blue eyes misted with memory. 'He was most gallant. A charming, sweet gentleman. But then you know that.'

Felicity sat like stone, wishing she could cut off the sound of the woman's voice but it slapped against her ears as relentlessly as the tide bore down upon the rocks at the Boca da Inferno, aptly called the Mouth of Hell. 'Did you not know that he was marr—— About Mama and me?' she felt compelled to ask, and Dee looked at her with a deep sadness as she tilted her head slightly in a self-deprecating nod.

'I knew. We never meant either of you to find out. I would have guarded his privacy to my dying day. He loved your mother still, you see. I know he did.' She was silent for a moment, drawing in a deep breath before continuing more briskly, 'But perhaps not enough, eh? Then matters got away from our control. Your father's old friend and sometime rival, Gilbert Farrel, discovered our secret when they both visited London one time. He saw us together and I'm afraid my eyes must have given it all away.' She sighed again. 'It all became very difficult after that. Farrel was most demanding. He wanted you, a girl young enough to be his daughter. And he wanted Hollingworth House, where he could found his own dynasty. He'd always envied your father and he longed for a slice of the aristocratic life for himself,' she said bitterly. 'But it takes more than a title to make an aristocrat or even a gentleman. When Joshua scorned his offer, Farrel began to blackmail him. Only a little at first, but then demanding more and more money, applying pressure to try to force him to change his mind or he would tell Carmella and you all about me. But Josh was prepared to go to any lengths to prevent that from happening, for all our sakes, even to ending our liaison.'

She smiled softly. 'That hurt, I can tell you, for I loved him dearly. By way of compensation he bought me the draper's shop, under his own name, of course. But I could not accept it.' She shook her head and Felicity saw how the tears welled in her eyes. 'I agreed to work there as a couturière only, in which I have some skill. But perhaps I should have given it more attention for it did not do well.' Delphine pushed the wild white curls back from the drawn face and held her cheeks between prematurely wrinkled hands and Felicity began to notice the evidence of a sad, hard life. 'The rest I expect you know. Josh was facing the shame of almost certain bankruptcy. He was a very private person, believing strongly in honour, duty and loyalty, all the things he should have owed and kept to your mother, but did not. Nor did he wish for me to be goggled at and our affair turned over like someone's dirty linen.' There was a harsh edge to the voice and Felicity surprised herself by feeling a sudden surge of pity for this proud, warm woman who had been so summarily abandoned, yet so well loved.

'But how did Jarle come to be involved?'

'After almost two years of not seeing or hearing any word from Joshua, he came to me at my little house in Manchester. I believe he came to England on the advice of his lawyer who was concerned about his financial affairs. But it was not a good time for him to come. Jarle and I were in mourning for our mother and Tommy lay close to death, it seemed, in the hospital.' She looked at Felicity directly now, all trace of reticence gone. 'I expect it sounds very callous to you but it seemed sensible since your father was a dying man, desperate to make reparation to his family yet with little he could do financially, for Jarle to step in. Josh had enormous debts but was determined not to sell to Gilbert Farrel, nor to agree to his marrying you. But he couldn't tell you his reasons for turning against the marriage. He explained all this to Jarle. My brother had plenty of money and had once made a bid for the store.' Dee's eyebrows twitched and her blue eyes glittered with a sudden show of humour remarkably reminiscent of her brother. 'Admittedly, Jarle had the working man's suspicion of the "gentry" but he found that he liked your father and perhaps felt a responsibility because of me.' She pushed back the curls from her damp forehead. 'Joshua returned to India a sick man, never to recover, but content that he'd done all he could for his family in the end.' There were no tears now, only a bleak acceptance.

Felicity sat without moving, lost in the ghosts of the past. The sweet smell of orange blossom wafted into the room, mocking the bitterness of disillusionment so strong within her. 'Does Jarle imagine that by destroying the sweet image of my father as a loving, honourable family man, that will somehow be good for our marriage?' she asked finally, pressed to express some of the misery she was feeling.

Delphine jumped to her feet. 'Your papa is not destroyed,' she retorted. 'He was a fine man, as good a husband and father as he was capable of being and a wonderful ambassador for his country. But he was a human being with failings like other human beings. He was no god, Felicity, no supernatural creature. He was a bad businessman, he wasted money, was weak and soft where women were concerned and was ashamed of these weaknesses. But he was no less a man for all that and I'll not sit here and have you say otherwise.'

Felicity was stunned by this outburst, filled with a sudden longing to be somewhere very private where she could rethink her values, try to analyse her bruised emotions.

'I think I should like to go home,' she told Jarle, who chose that particular moment to come back into the room.

'We'll drive back to the hotel at once,' he said, his concern making him reach out for her, but she backed away.

'No, no, I mean really home. To England.'

'England?'

'Yes,' she cried, eyes bright with unshed tears. 'I want to go home. Now, or at least as soon as a ship can be found.'

'Oh, there is no problem there,' put in Dee, 'since Jarle has his own ship to do his bidding. She is his latest pet project. A beautiful new cruise shop on her maiden voyage. But I wish, my dear, that you would not leave in this way.'

Felicity whirled to face Jarle, her thoughts once more in turmoil. 'Ship? Do you mean that ship was yours? Why did you not tell me?'

'I did not think of it. Is it important? It had to be tested so why should we not enjoy it?'

'Is it important?' Felicity shook her head, distraught with despair. 'The ship had to be tested, so what better than a new wife, your compliant, obedient business partner to try it out? Does everything have to be so practical, so utterly logical, for you? Even to arranging a honeymoon? And you chose the Portuguese Riviera not for its climate or its beauty but because you wished to crush the last remnant of my family pride, to tell me things I'd much rather not hear.'

He reached for her again but she pushed him away. 'It had to be done,' he said.

The tears were spilling over her lids now, rolling down her cheeks unchecked, drowning her heart in misery and disappointment, the shock of all she had just heard robbing her of reason. 'And you always do what has to be done, no matter what the cost to personal feelings, everything you touch a precisely ordered business deal based on the logic of figures, statistics, practicalities. Even me, your wife, and now this our honeymoon. I hate you, Jarle Blakeley. I hate you with all my heart.' She ran from the room before she entirely lost control of the last scraps of her dignity.

There was no option, however, but to climb into the open carriage, and, though she sat as far from him as she could and did not speak a word the entire drive, she was certain the driver was aware of the whole embarrassing scene.

Later, in the hotel room, she gave way to a storm of weeping. She lay on the bed and sobbed until her head ached and not another tear could be squeezed out. She was aware of Jarle quietly sitting in the wicker chair by the open window, but she did not speak to him.

'How shall I tell Mama?' she said at last into the gathering gloom.

'Is that necessary?'

'Hasn't she the right to know?'

Jarle came to sit beside her on the bed but stubbornly she edged away, not yet ready to forgive him for this unwelcome truth. 'Perhaps she knows already but prefers not to speak of it. Your father did not wish her to be told so I see no reason why the subject should even be mentioned. She is happy now, with Joe, and I am glad of that.'

'But you told me.'

'I thought it best that you knew, yes,' Jarle agreed. 'May I bathe your eyes? They look very sore.'

'No.'

He sighed softly, trying to still the urge to take her in his arms. 'I would do anything not to hurt you, Felicity, but apart from the fact that we agreed there should be no more secrets between us, there were other reasons why you had to learn the truth.' As she made no response he continued, 'I could not keep little Tommy and Dee a secret for ever. You see how your imagination had already begun to weave fictitious fantasies over her, or would you have preferred to find that it was I and not your father who had a mistress secreted away?'

Felicity had the grace to look abashed. 'I'm sorry about that. It was rather silly, I suppose.'

'I know you loved your father but somehow he always came between us, and I felt that to be a bad thing, don't you see?' Jarle said, his voice low and soft, and, encouraged by her lack of protest, he slid a hand across the counterpane to capture one of hers. She did not take it away, and she lay quiet now, though with her face deep in the pillow. 'Though I did understand Sir Joshua's efforts to make reparation to his family. Having failed my mother and Tom I didn't want to let Dee down as well.'

'Why did you not tell me that Delphine was your sister?'

'Would you have believed such a lame-sounding tale?' he asked. 'And you might have probed further and I couldn't decide if the time was right for that.'

'But how can I ever trust you?' asked the muffled voice. 'All men seem to be cheats, even my own father.'

He stroked her honey-gold hair. 'I am not your father, Felicity. Nor have I any wish to behave as he did. You must believe that I have no wish for a mistress. All I want is a wife. A beautiful, adoring, loving wife. I want our marriage to be a good one, open and fair and with mutual respect. I want you.'

She lifted her face from the pillow and turned to look at him. 'Do you?'

He gave a little nod. 'If I was wrong in my belief that the ghosts of the past had to be exorcised before we could hope for true happiness, then I hope you will find it in your heart to forgive me. And now I shall bathe your poor eyes, no matter what you say.'

He brought a bowl of cold water and began to dab at her eyes and her heated forehead with a cooling handkerchief. When he had done he dried her face very gently with a soft towel, and she sat unprotesting, her eyes never leaving his face.

'If you were a child I could kiss you better,' he said, smiling.

'But I am not a child.'

'No, my Felicity, you are not. Perhaps once you were, a sheltered, pampered child who was her father's darling, no matter how you might protest otherwise,' he warned. 'But you have grown up, and I like the new Felicity much better.'

She looked up at him through dark lashes, still spiky with the damp of tears and the cooling water. 'Will you tell me something?''

'If I can.'

'I can understand why you made the marriage contract in the first place, but since I had released you from it and you were no longer bound by it, why then did you agree to it the second time? Was it simply to prevent Gilbert Farrel marrying me?'

Jarle put back his head and gazed at the ceiling as if seeking patience from high. Then, wrapping both arms about her, he pulled her very firmly into his arms. 'You are the most trying woman I ever met. For all this new-found confidence and maturity you are still incredibly naïve in certain departments.'

'I dare say I may be,' she giggled. 'But tell me all the same,' and Jarle's eyes opened wide in disbelief.

'You minx. You know well enough. Have I not shown you these last weeks?'

'I want to hear you say it,' she whispered. 'For you have not yet done so.'

'Have I not? Then I'd best make up for lost time, my darling. I love you,' he whispered, kissing her upon her soft lips, then said again, 'I love you, Felicity. I love you, I love you, I love you. Is that enough?' he teased, squeezing the breath from her with each new declaration.

'No, it is not,' she murmured, sliding down upon the soft pillows with a telling smile. 'You must promise to give me constant reassurance. Besides, I am still on my honeymoon, so perhaps you wouldn't mind confirming what you say by showing me again.'

And, as Jarle lay down beside her, his hand already pulling the combs from her hair, he vowed it was a promise he would gladly keep.

The other exciting

MASQUERADE
Historical

available this month is:

A MARRIAGE MADE ON EARTH

Sheila Bishop

Poor investments by her elderly father had left seventeen-year-old Pamela's future in dire straits, particularly when her godmother willed her fortune to Lord Blaise, instead of Pamela.

Even so, when the unknown Blaise arrived, offering marriage, Pamela only reluctantly agreed. She didn't expect a great deal from the marriage, but it was a nasty shock when Richard always seemed to take the side of his childhood friend, Mrs Decima Strang, and to assume that Pamela's youth meant she was incapable of rational thought!

Yet despite all, Pamela *wanted* her husband's approval. The thing was, how to go about it?

ISABELLA
Janet Grace

Things were going drastically wrong for Isabella! Deprived of her poetical beau, and a season in town under her aunt's aegis, she was mortified to discover she was expected to accompany her young brothers to their tutor's home in the country. The next blow fell when her father announced her betrothal to the elderly roué, Lord Carton Crue.

Beseiged on all sides, Isabella wasn't best pleased to discover the tutor was no longer Me D'Estine, but had become Anthony, Viscount Alladay, heir to an earldom! Reviewing her life, and her perception of Anthony, Isabella's resolve strengthened – she *wouldn't* be a victim.

A PASSING FANCY
Deborah Miles

For the sake of his health, Cleo Montague and her father embarked from Plymouth for warmer climes. But the journey to Australia in 1858 proved too much for his strength, and Cleo found herself travelling on alone. Determined not to abandon her father's dream, and with superb millinery skills to earn her living, Cleo found herself setting up business in the goldrush town of Nugget Gully.

But this was only possible at the cost of accepting Jacob Raines as a silent partner. A decent respectable woman, Cleo knew that any hint about black sheep Jake would ruin her reputation in the community . . .

Available in January

TWO
HISTORICAL ROMANCES

Masquerade historical roman
bring the past alive with splendo
excitement and romance. We v
send you a cuddly teddy bear a
a special MYSTERY GIFT. Ther
you choose, you can go on to enjo
more exciting Masquerades every t
months, for just £1.75 each! Se
the coupon below at once to – Rea
Service, FREEPOST, PO Box 2.
Croydon, Surrey CR9 9EL.

&

TWO
FREE GIFTS!

--- **NO STAMP REQUIRED** ---

Yes! Please rush me my 2 Free Masquerade Romances and 2 Free Gifts!
Please also reserve me a Reader Service Subscription. If I decide to
subscribe, I can look forward to receiving 4 Masquerade Romances every tw
months for just £7.00, delivered direct to my door. Post and packing is free
and there's a free Newsletter. If I choose not to subscribe I shall write to yc
within 10 days - I can keep the books and gifts whatever I decide. I can
cancel or suspend my subscription at any time. I am over 18.

Mrs/Miss/Ms/Mr _____ EP93

Address _____

_____ Postcode _____

Signature _____

mps MAILING PREFERENCE SERVICE

Experience the thrill of 2 Masquerade Historical Romances Absolutely Free!

*Experience the passions of bygone days
in 2 gripping Masquerade Romances - absolutely free!
Enjoy these tales of tempestuous love from
the illustrious past.
Then, if you wish, look forward to a regular supply of
Masquerade, delivered to your door!
Turn the page for details of 2 extra FREE gifts,
and how to apply.*

An irresistible offer for you

Here at Reader Service we would love you to become a regular reader of Masquerade. And to welcome you, we'd like you to have two books, a cuddly teddy and a MYSTERY GIFT - ABSOLUTELY FREE and without obligation.

Then, every two months you could look forward to receiving 4 more brand-new Masquerade Romances for just £1.75 each, delivered to your door, postage and packing is free. Plus our free newsletter featuring competitions, author news, special offers offering some great prizes, and lots more!

This invitation comes with no strings attached. You can cancel or suspend your subscription at any time, and still keep your free books and gifts.

Its so easy. Send no money now. Simply fill in the coupon below at once and post it to - Reader Service, FREEPOST, PO Box 236, Croydon, Surrey CR9 9EL.

- - - - - - - ▬ NO STAMP REQUIRED ▬ - - - - - - →

Yes! Please rush me my 2 Free Masquerade Romances and 2 Free Gifts! Please also reserve me a Reader Service Subscription. If I decide to subscribe, I can look forward to receiving 4 brand new Masquerade Romances every two months for just £7.00, delivered direct to my door. Post and packing is free, and there's a free Newsletter. If I choose not to subscribe I shall write to you within 10 days - I can keep the books and gifts whatever I decide. I can cancel or suspend my subscription at any time. I am over 18.

Mrs/Miss/Ms/Mr _____ EP94M

Address _____

_____

_____ Postcode _____

Signature _____